Dacia Wolf
& the Demon Mark

A magical coming of age dark fantasy novel

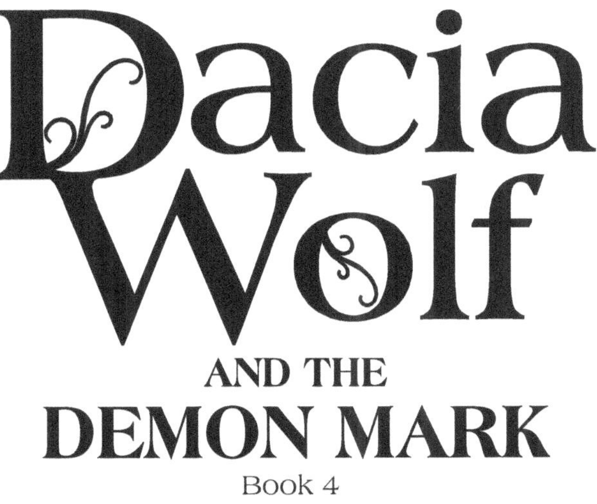

AND THE
DEMON MARK
Book 4

Visit Mandi Oyster online at
www.MandiOyster.com

Facebook: https://www.facebook.com/MandiOysterAuthor
Instagram: https://www.instagram.com/MandiOyster/

*This book is dedicated to everyone who has
ever called me Queen Mandi the Magnificent.
You're all royalty in my eyes.
Long may we reign!*

Chapter 1

New Students

They were in all of my classes. Beautiful and distant. They stood out. My classmates thought they were models. I knew they were other, but what exactly, I couldn't be sure.

I'd noticed the first one in the hallway outside my dorm room. She had long blonde hair that fell in waves down her back. People darted down the halls, but she stood absolutely still. Her gaze never left me as I walked to the bathroom. When I finished my shower and stepped back into the hallway, a second one had joined her. Dark lashes framed seafoam green eyes that drew me in and kept me from turning away.

I ran into another student.

She stumbled. "Watch where you're going," she grumbled.

I shook my head and stepped back. "I'm so sorry."

While my friends and I walked to Mythology class, the others watched me from beneath the trees and on the benches, men and women alike. They gathered together, following behind us.

When we got to class, Aurelia and Cody sat to either side of me, and Dan and Samantha sat in front of me, blocking me from the others.

Cassandra Nightshade and Bryce Sumac entered the room hand in hand. Cassandra nodded at me and took the seat next to Samantha.

My eyebrows pinched together, and I looked from her to Cody. With his jaw clenched, he glared daggers at the two of them. I twined my fingers with his, trying to soothe him. It would be a long time, if ever, until Cody forgave any of the Potato Heads for what they had done to him.

The beautiful people sat along the aisles and by the exits, effectively blocking my escape. They turned awkwardly in their seats to ogle at me.

Dr. Cedar walked into the room and came to an abrupt halt. He rubbed his chin while looking at all the extra students. "Anyone not prepared to learn about mythology can leave now."

He waited by the door, but nobody budged. I was tempted to get up to see if the beautiful people would follow my lead.

"Well"—he walked the rest of the way into the room, rubbing his hands together—"if you're all staying, let's get started."

About halfway through class, Cassandra tossed a folded piece of paper onto my desk. I stared at it. Part of me wanted to know what it said, and the other part wanted to ignore it. Curiosity ended up getting the best of me. I picked it up like it might explode, holding it by the edge. Cody put his hand over mine and shook his head.

Dropping it, I went back to taking notes, but the paper seemed to call my name. I snatched it up and read it before Cody could stop me.

What's with the entourage? And what happened to Damon?

Seeing his name made my heart clench. My throat felt painfully thick. I pictured Damon's tousled hair and cocky grin. I remembered his confidence and his humor. Tears pricked my eyes. I held my pen above the sheet, not sure if I should answer. Finally, I settled on:

I've never seen them before. He went home. He won't be back.

My hand shook when I wrote the last line. I needed to get over it, but I didn't know how. I never should have befriended him to begin with. I'd known all along that he was the demon, Mavros, but he'd been funny and charming, and even though he had said I never meant anything to him, I felt differently.

I held the note out, considering crumpling it up, but I tossed it back to her instead.

⁖3⁗

When class ended, Cassandra turned and looked at me. "I know there's more to them." She pointed at the watchers. "And her"—she nodded at Aurelia—"and Damon. You don't have to tell me. You don't have to trust me, but I might be able to help somehow."

Shoving my things in my bag, I contemplated ignoring her. I had no idea what to say. She knew about my powers. Like me, she had also been demon-marked. The difference between us was that I could defend myself from the monsters, and she couldn't. Maybe she deserved a second chance.

"Thanks. You did help." I smiled at her and Bryce. "Keeping them from sitting right next to me. Giving me a break."

"No problem." She tossed her ebony hair over her shoulder, grabbed Bryce's hand, and sashayed out of the room.

Samantha watched them leave, her mouth slightly open. "What was that about?"

"I have no idea." I rubbed my arm, wondering if I'd ever know what was going on.

The beautiful people loitered in front of the exits, watching me, waiting for me to make my move. Dr. Cedar sat upright at his desk, keeping an eye on everyone in the room. I was sure he could feel the tension. I wondered how he'd react if he knew creatures of legend stood in his room and others walked among us. Would it change the way he thought about his class? Would it change how he taught it?

Surrounded by my friends, I strolled past the beautiful people. They followed me out of the building, never too far behind. I shoved my hands into my hoodie's pouch. Even though the sun shone down on us, the mid-October weather was chilly, and the breeze warned of colder days to come.

Samantha fiddled with her bracelet and with her backpack straps. She cleared her throat like she wanted to say something but didn't.

After about the fourth time, Cody said, "What?"

She looked over her shoulder. "Dan and I need to go to his room, but I don't know if we should."

"You will be fine." Aurelia waved her arm at our followers. "They will not concern themselves with anyone but Dacia."

"Will she be okay?" Dan looked back at the mob trailing behind us. His hazel eyes filled with concern.

"Yes." Aurelia's form rippled, and for an instant, I swore I saw the dragon looking at me.

Dan and Samantha veered right toward Dracaena Hall. They turned back several times, whether watching to make sure we were okay or to make sure the others weren't following them I didn't know.

When we were almost to Wisteria Hall, several of the beautiful people broke off from the group, surrounding the building. As we ascended the stairs, more of them split off on each floor, blocking the exits.

I wondered if they knew I could turn invisible and walk past them or that I could just teleport out of my room if I wanteded.

They didn't talk to me, didn't try to touch me, but they scared me more than I wanted to admit.

My nightmares hadn't given me any clues as to who or what caused me to lose control, but somehow these beings had to be involved.

"Who are they?" I asked Aurelia as soon as Cody shut the door to mine and Samantha's room. "Why are they here?"

She tilted her head, and her long, golden hair fell over her shoulder. "They are Nephilim." She looked away from me.

"Why're they here?" Cody's posture was rigid, his blue eyes filled with worry.

Aurelia's pupils turned to slits. "They have come for Dacia"—her voice was a snarl—"but if they try to take her, they will have to deal with the dragons."

Plopping down on the vermillion couch, I pulled my hands through my hair, catching red, curly strands under my fingernails.

It had been less than a month since I had sent Mavros back to the Abyss. Even though I had said my goodbyes to Damon, even though I knew he was a demon, my heart still ached for him. I didn't know how I would withstand another trial so soon.

Fear and despair pulsed through my veins. I wanted a life with Cody. I wanted to be a normal teenager. I wanted peace. Instead, I got Nephilim.

Aurelia sat beside me, gently rubbing my back. "They are here because they do not know you as I do. They fear your power."

I envisioned all of them following me and sitting in the classroom. There had to be at least twenty Nephilim. What could I do against that many people? How could I stand against them? My heart raced, and my body trembled. I clutched my elbows, trying to hide my fear from Cody and Aurelia.

The terror grew. Clenching my heart. Twisting my gut. I imagined them taking Cody … and Samantha … and then Dan. Overpowering Aurelia. I envisioned using my powers against them and having my magic turn on me.

The room darkened. Lightning flashed immediately followed by thunder. I jumped, and my heart sprinted.

"You must regain control, Dacia." Aurelia clasped my shoulder. "Your powers are too strong to be unharnessed."

Cody sat on my other side, pulling me against him. "Little rain never hurt."

"No." I patted Cody's leg. "But a full-blown storm can." I closed my eyes and tried to calm myself. The wind gusted. Rain hammered against the windows. I held my head in my hands and focused on my breathing.

I pictured the mountain lake I'd used to calm myself so many times when I was learning to control my powers, but the details warped until it was a place I'd visited with Damon. Our picnic basket sat on the edge of the trees. I spun in a circle, hoping to see him and terrified that I would.

Thunder boomed louder than before. I jumped up and paced. My hands shook. I tucked them into my pockets.

Aurelia grabbed my shoulder, and a soothing burst of energy shot through my body, calming me. The winds died down. The rain slowed, turning to gentle showers before diminishing completely. Within minutes, sunlight brightened the room.

The door opened, and Samantha and Dan came in. Their clothes were soaked. Water dripped off their hair.

"We didn't know it was supposed to rain." Samantha tossed a towel to Dan and grabbed one for herself.

"Sorry about that," I mumbled.

Dan pulled his shirt off and wrung it out. "What brought that on?" He hung his tee on the side of the sink and continued drying off.

Samantha stared at him, holding her towel out in front of her. Water puddled on the floor at her feet.

"Nephilim." Cody watched me.

I ducked my head, hoping he didn't know why I hadn't been able to control my powers on my own, hoping he couldn't see my guilt. I had no idea how long Damon's ghost would haunt me, but Cody deserved better.

"We—" Samantha cleared her throat, removing the huski-ness from it "—need more information than that."

The night-darkened forest is the perfect place to find peace. I walk through the trees, letting go of the stress that had tightened my neck and shoulders.

The evergreens muffle the noise from campus. Wind rus-tles through the branches, occasionally, moving them enough for a stray moonbeam to caress my face or light the path.

A twig cracks behind me.

I turn, searching the trees. Seeing nothing there, I move on. The dorms are in sight. I could teleport closer or even into my room, but I need space. The longer I stay at Phlox University, the smaller my room becomes.

Another branch snaps.

Something's following me.

Without thinking about it, flames ignite in my palm. Their blue glow lights up the forest surrounding me. I spin around to face my stalker.

Squinting, I search the trees, knowing that unless it moves, I won't be able to see it. I slowly turn back, hoping it will show itself.

Nothing.

I close my hand to extinguish the fire, but the flames spread. Fire dances over my skin, climbing my body.

I concentrate on the inferno, willing it to die. It blazes higher. Sparks flicker through the sky, carried by the breeze.

My breathing accelerates. Quick, shallow breaths make me lightheaded. My heart races. I stumble back. My fingers and toes tingle.

Pressing my lips together, I try to regulate my breathing. Hoping that with a clear head, I can regain control.

Staring at the blaze, I imagine it extinguishing. The fire diminishes, and I fold my fingers over the dying flames. That was too close. If I would have lost control here, the whole forest could have become a raging inferno.

I press my palm to my chest, trying to slow my heartbeat and steady my breath. I startle at the sudden chill. Pulling my hand back, I stare at it.

Frost coats my fingertips, spider-webbing out, spreading along my palm and scaling my arm. It crawls up my neck.

I thrash, fighting against the chill. The ice covers my mouth and nose. Climbing over my eyes, blurring them. I crumple to the ground.

My lungs burn. I try to crack the ice, but it presses over my lips and scurries down my throat. My vision darkens.

Someone strides toward me, nudging me with the toe of a boot.

A twig snaps.

Chapter 2

Friday morning, Aurelia knocked on our door. When I opened it, I waved at the first two Nephilim I'd seen yesterday. They looked at me like I was bubblegum stuck on the bottom of their shoes. Closing the door, I leaned against it. "What do they want with me?"

Aurelia nodded at my friends. "Mavros manipulated you and wove tall tales about many things, but he did not lie when he said there is more to the prophecy."

"Right." I stood with my hands on my hips. "Are you ready to tell me yet?"

"I cannot." Aurelia's chin lowered to her chest. "The elders have forbidden it until they reach an agreement."

I stared up at the ceiling, trying to overcome the anger that built inside of me each time I was told I couldn't know something about my life. "What are they scared of?"

Aurelia tilted her head, and I knew she was having a conversation with somebody else. "I am sorry. I cannot answer." She sat down, looking defeated. "The elders have agreed to send extra protection for you."

"What do you mean?" Samantha positioned herself on the couch next to Dan.

"Some of the dragons that Dacia saved will be here later today to help ensure her safety."

"Dragons on campus?" Dan snorted. "Are they going to hide behind the trees? Everyone will see them. How are they gonna help?"

Aurelia's lips turned up on one side. "They will be in human form."

"You remember she's a dragon." Cody stepped behind me and wrapped his arms around my waist. "Won't be a problem, will they?"

"Only dragons who have volunteered as her bodyguards will be here."

I remembered Acacia's arrogance even after I'd freed him, the feel of the green dragon's claws tearing through my muscles, and the rotten-flesh smell of the black dragon's breath. I rubbed my forehead. "Which ones?"

Samantha shuddered. Her face was pale, and she looked smaller. Dan's hand ran the length of her arm, up and down, but she didn't seem to notice.

"I do not know yet." Aurelia's golden eyes softened. "Every dragon owes you a debt of gratitude whether they were under Draconian's spell or not. We were not safe while he existed."

The fear in Draconian's eyes and the feel of the blade plunging into his chest flashed through my memory. Dragons were better off without him, but I hadn't wanted to kill him. His death was something I would carry with me forever.

Cody massaged my shoulders. "Time to go."

The Nephilim followed me to Scientific Computing. They sat at tables surrounding us in the lunchroom. They stood outside the doors while I was in my Shakespeare class.

On the way back to my room, the blonde Nephilim walked alongside me. I stepped closer to Aurelia. She grabbed my arm and pulled me behind her, baring her teeth at the intruder.

The blonde narrowed her sky-blue eyes at Aurelia and backed up. When we got to the dorm, the Nephilim followed the same routine as they had yesterday, blocking all the exits.

I stepped into my room and slumped against the wall, pulling a trembling hand through my hair. "I can't do this."

"They are here," Aurelia said as soon as she closed the door. "Shall we go meet them?"

Cody looked over the back of the couch at us. "Where?"

"In the mountains." Aurelia lowered her eyes. "Where Dacia freed them."

"No." I shook my head, backing away from her. Unless creatures had eaten it, Draconian's headless body would still be decomposing there.

"They are waiting for us." Aurelia reached for my hand. "It is far enough away that the Nephilim will not find you."

Cody jumped off the couch and stood between us. "She said no."

Aurelia growled at him. "Do not test me today." Her pupils were thin slashes, and smoke rolled out of her nostrils. "The Nephilim have pushed my dragon very close to the surface."

Cody backed off, looking away from her.

Seeing that she wouldn't budge on this, I grabbed Cody's hand. "Are you coming with us?" I asked Samantha and Dan.

Samantha shifted uncomfortably, not meeting my eyes. "I'm sorry. I can't … I can't go back there, and if they're in dragon form …" Her voice trailed off. "I just can't."

"I understand." I nodded at her, hoping she could hear the sincerity in my voice.

Dan wrapped his arm around her shoulders. "I'll stay here with her."

Aurelia took hold of my hand and held her other one out for Cody to take. He stepped forward cautiously. As soon as he slipped his hand into hers, she teleported us to the mountain clearing. Darkness surrounded me. I felt like my body was being stretched out and squeezed together at the same time.

As soon as daylight hit me, I pinched my eyes shut. Sweat beaded on my forehead, and I fought the urge to throw up.

The wind rustled through the trees, but there were no birdsongs, no critters skittering through the undergrowth. I wondered if it was because we had arrived so suddenly or because of the taint of Draconian. Would his vileness forever corrupt this area?

"He's not here, Dacia." Cody's voice was soft. His hands skimmed my arms.

As soon as I opened my eyes, my gaze was drawn to the spot where I'd killed Draconian. I saw him, sitting against the tree, blood spilling from his lips, staining his beard, fear on his face when he realized he was going to die. I looked down at my palms expecting to see them covered in gore.

"Dacia," Aurelia said.

I didn't acknowledge her, I kept replaying Draconian's death, feeling his blood coat my hands, watching the life slip from his body, seeing the light in his eyes dim.

"Dacia." Aurelia's voice was urgent.

Cody stepped in front of me and lifted my chin so I was looking at him. "They're here."

I pressed my eyes shut and drew some strength from him. Then I turned around. My heart raced, and my legs weakened, but I fought to keep my face from showing the terror that threatened to consume me.

The dragons formed an imposing line next to Aurelia. All of them were in human form. A massive black man stood on Aurelia's right. He towered over her. Long cornrows ran down his back, and his bronze eyes bored into mine.

I staggered back, and Cody braced me. "Malus Tribulus." His name was little more than a whisper, but he heard it and nodded.

Extending his hand, he said, "Call me Malcolm." His voice was low and resonant and brought with it flashes of his dragon.

Taking a deep breath, I placed my hand in his, feeling dwarfed by his size and strength. "Thank you for volunteering."

"After the terror I imparted on you and your friends"—he lowered his head, and the beads in his hair clanked together—"it was the least I could do."

A blue-haired guy stepped forward and pulled me against him. He breathed in deeply and moaned.

I tensed, jerking back, trying to free myself from his embrace. He held on longer than was called for, patting my back when he finally let go.

"Call him Val," Malcolm said.

Val dropped his chin to his chest. "I wanted to tell her my name." He grabbed my hand with one of his and rubbed his other one down my arm. "Call me Val." A bright smile engulfed his face.

"Okay." I stepped away from him and tried to return his smile. "Thank you."

Next in line was an albino lady with lavender eyes and white close-cropped hair. She smiled at Cody before nodding at me. "Names, as you know, have power." Her voice was soft and lyrical. "While I'm here, please call me Arianna."

"Thank you for helping my friends."

She bobbed her head. "Thank you for freeing us."

A dark-skinned man with crimson hair nodded. "Russ'll do."

"Thank you." I shook his hand and moved on to the next.

He glowered at me. His black hair was streaked with purple. My heart felt like it slammed to a stop. This dragon was the one I wanted here the least. Even though he'd never attacked me, this was the dragon I still had nightmares about.

"I don't care what you call me, but if you say my true name out loud again *ever*, you'll regret it." He stepped close to me and breathed in deeply, closing his eyes. "I can smell your fear." He stepped back, smirking at me. "You'd do well to remember it in my presence."

"Why—" my voice shook "— why are you here?"

"I'll not owe a human." He spat at my feet and turned away.

"Cash." Aurelia growled. Her features shimmered, and her teeth lengthened into fangs.

He backed away from her, but his amethyst eyes narrowed on me. I shuddered and turned toward the last dragon. He was an enormous man. His long brown hair was braided and fell to the middle of his back.

I had no idea who he was until he bowed and said, "Trickster, I am indebted to you."

"Tai—" I stopped before saying his full name.

"Tye's good." He bowed again and stepped back.

"The dragons here"—Aurelia waved her arm at them—"will be enrolled in your classes. They will be your constant companions."

I tugged my hand through my hair. "Is all this necessary?"

"Yes," Tye said. In dragon form, his voice had been sibilant, but as a human, it was commanding. "We can't let you fall to d—"

"Tye." A golden haze shimmered around Aurelia, spinning like a vortex, lifting leaves and debris from the ground. She emerged from the miasma fully transformed. The rubble settled around her, and she prowled forward.

Cody's hand tightened on mine.

"Enough." Aurelia's tail swished through the air, and she pawed at the dirt. Deep claw marks gouged the ground.

Arianna stepped between Tye and Aurelia. "She deserves the truth."

"She does." Aurelia lowered her head. "For now, it has been forbidden." Her crest flattened, and she morphed into a human again.

The other dragons grumbled, until Malcolm finally said, "We'll agree to keep her in the dark unless it puts us in danger."

Aurelia tossed her hair over her shoulder and turned to me. "There are four other dragons here. They will keep an eye on you and your friends but have chosen to remain unseen."

All the dragons I'd faced flashed through my mind. There had been fifteen under Draconian's control and one we had warned to stay away. I didn't like that there were others here that I couldn't see or sense. The unknown was scary, especially when it involved invisible dragons who might be like Acacia and hold a grudge.

Chapter 3

The sun sank behind the mountains as Cody and I walked to the student center surrounded by Tye, Cash, Malcolm, and Val. When the breeze picked up, I shivered, and Cody pulled me against his side.

The other two dragons Aurelia had introduced me to this afternoon were with Samantha and Dan in Althea. Arianna had protected them when I fought Draconian, and Russ was a father who I'd returned to his son. I felt my friends would be safest with them. I wanted to keep Cash as far from any other humans as I could, but I hated having him with me.

He looked down on me like I was an insignificant ant that he was contemplating stomping to death. His posture and scowl made it clear he wanted nothing to do with anyone.

The Nephilim trailed behind us, constantly watching me. They stayed back from my bodyguards. Whether they feared them or didn't want a confrontation, I wasn't sure.

Val held the door to Sedum Hall open. As I walked past him, he clasped my shoulder and smiled at me.

I stood in line looking at the food and wondering if I could stomach any of it. Since sending Mavros back to the Abyss, I hadn't had much of an appetite, and it was starting to show. My cheeks were sunk in, and dark rings surrounded my eyes.

"Eat." Cody nudged me forward. "Please."

I scooped some garden pasta into a bowl and grabbed a slice of cheesy garlic bread. Cody frowned at my tray and piled extra food on his. We sat at a table against the wall so I could keep an eye on all of the people watching me.

Cash pulled out the chair beside me, but Malcolm grabbed his arm and pointed at the table next to ours. "Let them be."

Cash's pupils slitted, and his muscles tensed. Tye stood next to Malcolm, and Cash backed down but not before glowering at me.

The beautiful people sat at the tables surrounding us. There seemed to be more of them now than there were earlier. Eight people fit comfortably at each round table. The Nephilim filled four tables with more standing guard at the exits.

I pushed the noodles around in my bowl, feeling like I might throw up if I put them in my mouth. Shoving my tray forward, I laid my head on the table.

"Dacia." Cody rubbed my back. "You've gotta eat."

I shook my head. "I can't." I sat up and looked at him. "What do they want? Why's it so bad that nobody can tell me?"

"Don't know." His hand stopped moving along my spine. "Grabbed this for you." He lifted a chocolate chip cookie off his tray. "It's your weakness, remember?"

I took it from him and to make him happy, nibbled on it. "They always have been." That wasn't the truth anymore, though. Draconian, his dragons, and Mavros had all proven to me that my true weaknesses were my friends. I'd do anything to keep them safe, including letting the world burn.

Cassandra and Bryce stopped at our table, pulled out chairs, and sat. Alvin and Vanessa, two of their closest friends, kept walking. They looked over their shoulders at us and whispered to each other. In my first semester here, I'd dubbed the four of them the Potato Heads because they were always together and always giving me grief.

"What's with all this?" Cassandra waved her fork at the dragons. "Are you trying to start a gang war?"

I tilted my head, shaking it at her. "Why are you sitting here?" The desperation in my voice was obvious even to me. I pointed at several empty tables and the one her friends had chosen.

"I'm sorry." She set her fork down and leaned forward, looking first at me then at Cody. "For all of it." Her voice lowered. "I don't remember everything, but what I do …" She cleared her throat. "I was horrible. Because of some dreams. Because of a … a monster?" Her voice rose at the end, turning it into a question. She looked at me like she hoped I could answer it for her.

"Really don't remember?" Cody asked.

She peeled the wrapper off of her straw and shoved it into her glass. Then she picked up the wrapper. She folded the paper, smoothed it out, and folded it again. I couldn't remember ever seeing her so insecure. "Bits and pieces." She glanced at the other tables. "Enough to know this can't be good."

"For what it's worth"—Bryce's voice was quiet—"I'm sorry, too."

Cody shook his head. "Unbelievable." He leaned back in his chair, moving as far from them as he could without getting up. "Think you're forgiven?"

"No." Bryce shook his head and laughed somberly. "I don't deserve your forgiveness. But, if it makes you feel any better, my hand is in constant pain. Especially when it rains."

"Good." Cody's voice was harsh, his eyes cold. This was not the Cody I knew. This was anger and hurt and betrayal that had festered inside of him for far too long.

I remembered the pain in Bryce's scream when I'd crushed his hand. It had stopped him from punching Cody again, but I hadn't known what I was doing, and I'd never forgiven myself for it. "Let me see it."

Bryce slid his hand over the table. I set mine on top of it, and his muscles tightened in response. Thinking about life, I sent my power into him. His body relaxed, and he sighed. He wiggled his fingers, stretching them, then clenching them into a fist. He held his hand in front of him, massaging it. "Thanks, but why would you do that?"

"I told you—" I looked down at the table "—I never meant to hurt you."

"You should have." He opened his Gatorade. "I'd planned to hurt you." He screwed the lid back on and slid the bottle from hand to hand across the table. "I kept hearing a voice telling me you were evil and you needed stopped." He caught his drink and looked up at me. "I don't know why I listened."

"Demon—" Cody leaned forward "—controlled Cassandra. Maybe you."

Cassandra crumpled the wrapper and clenched it in her fist. "A demon controlled me?" Her voice rose, and Bryce clamped his hand down on her arm.

"Yes." I massaged my forehead, not really understanding how I'd gotten into this conversation with them. "He tried to kill me. I won. Yay me."

Bryce leaned so far over the table he was practically lying on it. "You killed a demon."

Cody lifted up two fingers.

Pushing them down, I said, "None. I returned them to the Abyss."

"So, what happened to Damon?" Cassandra's ice-blue eyes were alight with interest.

My throat went dry. She'd been my enemy since the first day I arrived on campus. How much did I want her to know? I took a long drink of water, partly to wet my throat and partly to avoid the question.

"Abyss." Cody squeezed my thigh.

"But—" Cassandra's perfectly plucked eyebrows pinched together "—I thought you liked him."

I slammed my chair back and jumped up. "I gotta go." I darted for the doors. I heard other chairs scrape across the tile floor and footsteps keeping time with mine, but I didn't turn around to see who was following me.

Pushing through the cafeteria doors, I ran out into the evening. As soon as the cool air hit my face, I stopped. Tears wetted my cheeks. I clutched my stomach and sobbed. Strong arms wrapped around me, pulling me close.

I started to settle back against him before realizing it wasn't Cody. "Let go!"

The arms pulled back, and I spun around. Val lifted his hands in the air, backing away. "Sorry. I thought it would fix you." He pointed at the corner of his eye.

Wiping my tears away, I said, "Nothing's going to fix me."

Cody walked up with Malcolm and Cash. His face was the stony mask he'd worn so often when Mavros was on Earth.

"The girl apologizes." Malcolm growled.

The Nephilim gathered outside the student center. I had no idea what they were capable of or what they wanted, but their sheer numbers terrified me.

I nodded at the Nephilim, drawing my guards' attention to them. "Let's go before they realize they outnumber us six to one."

Cash stood with his arms folded over his chest, glaring at me. "You don't think very highly of us if you think they can defeat us."

Stepping closer to him, I shoved my finger into his pecs. "Not of you," I said through clenched teeth. "You can't be grateful that I freed you because you're too arrogant to admit you needed help."

"You worthless human." He shoved my hand away.

I turned my back on him, knowing it would infuriate him. "We can't cause a scene unless you want every human to know about you all."

Val laughed, a deep rumble that started quiet and built up. "She got you there."

Tye ushered Cody and me in front of him, keeping himself positioned between us and Cash. Then he herded us back to the dorm.

As soon as we were in our room, I said, "I'm sorry, Cody."

He walked past me and plopped down in Cookie Monster. "Yeah, hear that a lot."

Knowing he didn't want me near him, I sat in Big Bird. "I didn't expect the questions or the guilt. I did like him, and I sent him to Hell."

"He planned to kill us, Dacia." The vein in his neck bulged, and his lip curled up.

"I know." I stared at my hands. He had every right to be mad at me, but I couldn't help the way I felt. "Why do you stay? All I do is hurt you."

"Parta me gets it. Had friends with bad intentions. Was okay when they kept it from me." He leaned back, looking any-where but at me. "Parta me wonders if he has a hold on you still." He let out a deep breath. "Every time you grieve for him, it cuts deep."

My head dropped further, and tears spilled over, blurring my vision. "I'm trying, Cody. I really am." A tear dripped off the tip of my nose. "She caught me off guard."

"Falcon Lake?"

"Really?" I snorted. "With Cash?"

He scooted to the edge of the chair. "No. You promised. Remember?"

He was serious. I could see it in his face. I remembered telling him that no matter what monster I was facing, we needed to make time for ourselves. We needed that time away to recharge. "Give me your hand." As soon as his fingers grazed mine, I teleported us to the trees surrounding the lake.

The half-moon brightened the night sky but not enough to cover the stars. Millions of them lit up the heavens. Their tiny flickering lights eased the knot of tension between my shoulder blades.

I slid my arm around Cody's waist. "The dragons will be pissed when they find out about this."

"If."

A smile lifted my lips. "Yeah … if."

We walked hand in hand to the water's edge. It gently lapped against the rocky shore. The smell of moss and pine helped relax me further.

I slid my hand out of Cody's and into his back pocket. "Thank you."

"For what?" He stopped walking and looked down at me.

Waving my arm at the mountains and lake, I said, "For this. For thinking of getting away."

The breeze blew my hair across my face, and Cody brushed it back, letting his hand linger, gently caressing my cheek with his thumb. His eyes sparkled even in the darkness.

Lifting onto my toes, I wrapped my arms around his neck and swept my lips over his. One of his hands slid around my waist. The other twined through my hair. He pressed his mouth down on mine. A low moan escaped from deep in his throat, sending a flash of desire through me. He clutched me tighter, pressing our bodies together. His hand slid under my sweat-shirt. Tingles followed his touch.

He lifted me, and I wrapped my legs around his waist, tangling my hands in his hair. I nudged his head back and trailed kisses over his chin and along his neck.

Cody knelt, laying me on the ground. He hovered over me, and I pulled him down, sliding my hands under his shirt, running them over his ribs and up his back. He kissed along my jawline to my ear.

"I love you," he breathed. His teeth grazed my neck.

My eyes shot open, and my heart raced. I half-expected to find Mavros kissing my neck. When I saw it was still Cody, I said, "I love you, too."

Somebody cleared their throat. Cody rolled to the side. I clutched his hand and looked up at the blonde Nephilim.

"And, I love that you're finally alone." She knelt beside us, not close enough to touch me, but closer than I'd like. Looking at Cody, she added, "Well, not alone, but no dragons."

I sat up, never losing contact with Cody. If I needed to, I wanted to be able to teleport us away. "What do you want?"

She cocked her head, pursing her lips. "The dragons haven't told you?"

"No." I heard the frustration in my voice. "The elders won't allow them to."

"Interesting." She sat back, wrapping her arms around her legs.

I felt like the move was deliberate, intended to show me she meant no harm, but I didn't trust her.

"What?" Cody asked.

While she focused on him, I tried to read her aura. A blinding light filled my vision, and my power was repelled.

She narrowed her eyes at me. "That won't work."

"It helps me tell if people are good or evil." I shrugged.

"You'll have to let my actions determine that." She smiled at me, and if I hadn't met Mavros, I might have believed the sincerity in her expression. "The prophecy says: The chosen will emerge with powers unrivaled in this world. To fight a demon from the Abyss is the savior's onus."

She paused, and I said, "Been there. Done that." I held up two fingers. "Twice."

She nodded slowly. "Fail and the world will perish. Succeed and 999 years before the cycle begins anew."

"Right." Cody scooted closer to me, draping his arm over my shoulder. "We know that."

"Patience is a virtue." She picked up a rock, studying it, even though it was too dark for a normal person to make out any details.

I rested one hand on Cody's knee and shoved the other into my hoodie's pouch. "We're both running low on patience lately. Demons, Nephilim, dragons. They'll do that to a person."

"One champion reigns amassing powers unparalleled." Tossing the rock over her shoulder, she pointed at me. "That's you, by the way. Evil endeavors to corrupt the savior's soul."

I shivered. Was that why Draconian and Mavros had entered my life so soon after I defeated Nefarious? Draconian hadn't wanted to kill me. He'd wanted me to be his protégée. Mavros had wanted me by his side, not dead.

"Victorious, the powers of light"—she pointed at herself—"fade to shadow. Darkness reigns over the Earth."

I leaned against Cody. "Great."

"We are not here to hurt you." Her voice was soft and understanding. "We have several sanctuaries where you would be safe. You could live your life without these trials."

Cody rubbed my arm. "Don't wanna hurt her, just imprison her."

"Her safety is our priority." She tilted her head to the side and looked at him like he should have realized that.

To not have to fight monsters would be a dream come true, but one thing I'd learned since starting college was not to trust everyone who offered their help. "At what cost?" A cloud blew in front of the moon. "And what is your name anyway?"

She smiled. "Diana."

"Cost?" Cody's voice was lower than normal. He obviously wasn't buying what she was selling.

"A cost I'd think you'd both like to pay." She picked up another rock. "Safety. Peace. No more fear."

I snorted. "Death offered me the same. I turned him down, too."

Her mouth went slack, and her eyes widened. "You'd rather have your freedom than save the world."

"No." I shook my head. "I prefer both." I tightened my grip on Cody's leg and teleported us back to my room.

Chapter 4

Aurelia's Wrath

Cody and I landed on the floor with a thump. I blinked back the bright fluorescent lights and climbed to my feet, brushing off my jeans, then held my hand down to Cody and helped him up.

A low growl rumbled through the room, alerting us to Aurelia's and Malcolm's sudden but not unexpected appearance in my room. They stood between us and the door. Even though he dwarfed her, she seemed to take up more space. Her pupils were slits. Gold scales peppered her arms and cheeks. "Where have you been?" Her voice sounded more like her dragon's than her human's.

"Falcon Lake." Cody's eyebrows lifted.

I sat on the couch, not wanting to have this conversation but knowing it couldn't be avoided. "Talking to Diana."

Malcolm chuckled. "So … you know the prophecy?"

"Yep." The p popped out of my mouth.

"Good." He nodded and pointed at Big Bird.

I waved my hand at the chair. "Sure."

He sat down and pulled the sleeves of his tan sweater up to his elbows. Then folded his hands together, steepling them against his chin.

Aurelia paced from the door to the window and back again. Her scales slowly diminished.

I leaned my head against the back of the couch and stared at the ceiling. "When Mavros was here, Cody and I made a pact that we would get some time to ourselves no matter what creatures were tormenting me." I let out a huff of air. "I figure I can keep myself and somebody else safe most of the time."

"Maybe." Aurelia's voice was closer to normal. "What if your dreams come to fruition? How will you protect him if you cannot control your powers?"

I jumped up. "What do you want from me? I know what the Nephilim want now … to cage me. Is that what you want?" Tears burned the back of my eyes.

She plopped down in Cookie Monster and dropped her chin to her chest. "No, Dacia. Please do not think that about me. I thought they had taken you." She wouldn't look me in the eyes. "I thought we had failed you."

Malcolm nodded at me. His expression was grim. "Past experience should've made me realize it'd be hard to keep an eye on you." He smiled, and for the first time, I realized he had fangs. "But, if you'd have been injured, I could've smelled your blood thirty miles away."

Cody's face paled, and my stomach rolled. "Really?" I gulped down a lungful of air. "Thirty miles?"

He shrugged. "I've tasted your blood. Maybe fifty." His eyes flashed. "Same with the boy."

Cody sat up taller, narrowing his eyes at Malcolm.

"I mean no offense." Malcolm chuckled, a deep, rumbling sound. "You're at least two thousand years younger than me, maybe more. I forget how old I am."

"You tasted my blood?" My lip curled in disgust.

"Licked it off my claws." He put his fingers to his mouth and kissed them, opening his hand as he pulled it away. "That … I won't forget … ever."

"Malcolm." Aurelia growled.

I shivered. Cody's hands clenched, and he glared at Malcolm.

"I'm a dragon, and your blood is powerful." He buffed his fingernails on his sleeve, then held them in front of him. "Waste not, want not."

Pink blossoms cover the trees. The air smells sweet. Gray clouds promise spring showers. I put my hand on Cody's arm, and we stroll along the path. There's no fear of attack. No monsters hunting me. Nothing haunting my dreams.

My days run together, one blending into the next. I spend my time wandering the massive grounds, staring at the rolling hills, trying to figure out where I am. I paint and read, but without purpose, I feel lost.

The Nephilim allow Cody to come and go as he pleases, but they guard the exits, keeping me trapped inside. I cannot force my way out. My magic is bound here, and without it, I no longer know who I am.

The loss opens a hole inside of me that fills with hopelessness and despair. Each day it builds up, pushing out any happiness I might have found here.

Cody leads me to a bench that overlooks a pond. Swans swim languorously across the water, creating ripples on the surface. It's a beautiful setting, but anger eats at me from the inside, hardening me, taking everything that should bring me joy, and twisting it.

He brushes the back of his hand along my cheek. "You don't smile anymore."

"I should be happy." I lift one shoulder in a half-hearted shrug. "But I feel so … broken."

The alarm clock rang, startling me out of my dream. I reached across Cody to turn it off. Once I did, he pulled me on top of him. "How'd you sleep?"

I laid my head on his shoulder and ran my hand over his chest. "I dreamed about the Nephilim's sanctuary."

"And?" There was something in his voice. I thought it might be hope, but was it hope that I'd go there or that I wouldn't?

"It's beautiful, peaceful"—I pinched my eyes shut, hoping he would understand—"and all wrong for me."

He held his hand over mine. His heart pulsed against my palm. "Will they leave you alone?"

"I doubt it." I sat up. "I'm gonna shower. Then we can figure out what to do today." Grabbing my stuff, I looked into the lofts and realized Samantha and Dan weren't there. *Aurelia.* I projected the empty beds to her.

They are in Cody and Dan's room. Arianna and Russ are watching them.

Thank you.

I stepped into the hall, and somebody grabbed my arm, spinning me around.

Cash glared at me. "That stunt you pulled last night." He tightened his grip. "Don't let it happen again."

Diana and the dark-haired Nephilim watched us from near the staircase, but the rest of the hallway was still empty.

"Let go of me, Cash." I froze my arm.

He yanked his hand back. His nostrils flared, and the veins in his neck bulged.

I turned my back on him and strolled down the hall, trying to look strong and in control. I waved at the Nephilim as I walked past. As soon as I shut the door to the bathroom, I crumpled against the wall. Cash was dangerous, volatile. I needed to show him I wasn't afraid of him so he'd back off. But in truth, I wasn't scared of him. I was petrified.

By the time I finished my shower, Val had replaced Cash as the hall monitor. He threw his arm over my shoulders and leaned in, sniffing my hair. "You smell good." I pulled my head back, but he pressed closer. "So, uh, last night you learned about the prophecy. Didn't ya?" He patted my arm like an excited little kid. "Pretty cool, huh?"

I ducked under his arm, wishing he knew something about personal space. "What about it is cool?"

"Really?" He stood with his hand on his hip, tilting his head until it practically rested on his shoulder. "You're like the most powerful human on the planet. It's awesome." The last word was practically sung. He stepped inside my bubble again and rubbed my head. "Don't you think?"

I pulled away from him. "I just want to be normal."

"We can make that happen," the dark-haired Nephilim said in a voice like an angel's.

I jabbed my finger at her. "No." The word came out low and harsh. "Leave me alone." I stormed down the hall and into my room, slamming the door behind me.

Aurelia and Cody stared at me.

"You okay?" Cody asked.

I dropped the bathroom bag on the floor and slid my hand through my wet hair. "I've had it with Nephilim and dragons."

Aurelia sat up straighter. "What happened?"

"Cash scares me." I plopped down next to Cody. "Val is touchy, feely. And the Nephilim … they won't leave until I go with them."

Cody drove his car along the mountain road, hugging the curves. I stared out my window, wondering which dragons were trailing us and how many Nephilim we'd have to contend with.

We parked in front of The Avalanche and walked inside hand in hand. Cody's thumb rubbed along mine but did nothing to ease my nerves. The hostess led us to a table too close to the door for my liking. Every time it opened, I was momentarily blinded when I glanced at the silhouette standing there.

My leg bounced up and down. I jumped when our waitress set my pop on the table. She smiled and shook her head as she took our orders.

One side of Cody's mouth lifted, and he softly huffed. "Relax." He reached his hand across the table, and I placed mine in it. "Nothing'll happen while we're eating."

I closed my eyes and breathed deeply, nodding at him. He was right. Neither the dragons nor the Nephilim wanted their existence known.

After I ate about a third of my chicken wrap, I pushed my plate away. Cody shook his head. "Please eat."

I dragged my plate back and picked at my food. I knew Cody was worried, but even the smell of food made my stomach roll. I'd already eaten more today than in the last few weeks. He watched me, analyzing every nibble.

When the waitress came by again, Cody ordered a brownie sundae with two spoons. She brought it by a few minutes later and put it in the center of the table. "Enjoy." She cleared the empty dishes off the table, not even reaching for mine.

Cody watched me. His spoon sat untouched in front of him.

"Aren't you going to eat it?" I asked.

He nodded toward my spoon. "You first."

It looked delicious, and I hated to see it go to waste. So even though my stomach protested, I took a bite. When Cody still didn't reach for his spoon, I took a couple more.

He grinned and shoved a big bite into his mouth. Whipped cream coated his lips.

The smile that crossed my face in response was genuine. I loved seeing the sparkle in his eyes.

After lunch, we walked around town, looking in shop windows. There were enough people out and about that it wasn't blatantly obvious the Nephilim were following us. We turned onto a side street, and the crowds thinned. My grip on Cody's hand tightened, and I pulled him to a stop. My heart pounded against my chest, and my stomach dropped.

Three men strode toward us. They were tall and muscular, dressed in black leather jackets and jeans. Their expressions were grim. The dark-skinned man in the middle slipped his hand inside his coat. The other two flexed their fingers.

Nephilim. The word reverberated through my skull, a warning from one of my guards.

I looked over my shoulder. Three more strolled along the sidewalk, closing in on us. I pulled Cody behind me and backed up against the side of the nearest building. Looking up and down the street, I didn't see anybody else. I pictured Cody's car and clenched his hand in mine.

Nothing happened.

My heart thundered in my chest, drowning out all other sounds. *No, no, no. Not now. Please, not now.*

I tried again.

My heart pulsed faster. My breathing accelerated.

Nothing.

I reached for my powers, trying to call a flame to life. Not even a spark responded to my plea.

"Cody—" my voice caught "—they're gone."

"Who's gone?"

I watched the Nephilim approach and wondered how I'd get us out of this. "My powers."

"Relax." He massaged my shoulders, kneading the tension there. "Try again."

Taking a deep breath, I closed my eyes and pictured the boardwalk in front of The Avalanche. Nothing. Not even a flicker.

Cody's grip on my shoulders tightened, and I opened my eyes. Malcolm, Tye, Val, and Cash surrounded us.

"She isn't going with you." Malcolm's deep, rumbling voice reminded me of a roar.

The dark Nephilim pulled his hand out of his jacket and held it out in front of him. "She will eventually. We cannot allow her power to remain unchecked."

Tye grabbed my arm. *Be ready.* His voice broke into my thoughts.

I slid my hand along my shoulder until bumping against Cody's warm skin. Then I slipped my fingers into his.

"What happened to free will?" Malcolm asked. "Isn't that why your ancestors fell?"

"Free will shouldn't be given to everyone," a Nephilim from the other group answered. His honey-colored hair was pulled back in a tight ponytail.

"Why?" Cody sounded angry. "She fought evil, freed dragons, protected everyone. Doesn't she deserve the life she wants?"

The dark-skinned Nephilim lowered his head, shaking it. "We cannot take that risk."

Tye squeezed my arm, and I tightened my grip on Cody's hand. My body was sucked in and stretched out. The world spun, and when I opened my eyes, the three of us stood in my room.

I stumbled to the couch, nearly falling onto it. My body shook from the adrenaline rushing through it. "Thanks," I said to Tye. "My magic failed."

He cocked his head, and his braid slid over his shoulder. "Magic doesn't fail."

"Hers did." Cody sat beside me, wrapping his arm around me and drawing me closer.

"No." Tye shook his head. "Magic doesn't fail. Somehow somebody blocked it." He looked me in the eyes. His were green with brown flecks. "Trust no one."

Chapter 5

Dream Come True Or Nightmare?

*M*y bodyguards are nowhere to be seen as I stroll across campus. For once, I feel like I can breathe. Leaves litter the path, blowing and tumbling over the sidewalks, collecting in deep mounds. I kick up a pile of them and watch as the wind carries them away.

I look at the ground as I walk, stuck in my thoughts. I know that I can't let the Nephilim take me, but I don't know how to keep it from happening. And, to be honest, sometimes the life they're offering appeals to me.

I see a pair of black boots in front of me and look up to avoid running into their owner. My heart and feet slam to a stop at the same time.

Mavros smiles at me and slides his arms around my waist. "I've missed you."

I can't stop the snort before it escapes my mouth. "You said I never meant anything to you." I step away from him. "You said it was a game."

"That was before I knew better." He tucks his hands into his pockets and looks at the ground. "I stayed with you until the Abyss sucked me back into it." His features distort until he looks like Damon. "I tried to save you."

I swallow a sob at seeing my friend alive.

"My gift isn't life. I couldn't bring you back from Death's clutches." His black eyes moisten. "I've never tried to save someone before." He tucks a strand of hair behind my ear.

His touch sends a bolt of electricity through me. I back away from him before I forget myself. "I can't believe you." I cross my arms. "I can't trust you."

"I know." His voice is soft and disappointed.

I walk a couple steps away, then spin around. "Why are you here? How?"

"I was—" His mouth flounders but nothing comes out. A snarl lifts his lip. "Think, Dacia."

Cocking my head, I look at him. My eyebrows pull together as I try to figure out what game he's playing now.

"There's only one way I can be."

I press my fingers over my lips. "Who? Who summoned you? Why?"

He steps closer to me. "That's what you need to figure out." His fingers slide along mine. "Soon. Before the imbecile makes me hurt you." Leaning in, he whispers in my ear. "I don't want to watch you die again."

Walking away, he shifts from Damon to Mavros to the panther. Darkness swallows him.

My eyes snapped open. "No." The word was a panicked whisper, but Cody heard it.

"You okay?" he asked as he sat up.

I told him about my dream, not surprised to watch him slip his mask back into place.

"Never gonna end." He combed his fingers through his hair, and when he finished, it looked perfect. Mine would've looked like a clown's wig. "Thought you'd move on. Not if he's back."

Staring into his eyes, I cupped his cheek. "I don't want him, Cody. I want you."

"Yeah." He shook his head. "But you mourn him."

I tucked my chin against my chest. "I don't want him here, though."

Cody, Samantha, Dan, and I stayed on campus all day Sunday. I'd had enough excitement Saturday, and with the possibility of Mavros hanging around, I didn't want to press my luck. We went to Lupine Fieldhouse, and my guards joined us in a game of basketball. For being new to the sport, they caught on quickly.

Russ dribbled the ball down the court with me guarding him. "You doing okay?"

"Yeah." I looked over my shoulder, then back at him. My eyebrows pinched together. "Why wouldn't I be?" I swatted at the ball, and he dribbled it behind his back.

"Nice try." He slowed, keeping the ball out of my reach. "Your powers."

"Oh." I stopped, and he plowed into me. I fell, sliding on my butt across the floor.

He passed the ball to Arianna and lowered his hand to me. "Sorry." His amber eyes met mine, and I saw flashes of his life. His hatchling flying through the clouds beside him, his time with Draconian, him prowling toward me against his wishes, then flying away free.

Blinking back the images, I sensed his loyalty and gratitude. "I'm sorry. I didn't mean to intrude."

"You couldn't have done it without my consent." He hauled me to my feet and leaned closer, whispering, "I want you to know you can trust me." Louder, he added, "Looks like your powers are working."

Cash passed the ball to Russ. I knocked it down and sprinted after it, beating them both to it. I took off down the court, picked the ball up, lifted my arm to make the layup, and dropped it. I skidded to a halt, staring into the hall.

Nobody was there, but I swore I'd seen Mavros. I bent over to catch my breath and steady myself.

Cody rested his hand on my back. "Okay?"

"Yeah." My breathing was heavy. "I thought I saw him." I pointed to where he'd been watching me.

His fingers clenched against my back. "Wanna go?"

"Do you need to rest, or are we going to play?" The condescension in Cash's voice was a challenge I refused to back down from.

I stared into his eyes. "Let's go." I stood in front of him while he threw the ball in.

He passed it to Dan, then shoved me out of his way when he ran in. "Pathetic."

I jogged down the court alongside Malcolm. His cornrows bounced against his back.

"Where's Aurelia been?" I asked him.

He looked at me out of the sides of his eyes. "Guarding you with the others, with the elders, or trying to save you from the Nephilim." He ran off to play post position.

I guarded Arianna. "How is Aurelia trying to save me?"

She looked from me to Malcolm. He shrugged and grinned at her, showing his fangs. She shook her head. "You'll have to ask her."

"I've tried." My insides felt hollowed out. "She never answers."

Chapter 6

Back To It

When classes resumed Monday, they followed the same pattern as the week before. Nephilim trailed behind me, blocking the exits to every building, every classroom. Dragons surrounded me. Cash glared daggers at me, and Val constantly moved into my personal space. Aurelia was nowhere to be seen, and when I tried to contact her, I got no response.

Bryce and Cassandra joined us for lunch like it was the most natural thing in the world for them to sit with us. Bryce smiled at me, flexing his fingers. "My hand's as good as new. Maybe better. Thanks."

I didn't know how to react to that. If not for me, it wouldn't have been crushed in the first place. "I'm sorry I didn't fix it sooner."

"No worries." He smiled before biting off a chunk of his sandwich.

Cassandra leaned in toward me. "So, there's this tall, dark, and handsome guy wandering around campus."

I looked at Bryce and raised my eyebrows.

"No, no, no." She shook her head, and her black ponytail whipped from side to side. "He looks like one of yours." She waved her hand toward the Nephilim and the dragons.

The dragons tilted their heads ever so slightly but showed no other sign that they were paying attention to the conversation at our table.

My stomach plummeted. "If I didn't know any better, I'd guess Mavros, but—" closing my eyes, I rubbed the back of my neck "—it couldn't be him. He can't be back. Can he?"

Cody shook his head. "Hope not."

"So, who's he?" Cassandra tilted her head.

"Demon." Cody dropped his fork on his tray and donned his impenetrable mask. "Stay away."

She narrowed her ice-blue eyes at him. "I haven't seen you look that way since Damon was here. So, what gives?"

"Butt out." Dan didn't look up from his food.

Bryce straightened. A muscle in his jaw ticked.

"It's a long story." Samantha sighed. "This isn't the place for it. And, it's Dacia's to tell."

I rested my hand on Cody's leg. Samantha was right that this wasn't the place for it, but if I didn't say something, the questions would keep coming. It would be better to just get the conversation over with so that Cassandra and Bryce wouldn't keep bringing it up. "Mavros is Damon."

"What?" Cassandra's mouth hung open.

Bryce rubbed his chin. "I thought you got rid of him."

"I did." A weight settled over me, making me feel like Atlas. "If it's really him, then somebody summoned him here."

Samantha's eyes were filled with sorrow. "At least if he's back, he probably won't be after your heart this time."

"Nah." I pulled my hand through my hair. "If he's here, he's here to kill me."

"You don't know that." Cody dragged his hand down his face.

I opened my mouth, and he held his hand out. "Don't. Just don't. Seen what he can do to you."

"Well"—Cassandra stood and grabbed Bryce's hand—"it's obvious there are a lot of things we don't know. If you wanna talk, we'll listen."

Samantha held her sandwich in front of her and watched Cassandra sashay away. "What exactly is going on with them anyway?"

"Yeah." Dan nodded. His auburn hair brushed his eyebrows and curled at the nape of his neck. "I've seen a lot of weird things since meeting you all, but that"—he hooked his thumb over his shoulder—"beats them all."

I pushed my food around with my fork. "I need to read their auras. Figure out what to do." And pray that Mavros isn't back.

After lunch, my entourage, minus Russ and Arianna, followed me to Shakespeare. Malcolm walked beside me and put his hand on my shoulder. "We need to talk."

Pressing my eyes shut, I lowered my head. I didn't want to talk to Malcolm about Mavros. Even though Aurelia trusted him implicitly, I wasn't sure what to think of him. He'd tasted my blood and enjoyed it. He'd wanted to kill me and my friends. He was with me or watching me constantly. I wanted to trust him, but I wasn't there yet. "Okay, shoot."

"Is he back?" He stared down into my eyes, and I wondered if he could somehow sense the truth.

I shook my head. "I hope not." I thought about Cody's mask and what Mavros' return would do to him.

"You'll let us know." He squeezed my shoulder harder than was necessary. "Won't you?"

I tried to pull away from his grip, but he held on. "If I see him, you'll be the first to know." Narrowing my eyes at him, I said, "Now, let go of me."

He smirked at me, letting his fangs show, reminding me who he was, and dropped his hand.

I walked to my desk wondering how much longer I could hide the truth from Malcolm, but before I said anything to him, I wanted to either be positive Mavros had returned or talk to Aurelia.

Val and Cash sat to either side of me. Cash angled himself away, clearly not wanting to be near me, but I didn't think he trusted me enough to sit in front of me with his back exposed. Val sat so close to me that his arm brushed against mine. Malcolm and Tye took the chairs in front of me. Their broad shoulders formed an impenetrable wall.

Val leaned closer and sniffed me. I pushed him back while pulling my head away from him. He was nice enough, but he made me uncomfortable.

"Sorry." He was still too close. "You just smell so good. Is it your perfume?"

My nose scrunched up. "I don't wear perfume."

"It's her power, you imbecile." Cash shook his head and huffed.

I turned away from Val and stared at Cash. "You can smell my power?"

"A few of the lucky ones have even tasted it." He leaned in and breathed deeply like he was smelling a juicy steak. "I wouldn't have wasted a drop." Menace radiated off of him.

My eyes widened, and I pulled away from him, crashing into Val. The room seemed to shrink in on me.

Cash's mouth turned up in a sneer. "I don't know how Malcolm resists taking more." He licked his lips, and his pupils elongated.

"Cash." Malcolm's voice was the rumbling of distant thunder, low, menacing. He didn't turn around, but the single word was enough to make Cash pull back and look away from me.

I shivered and stared at Malcolm's back, wondering if he thirsted for my blood.

"I made a promise to protect you." Malcolm turned around and looked at me, and I wondered if he could read my thoughts.

"I don't break my vows. Now, quit worrying. You reek of fear, and it makes you smell even better." He faced forward.

Val slung his arm around my shoulders and pulled me against him. "You don't need to worry about him." He nodded at Malcolm. "He's honorable."

Even with four dragons surrounding me, Diana approached. "Dacia"—she stood between Malcolm and Val—"we really need to talk."

Malcolm bared his fangs at her, but she didn't back down. I couldn't help but wonder how she'd react if he was in his dragon form. Val lifted his arm and positioned himself so his body blocked me.

I peered at her over his shoulder. "Why?" I grabbed my book, notepad, and pen from my bag. "I don't do well in cages. It won't work for me."

She leaned closer and whispered, "Don't you care about the consequences?" Her face slackened, and she slowly shook her head. "Are you really selfish enough to put your happiness above the fate of the world?"

My mouth dropped open, and I stared at her. She knew what I'd been through to save the world and everyone in it. How could she think for one minute that I didn't care? I'd nearly died to save the planet from Nefarious. My friends had been taken prisoner and nearly killed by Draconian before I ended his life. Then less than a month ago, I'd killed myself to make sure life would go on for everyone else. I hadn't known Death would give me a reprieve, and even so, I'd sacrificed everything.

Cash growled, a deep, ominous sound, and Diana backed up a step. His pupils were slits in his amethyst eyes. "She cares more for this godforsaken planet than you and yours ever will." He started to get up, but Tye pressed down on his leg. "Where were you when Draconian was seizing control of the dragons? None of you fought to help us." He clutched the desk. "How many of you are there? But this lone girl who'd barely been trained freed us."

For the second time in less than a minute, I was flabbergasted. Cash stood up for me? The world might end sooner than expected. I cleared my throat, hoping my voice would work. "Diana, you might want to leave now." I looked at Cash, but he didn't spare me a glance. "Strange forces seem to be at work here."

Val laughed, and everyone in the room turned to stare at us. Heat crept up my neck and onto my cheeks.

As Diana walked away, she looked over her shoulder. "Think about it, Dacia. You could be safe and happy with us."

I knew differently, though. No matter what the Nephilim thought, I wouldn't be happy being trapped. I wouldn't be myself without my powers.

When class ended, the Nephilim didn't follow so closely. Cash walked in the grass beside me, keeping more space between the two of us than any of the others did. It was a warm day, the sun shone, but when the wind blew, I shivered.

I looked at Cash again, not sure what to think of him or how to get through his hard shell. I bit my lip, pulling it into my mouth, debating whether or not to say something to him.

"Don't," he growled. "I can't stand self-righteous angel spawn. I didn't say it so we could be friends." He pointed at himself then at me. "We will *never* be friends."

"Thanks anyway." I shrugged.

Val wrapped his arm around my shoulders, roughly pulling me into his side. "Keep at it. You might just get through his tough hide."

The dragons dropped me off at my room, then disappeared into Aurelia's. Even though I knew they were still watching me, it was nice to get a break from them.

My friends and I hung out there until going to dinner. Six dragon guardians escorted us, but only Diana and the dark-haired Nephilim from the first day trailed us.

Cody looked over his shoulder several times on the way to Sedum. Finally, he said, "Just two?"

"Yeah." I squeezed his hand. "I think Cash made them a little nervous earlier."

Malcolm opened the door to the cafeteria, and all the smells hit me. Pizza, burgers, bread, cookies, fries, garlic, onions, spaghetti sauce, soups. They wafted through the air, and my stomach growled in response.

Cody smiled when I put fried chicken, mashed potatoes, rolls, and steamed vegetables on my plate. He walked with me to our usual table in the back of the room. The dragons sat at one next to us. Their plates were heaped with meat of all types.

The Nephilim sat as far from us as they could at the closest table to the door.

I was about halfway through my dinner when Cassandra and Bryce sat down across from me. "So"—Cassandra flipped her hair over her shoulder—"where are the rest of them?" She pointed her fork at the Nephilim.

Samantha started to answer, but I held my hand up. "I don't know if I can trust you, but if you let me read your auras, I'll find out."

Bryce looked from me to Cassandra and back again. "So, what does that entail?"

"She'll look into your eyes," Dan said, "and see some of your memories."

"You'll see them, too." Samantha smiled reassuringly. "No big deal."

Feeling like I should be completely honest with them, I added, "It'll make it so I can sense your presence, too."

"That doesn't sound too bad." Cassandra looked at Bryce and shrugged.

"I have no control over the memories I see." I picked off a piece of my roll and stuck it in my mouth. Everyone at the table stared at me, making me extremely uncomfortable.

Finally, Cassandra nodded. "Okay. Let's do it. What do I need to do?"

Samantha stood. "Sit here." She moved to Dan's other side, taking her food with her.

For only the second time since I'd met her, Cassandra didn't look confident. She pulled the chair out and sat, folding her hands in her lap, staring at them. "What now?"

"Just look into my eyes."

She lifted her head. Fear shone in her ice-blue irises. I stared into them. The first memory that flashed through her mind was when I froze her hands together. Then I saw her dumping her coffee in my lap. Then I was sitting on a bench with Damon. He looked different in her memory, not quite as handsome, a little harsher. I told her she should think about dating Bryce.

I felt her insecurity, her fear, and her desire to help. I was surprised and relieved.

"That's all?" she asked.

I nodded.

"That wasn't bad." She smiled and stood up. Resting her hand on Bryce's shoulder, she said, "Your turn."

He sat down next to me. I had to look up to gaze into his pale green eyes. I'd never really been this close to him, face to face. His eyelashes were so light that even from here, I could barely see them.

The first image that floated through his memory was me healing his hand. It was quickly replaced by me crushing it. Pain flared. Then I saw him swing his bat at Cody, driven by some unseen force. I flinched back, and my connection with him flickered. The last memory I saw must've been from a dream. In this one, I looked maniacal.

Bryce's remorse and gratitude flowed through me. "Sorry." He looked at his feet. "Not my best moments."

"We've all done things we regret." My voice sounded gravelly. I remembered sending Mavros back to the Abyss and killing Draconian, crushing Bryce's hand, and hiding the truth about myself from my parents. I thought of Jonathan, my little brother, who'd been my first victim. I could barely remember his life, but I would never forget his death.

He lowered his head further, and his hair hid his eyes from me. "Before—" he cleared his throat "—Cody's a good guy. If I'd been myself, I wouldn't have done that."

Even though his voice was quiet, I figured Cody heard him. "We can't change the past." I patted Bryce on the shoulder. "You both seem to have good intentions now."

Cassandra smiled, and Bryce went back to his chair. I took a bite of my potatoes while I decided how much to tell them. I wasn't ready for them to know everything that I'd been through and everything that was going on.

After taking a drink, I nodded at the Nephilim. "They want to cage me." I rubbed my hand over my eyes. "Though to be fair, they don't see it that way." I hooked my thumb at the dragons. "They're trying to make sure that doesn't happen. They got into it today, and for some reason, fewer are following me now."

"They want to cage you?" Cassandra leaned closer.

"Wanna keep her in a sanctuary." Cody's face was stony, and I finally knew where he stood on me going with them. "Never let her out."

Bryce looked at each of us. "But why?"

"Because this'll never end." I set my fork down and pushed my plate away. "Evil is drawn to me."

Chapter 7

"*I* tried," Mavros says. His eyes plead with me to believe him. "I wanted to tell you who summoned me when I came to you in the first dream, but even here I'm bound by the constraints put on me."

"Why?" I swallow a sob. "Why are you trying to help me?"

He brushes the tears off my cheeks with his thumbs. His touch is gentle, tender. He no longer tries to control me. "Demons don't have friends. We have enemies, competitors, and coconspirators. You were the first person to ever show me compassion, and I—" he rocks back on his heels "—I liked it. Okay?" His eyes turn flinty, and his voice hardens. "And, I hate the being that summoned me. Nobody should have that kind of control over someone else."

I can't help the laugh that escapes from me.

He turns toward me with hatred in his eyes, and I sober. "I'm sorry, but for nearly forty-five days, you tried to control me. It's a bit ironic."

"When this is over—" he takes my hands in his "—I would trust you to summon me. You wouldn't use me."

I pull away from him and rub the back of my neck. This seems like the kind of thing the Nephilim are afraid of.

"I could give you my name, and you could put restrictions on me." He smiles, and it's an angel's smile. "Don't decide now."

I kick at the ground, knocking a rock loose. "What happened to 'We're all evil. If you live through this, you'll do well to remember that.' Those words are burned in my memory. I thought I'd meant something to you then. Now, I don't trust you."

He lowers his head. "Trust no one, Dacia. When it comes to you, everyone has an agenda."

"Yeah, I've noticed."

Mavros steps closer, cupping my face. "Remember the promises you made last time I was here."

I nod at him.

"Dacia Wolf, I release you from your vows."

My eyes popped open. I knew from past experience that Mavros could bind me in a dream. Could he also release me from my promises in one? Why would he? Could I trust that he had?

Sunlight streamed in between the crack in the curtains. I rolled over, hoping to ignore it, but it was too late. I was awake. I opened my eyes to see Cody propped up on his elbow, looking down at me.

He smiled and brushed his hand along my cheekbone. "Morning."

"Morning." I pulled myself against him, running my hands along his back.

"Heard Bryce."

I closed my eyes, not wanting to have this conversation. "Yeah."

"Need to forgive them." He dragged his finger in a line from my forehead to my lips.

I kissed the tip of it and nodded. Relief loosened the knot that had formed in my stomach. "They couldn't help it."

"I know."

I couldn't force Cody to forgive them any more than he could make me change my feelings toward Damon. I was proud of him for trying, though. Forgiveness would help him heal, too.

His muscles tightened, and he rolled over, pulling me on top of him. "It'll take time."

I straddled him, running my hands along his body. His eyes were bright with excitement. He held onto my waist while I traced his muscles and along his ribs, over his chest, and onto his shoulders. I trailed my fingers over his collar bones and up his neck. His eyes fluttered closed. I grazed my lips over his and drew back.

He pulled my head down, and I kissed him hungrily, flicking my tongue against his lips until he opened his mouth to mine. He slid his hands under my shirt, massaging my back. He moaned, and heat shot through my core. I deepened the kiss.

He held me with one arm and rolled us over using his other. His elbows pressed into the couch on either side of me. His eyes roved over me ravenously, looking at me like a blind man who was seeing for the first time.

"You know I love you." He kissed the tip of my nose. "Right?"

I nodded. "But not as much as I love you."

"More." He lowered himself and kissed me slowly, passionately. I gasped and arched into him. His lips slid onto my chin, then my neck. I clamped my hand against his head, twining my fingers through his hair. His blue eyes practically glowed with excitement.

I dragged his mouth onto mine, wrapping my legs around his waist, clutching his back, pressing our bodies together. I moved my mouth from his, kissing his jaw, his neck, and nipping at his earlobe.

He slid his arm under me, clasping my hips, pulling me against him. I gasped, and he covered my mouth with his, sliding his tongue against mine, biting my lip. My fingernails dug into his skin.

I arched my back, and he slid his hands down my arms, entwining our fingers.

Laughter echoed inside of my head followed by Malcolm's voice. *Skipping class this morning?*

My chest tightened, and my face was impossibly hot. "Oh, God. They're watching. Always."

Cody pulled the blanket over us, then slid to the side. "Shoulda thoughta that."

"Shoulda." I hopped up off the couch, grabbed my bag, turned invisible, and unable to face the dragons, teleported to the bathroom.

While I showered, I wondered if they watched me in here, too? Hopefully, they just made sure the Nephilim didn't come in. The thought of being under constant surveillance gave me the heebie-jeebies.

When I finished my shower, I walked to the door, made sure nobody was watching, and turned invisible. As soon as I stepped into the hall, Malcolm lifted his head, sniffing the air, then looked right at me. He smiled, showing his fangs, and walked alongside me to my room. He kept looking down, smirking at me.

"Oh, shut up." I fought the urge to punch him.

He laughed and opened my door for me, then leaned closer. "Stay away from Val if you can. Your power, anger, and lust combine for an even more intoxicating aroma."

I slammed the door shut in his face and heard his laughter through it. Before I'd even removed my invisibility, Cody had his arms around me. "I'm sorry."

"It's not your fault." I turned to face him. "I was enjoying myself, too."

"Someday we'll be alone."

I tried to imagine that future, but I doubted it existed. If the Nephilim had their way, I'd be guarded and imprisoned until I died of old age—if that could even happen. If the other beings had their way, I'd be fighting one monster after another until one finally killed me, or I'd stand by evil's side and watch the world burn.

As soon as Cody and I stepped into the hallway, we were surrounded by dragons. Arianna replaced Val as one of my guards. The other students stepped to the side as we walked by, throwing looks of confusion and annoyance our way.

When we stepped outside, I was struck by the beauty of the morning. Frost coated every blade of grass, every pine needle. The air smelled crisp and cool. My breath plumed out in front of me. I shoved my hands into my pockets, wishing I would've grabbed my gloves.

Cody walked on one side of me, and Arianna strode along on the other, looking like she wanted to say something.

"What?" Curiosity got the best of me.

The boys will tease you—even in my head her voice sounded lyrical—*but there is no need to be embarrassed.*

HHeat rushed up my neck and flooded my cheeks.

They do not desire to copulate with humans. It means little for them to see you mating.

My entire face burned. "We weren't …" I let my voice trail off.

Malcolm stopped walking and lifted his face, sucking in a deep breath. The others followed his lead.

Cash looked over his shoulder at me. "Good thing Val's not here." His voice was gruffer than normal.

"He'd eat her alive." Tye smacked him on the back, and they started walking again.

I repositioned my backpack just to give myself something to do. "Do they mean that?"

"Val is a creature of instincts." Arianna looked at me over the top of her sunglasses. "He has difficulty controlling his base urges, but he vowed to protect you, and vows are sacred to dragons. We do not make them or break them lightly."

Chapter 8

Thursday morning, I sat in class, trying to figure out why the Nephilim hadn't turned up yet. They showed no sign of backing off. Diana and the dark-haired one stood in the hall-way this morning, watching my every move, but they didn't follow me across campus.

I wondered what they were up to. Whatever it was couldn't be good.

Where are they? I thought to Malcolm.

He shrugged his massive shoulders. *Enjoy the reprieve. We'll deal with whatever comes next.*

It was good advice, but unfortunately, I couldn't take it. I sat on the edge of my seat, bouncing my leg up and down, staring at the door, waiting for the inevitable.

Creative Writing ended without the Nephilim showing up and without me having heard a word of Professor Fisher's lecture. I waited for the other students to leave before getting up. I wanted to talk to my guards without being overheard.

I shoved my stuff into my backpack. "I hate this."

"It'll be all right." Tye squeezed my shoulder. Of all my guards, his was the most comforting presence. He was a huge, imposing man, but he didn't use his size to try to intimidate me. He was more of a gentle giant.

As soon as I hung my bag on my shoulder, we walked out of the classroom and into the hall. The dragons encircled me, a solid mass of muscle surrounding me. I felt dwarfed by them. Tye led the way outside. Cash and Arianna stood on either side of me, and Malcolm guarded me from behind.

When we stepped outside, Tye stopped so quickly that I ran into his back. "Sorry, I can't see around you."

He leaned to the side a little. All of the Nephilim stood in a half-circle, blocking our escape. I looked around, wondering where the human students were and hoping they were safe from whatever was about to happen.

"They're behind us, too." Malcolm's voice edged closer to his dragon's than I cared to hear.

I put my hand on Tye's arm, nudging him to the side. "Why can't you just leave me alone?" I widened my stance, ready for a fight. "I've done nothing wrong."

The dark Nephilim from the side street in Althea tapped his head. "We have seen instances where you fall to darkness."

"Have you seen instances where I don't?" I shook my head, unable to believe his response. "I saw the world burn because of Nefarious and Mavros, but it didn't." I took a step closer, knowing the dragons would protect me and not wanting the Nephilim to see me as weak. "I saw myself as Draconian's protégée, but I wasn't."

"We have seen many paths that you may follow, but we cannot leave the fate of the world to chance." He stretched his hand toward me.

"Yeah … that's not a good answer." I rubbed my hand down my arm. "I've already saved the world twice, so it's a good thing you didn't try to imprison me earlier." My chest tightened, and a heavy weight dropped into my stomach. I couldn't believe they'd seen multiple futures and still believed the worst. "None of the other creatures of light are trying to capture me, so why are you?"

Malcolm stepped up behind me, close enough that I could feel his breath ruffle my hair.

"We"—Diana waved her arm, encompassing all of the Nephilim surrounding me—"are the ones who fight the evils of this world. We are the ones who will battle you when you fall to darkness. We have a higher stake in this than any of the other creatures." More Nephilim arrived on campus every day, and I wondered how many of them would have to be here before they challenged the dragons, or if that time was now.

"If you fight the evils of this world, where were you when I battled Nefarious, Draconian, and Mavros?" I clenched my teeth, feeling anger and hatred bubble up inside of me. These righteous creatures had allowed an inexperienced teenager to fight their battles for them. "Why didn't you free the dragons?"

A Nephilim I'd never seen before spoke up. A black tattoo ran down the left side of his face from his scalp, disappearing under his overly tight shirt. "We cannot fight every battle. We must choose the ones that will help those who deserve it the most."

Rage simmered in the dragons surrounding me, and that same anger flared inside of me. "Who makes that choice?"

He shook his head like I was an imbecile. "We do."

"So, the dragons didn't deserve your help?" I clenched my fists, trying not to show my outrage.

"Most of them are not noble creatures." Diana crossed her arms over her chest. "You don't truly trust your guardians. Do you?"

My lips curled with disgust. "Whether they're noble or not, they were being controlled by a madman who used them against his enemies."

"It's time for you to join us." She stepped forward, stretching her hand out to me.

"No." I slid my hand into Malcolm's just in case somebody tried to take my powers away from me. *Be ready to teleport away if we need to,* I thought to all of the dragons. "If you're so righteous and noble, isn't it your responsibility to help everyone, regardless of their worth?"

Cash tilted his head, looking at me like he was seeing me for the first time.

The dark Nephilim from Althea clenched his hands at his sides. I remembered him reaching into his coat the last time I'd seen him, and I wondered if he was fighting the urge to go for whatever weapon he had hidden there. "Do not pretend to understand the world when you cannot fathom your own intentions."

"I understand my intentions just fine. Thank you." I shook my head and hoped he could see my disgust with him and his kind. Then I whispered, "Now." My dragon guardians and I teleported to my room.

I pulled my hand out of Malcolm's grip and walked to the window. "I can't believe they want to imprison me based on one potential outcome."

"Did you mean what you said?" Cash's posture was less rigid than normal, and he rubbed the back of his neck.

"I always mean what I say. Lying just leads to problems. It's not worth the hassle." My gut tightened. I didn't want to argue with him right now. I wasn't in the mood to deal with his aggression or hatred. "Which part?"

He opened his mouth, then shook his head. "About the dragons. About helping everyone, regardless of their worth."

"Yes." I huffed out an impatient laugh. "Haven't you seen me try to help Mavros? Didn't you notice that I tried to spare Draconian?" Once again, I felt the blade slice through his flesh, piercing his chest. I would never rid my soul of the stain of his death, but I would live the best life I could in the hopes of eventually wiping my slate clean.

"I—" his voice caught "—I gotta go." He walked out into the hall.

I looked back out the window. I felt like everything was slipping through my fingers. Juggling the Nephilim, the dragons, and Mavros, one of the balls would eventually fall, and then what would happen?

"What is it, Dacia?" Arianna's voice was soft, soothing. "We can sense your anguish."

I slid down the wall to the floor. "Should I go to class this afternoon or skip?"

"Go," Tye said. "We'll keep you safe."

As soon as my friends returned with their guards, we went to Sedum Hall for lunch. The Nephilim now filled six tables with more standing by the doors and watching from the hallways.

My head swam. The beat of my heart reverberated throughout my body, a steady rhythm that grew louder and louder until it was all I could hear. I pressed my hands against my ears, and the sound became deafening. The edges of my vision grew shadowed and hazy until the only person I could focus on was Diana. She stared back at me. My breaths became shallower and faster, increasing with my pulse and the noise until I wanted to scream.

Something pressed against my back. A voice whispered in my ear. Then another in my other ear. Someone smacked my cheek, and I shook my head. Noises slowly filtered in through the haze.

My friends and guardians all stared at me. "You okay?" Cody asked.

I laid my head down on the table and tried to catch my breath. "I think I'm gonna throw up."

Chapter 9

Homecoming

Malcolm kept Val as far away from me as he could for the rest of the week. The only time we were together was at meals or on the rare occasions that Samantha and Dan walked to classes with us.

I didn't like the idea of him guarding my friends. If his instincts dominated him, I didn't want to put them into a dangerous situation. I trusted Russ with them, but I'd feel more comfortable dealing with Val myself.

Friday night, instead of going to the student center for supper, Cody and I decided to go to the homecoming bonfire. I left a note for Samantha in case she and Dan came back to our room. Since they had their own guards, they'd taken to spending more time alone. I missed seeing them, but I could understand why they'd want to stay away from my craziness.

As Cody and I walked across campus with our bodyguards, the smell of roasted meat wafted toward us. Laughter and music filled the air. Clouds covered the night sky, hiding the moon and stars from us. An uneasy feeling settled in my stomach, and the closer we got to the festivities, the more I wondered if my presence would put others at risk.

Malcolm slowed. Leaning close to me, he whispered, "What are you scared of?"

Cody gripped my hand tighter, likely concerned that something was about to happen. I tilted my head, and my eyebrows scrunched together.

"I can smell it on you." Malcolm inhaled deeply, and his eyes fluttered like he had caught a whiff of his favorite food.

Heat rose to my cheeks. Every emotion, every desire shouldn't be sensed by my bodyguards. I felt completely exposed and helpless around them. I turned away from him, knowing he'd still hear me, but not wanting to see his smirk at my reaction. "I don't want to endanger anyone."

"The Nephilim won't bother you with so many people around." He straightened up.

I twirled a strand of hair around my fingers. "There's more to worry about than Nephilim."

All of the dragons glanced at me. Malcolm grabbed my arm. "What do you mean?"

I hadn't told them. I'd wanted to talk to Aurelia about it first, but she'd vanished. "I—" my voice caught "—I think Mavros might be back."

Cash tipped his head back and laughed. "He can't come back. He'd have to be—"

"Summoned." I finished for him in a flat voice. "I know. In my dreams, he told me he was, but he couldn't tell me who did it."

Malcolm growled. The sound raised the hairs on my arms. "You said you'd tell me."

"I haven't seen him. I don't know that he's back for sure." I told them about my dreams.

The dragons listened to every word I said, cocking their heads toward me. Their bodies went from relaxed to tense, ready for a fight. Malcolm rolled his head, cracking his neck. "Tonight might be a good time to find out. It would take someone powerful and experienced to bring a demon of his magnitude back to Earth so soon after he departed."

"Yeah." I agreed as we stepped to the edge of the festivities and stopped.

Cody tugged me forward. "Think you'll be safer near people."

Students packed the grassy area surrounding the bonfire pit. Flames leaped into the air, casting moving shadows over everybody's faces.

We made our way to the food line. The culinary arts classes had made potato salad, coleslaw, baked beans, pasta salad, and desserts to go with the roasted pigs. I plopped some food on a plate, but my stomach roiled at the thought of eating it.

The dragons sat with Cody and me. Their plates were heaped with meat. They surveilled the area even while shoveling pork into their mouths. I pushed my food around on my plate and only took a bite when Cody set his fork down, folded his arms over his chest, and frowned at me.

When it was obvious that I wasn't going to eat anymore, Cody picked up my plate and threw it away. Then he came back and took my hand, leading me to where several students were dancing. The music was fast, but Cody pulled me against him and swayed. I rested my head on his shoulder.

Malcolm, Cash, Tye, and Arianna surrounded us. Students sashayed by, accidentally brushing up against them, trying to draw their attention, but the dragons didn't spare them a glance.

Some of the students watched me with curiosity burning in their eyes. I knew several rumors had spread about me and my need for bodyguards. Some people were sure my parents were drug lords in the midst of a turf war. Others were certain I was in the witness protection plan, and some even believed I was royalty. I couldn't help but wonder what they'd think if they knew the truth.

The song changed to a slow one, and I closed my eyes to block out the stares.

Cody's grip tightened on my waist, and one of the dragons growled. The sound could be felt more than heard. I sucked in a deep breath and opened my eyes. Mavros stood next to Cody. Claws tipped his fingers. "If you want him to live, dance with me, Dacia."

Cody opened his mouth to protest, but I said, "I'd love to." I stepped out of Cody's arms, and as Mavros pulled me against him, his claws morphed into fingernails. He smelled like warm summer nights, and now that he wasn't trying to control me, I could make out the other scent that was mixed with it. Sulfur.

The dragons stepped closer, forming a ring around us. Beyond them, I saw the Nephilim gathering. Their eyes never strayed from me.

I pressed my hands against Mavros' shoulders, holding him back a little, hoping he wouldn't try to control me. Praying that he wouldn't make me kiss him in front of Cody, in front of the Nephilim, and all the other witnesses.

"What do you want, Mavros?" I asked without looking into his eyes. The music thumped, making the students yell over it, keeping our words private.

His hands slid lower, and he pressed our bodies together. "To be left alone, but M—" his eyes bulged, and he choked on the word "—someone summoned me."

"So now what?"

He lifted one shoulder slightly. "I do whatever I'm told or I suffer."

"And, what have you been told?" I pulled away from him, still in his arms but with room to breathe.

A grin spread over his features, and I heard his voice in my head. *Now would be a good time for ice.* "Nice try, but I can't tell you that."

I thought about ice, trying to concentrate it on my fingertips. A slight chill spread to my hands but nothing more.

I can't wait forever, Dacia. Do it!

I stepped back, but he clutched my waist. "I … I can't." I held my hands between us and glanced from them to him. "What'd you do?"

The dragons stepped even closer.

"Nothing." He tilted his head and looked at me. "I swear it. I don't want to hurt you." *Tell them to grab me.*

I looked at Malcolm. "Get him away from me."

The dragons grabbed Mavros, roughly jerking him back. He didn't try to stop them. He just sneered at me. "This isn't over."

All four dragons followed Mavros, blocking his return to me. The Nephilim looked between the dragons and me. A few of them stepped forward, but Diana held up her hand and shook her head. Apparently, kidnapping me in front of so many witnesses was against their rules.

Cody cupped my cheeks and tilted my face so I looked up into his eyes. "Okay?"

"Yeah." I slid my trembling hands into his back pockets. "You?"

"Fine." His jaw was tight. "What'd he want?"

I bit my lip and lowered my head. Cody would never believe anything good I said about Mavros. Blowing out a quick breath, I said, "I think he wanted to protect me."

"Right." His hands slipped onto my shoulders. "Wants you to think that."

"He was talking in my head … helping me get rid of him." I rubbed my finger and thumb over my eyes, then pinched the bridge of my nose. "I know you don't believe it. I'm not even sure I do."

Cody's hands dropped to his sides, and he donned his mask.

"I don't trust him, Cody." My shoulders drooped. "I did that once."

Once again, my guards surrounded me. "The demon slipped away from us at the edge of the festivities, almost like he'd allowed us to drag him off." Malcolm's voice was gruffer than normal.

"You're falling for it, too?" Cody's body went rigid, and he laughed grimly.

The dragons' postures were all stiff and alert, their eyes watchful. Malcolm grabbed my arm above my elbow. "Are you planning to stay here longer?"

I shook my head. "I think we should go back. Whoever's controlling him won't be happy they didn't get what they wanted."

Malcolm and Arianna walked on either side of me. Cody trailed behind. Whether he was mad at me or didn't want to hear me talk about Mavros, I wasn't sure.

The full moon broke through the clouds, illuminating their edges, making me itch for a paintbrush for the first time in months.

The dragons followed me into my room. It was too small, too close. The walls squeezed in, sucking the oxygen out. I stumbled to the window, pulled it open, and frantically gulped in fresh air. I folded my arms on the windowsill and laid my forehead on them, fighting my rising panic. Cody's fingers gently climbed my spine. He murmured something, but I couldn't make out his words. The repetitive motion and the feel of his hand helped calm me.

When I could breathe easily, I stood up and turned around. Aurelia appeared in the middle of the room, and relief spread through my chest. She'd helped me battle Draconian and Mavros. She could help me through this, too.

Before I had a chance to say anything to her, Cash stepped forward. His nostrils flared, and his form rippled. "We agreed to protect her from the Nephilim. We did not agree to fend off a demon."

"Cash"—Aurelia's voice was more dragon than human, the warning in it clear—"back away."

He stopped and looked down at his feet.

Aurelia waved her arm at the couch. "Shall we sit and be rational?"

Arianna pulled the desk chair over and sat on it. Aurelia sat in Big Bird. The other three dragons sat on the couch. I motioned for Cody to sit in Cookie Monster. I planned to stay where I was, but he grabbed my wrist and pulled me onto his lap.

I looked at Aurelia, intending to tell her how glad I was to have her back on campus, but when I opened my mouth, that wasn't what came out. "Where've you been? Why won't you respond to me? How could you leave me with no explanation?"

She lowered her head, and the other dragons seemed to shrink in on themselves. Suddenly, the room didn't feel quite so crowded.

"I had no choice." Aurelia's voice was soft and wholly human. "I have been in conference with the Nephilim, trying to convince them of your worth."

"So." Maybe the dragons' anger had diminished, but mine hadn't. "Couldn't you have told me? Couldn't you have responded? I wanted to tell you about Mavros. I needed you." A strong burst of wind blew in through the window.

Cody trailed his fingers from my temple to my chin. "Breathe."

I pinched my eyes shut and focused on controlling my emotions. Other students were still outside, enjoying themselves. They didn't need me ruining their evening for them, whether they'd blame it on me or not.

"They are afraid of you." She looked directly into my eyes. "They would not let me communicate with you for fear that you would control me."

My thoughts seemed to freeze. I shook my head. "Control you? How would I control you? Why would I?"

"You know my true name, Dacia." She looked pointedly at all the dragons. "You know all of our true names. You could control all of us."

My shoulders slumped forward. "But … I wouldn't."

"I am aware of that and have been trying to convey that sentiment to the Nephilim." She sat up straighter and glanced at Malcolm. "When I found out about Mavros, I told them I needed to leave. We need to figure out who summoned him before he can enact some wretched plan."

Malcolm walked to the window and stared up at the moon.

The doorknob rattled, and Cody and I tensed. Dan and Samantha walked in, and Russ and Val stood in the hall. Samantha's laugh stopped immediately when she saw us. "This can't be good."

"You may as well come in," Aurelia said.

As soon as the door shut, Malcolm turned his back to the window. "Mavros didn't seem to want to hurt Dacia. It seemed like he wanted to protect her."

Cody snorted, and Malcolm shrugged at him. "Demons are deceitful, but they can't change the smell of their emotions. Even though they were coated with the scent of sulfur, I could smell his resistance to whatever orders he'd been given, his pain at not following them, and his concern for Dacia."

Cash crossed his arms over his chest and nodded. "As could I."

"Me, too." Arianna and Tye both agreed in turn.

"Why would he want to protect me?" I asked.

Cody's arms tightened around my waist. "Wants you for himself."

"I don't think so." Arianna shook her head. "He didn't seem to have selfish intentions."

Cody covered his face with his hands. "You've gotta be kidding me." He nudged me. I stood up, and he paced. "For forty-five days, I heard he wasn't as bad as I thought." He pointed to himself, then to Samantha and Dan. "He planned to kill us."

"Right," Arianna agreed, "but circumstances have changed now. He's not here to win Dacia over, and whatever his master wants from him, he's fighting it."

I stood in front of Cody with my hands out. He stopped, not touching me. I looked over my shoulder at Aurelia and said, "We'll be back." I grabbed Cody and teleported. My normal go-to place would have been Falcon Lake, but I didn't want Nephilim, dragons, or Mavros to follow me. I thought of what

Malcolm had said about being able to smell me within fifty miles, so I took a risk and teleported us further away.

Cody spun in a circle when we arrived. Unfamiliar trees surrounded us. "Where are we?"

"Cougar Lake." I grabbed his hand and led him through the tall pines to the water. The moon reflected over its calm surface.

He stepped up beside me. "Why?"

"Hopefully, it's far enough away for privacy." I slid my arm around his waist, hoping he wouldn't pull away from me. "I understand why you don't want to believe anything good about Mavros. I don't know why, but he seemed like he was trying to help me. I don't trust him. I don't want him here." I turned so I was facing him. "But he was struggling against the hold on him. He tried to get me to use ice to fight him off. Then he told me to make the dragons take him away. He could've fought them, and the way Cash acted, he might've been able to win, but he didn't even try."

Cody dragged his hands down from my shoulders, skimming over my arms. "I know." He rested his forehead against mine. "I'd rather have Nefarious or Draconian back."

Chapter 10

Knowing

*M*avros stands in front of me. His fingers are tipped with claws. *Please, Dacia ... don't let me hurt you.* Pain flashes across his face. His eyes plea with me.

I think about ice, funneling my energy into my hands, but nothing happens. Sweat drips along my temples.

My master knows. I can't keep fighting. Do something! The muscles tighten in his neck and jaw. His hands clench and unclench. He roars and slashes his hand across my chest.

Blood wells up, cresting before spilling over the edges of the cuts. Searing pain rips a scream from my throat.

Mavros presses his palm to my chest and pulls me against him with his other hand.

My body is limp in his arms. The pain is dragged from my wounds into Mavros' fingers. As he draws the poison out and heals the slashes, he mumbles over and over again, "I'm sorry. I'm so sorry. I didn't want to do this."

I stare at him, unable to comprehend why he's healing me, why he says he doesn't want to attack me, why he's helping.

Why won't you use your powers against me?

"I can't." My voice was weak even though he'd healed my wounds. "Nothing happens." As soon as the words are out, I regret saying them. Somehow, he'll use the information against me.

Try! He sounds desperate. *I can't fight much longer.*

I call on my powers. Ice begins to spread from my fingertips along the back of my hand and up my arm. Tears wet my eyes as a lightness settles over me.

Use it, Dacia. There's an urgency to his voice that startles me. *Hit me in the chest.*

I reach out, and flames spring up where the ice had been. They dance across my skin, flaring up as they climb higher.

Mavros stares at me as I fight against my own magic. *Someone else is controlling it. How?*

The flames leap onto my neck. I lean my head back, delaying the inevitable. The fire ascends, blocking my nose and mouth, stealing my oxygen. I gasp, sucking in flames. They burn my throat and lungs.

I popped up, wheezing for air. It took several breaths before my lungs accepted any oxygen into them.

Cody sat propped up beside me, rubbing my arm. When my breathing regulated, he said, "You okay?"

I nodded.

"Bloody." He pointed at me. "Shirt's shredded."

I went to the sink. While it filled, I grabbed a washrag and towel. Then I slipped my shirt off and washed away the blood. Wrapping the towel around my body, I went to the closet and got a new shirt. I knew Cody and most likely a dragon or two were watching me, but I didn't have the energy to care. I let the towel fall to the floor and pulled the shirt over my head as I went back to the couch.

Cody slid against the back, making room for me. "Wanna talk?"

I lay down beside him, pressed my hand to my neck, willing him to understand that I couldn't, and shook my head. My throat ached like flames still smoldered in it.

Cody traced circles on my arm until he fell asleep.

Cody's body was warm. I pulled myself against him, snuggling closer. I wasn't ready to open my eyes and face a new day. Whoever controlled Mavros had no qualms with sending him after me in highly populated areas, so the only safe places were mine and Cody's rooms. They'd both been blessed to keep Mavros out.

The dragons hadn't been too pleased with me when I'd returned with Cody last night. I'd refused to tell them where I'd taken him. Sometimes we needed privacy, and they needed to realize that, whether it thrilled them or not.

I sensed Samantha, Dan, and Russ a moment before the door opened. Samantha looked terrific. Without my nightmares keeping her up all hours of the night, she was probably getting way more sleep than she had since becoming my roommate. When we'd first met, her hair had fallen just below her shoulders. It now went to the middle of her back. She'd curled the ends this morning and had makeup on, so I knew she had plans.

"Hey, guys." I sat up. "What's going on?"

Russ waved from the hallway as Dan shut the door.

"We were thinking Althea for lunch." Samantha waited for Dan to sit in Big Bird, then positioned herself on his lap. "Then the homecoming game."

Cody grabbed his shirt from last night off the back of the couch and pulled it on. "Have fun."

"You're … you're not coming?" Samantha's shoulders slumped, and she looked down at the lavender carpet. "We never hang out anymore."

I massaged my temples. "It's not that I don't want to."

"Then what?" Dan asked.

I walked to the window and looked outside. The sky was bright blue with white puffy clouds dotting it. "Whoever is controlling Mavros doesn't seem to care about collateral damage. I can't be responsible for that many people."

"How 'bout lunch?" Cody stood behind me, rubbing my shoulders. "We'll have guards."

I nodded. "Sure."

"Lunch is better than nothing." Samantha bounced up, and I couldn't help but smile at her enthusiasm. I had missed seeing so much of them, but I'd assumed they were enjoying time alone together.

I gathered my clothes and gave Cody a quick peck on the cheek. "Be careful." Malcolm and Cash met me in the hallway. The Nephilim watched us walk to the bathroom, and I wondered if they ever slept.

As soon as I got back from my shower, Samantha walked over to me and held my wrist. "I noticed the pajamas in the trash." She flicked a glance at them. "How bad have your dreams been?"

I tried to smile at her. "That's the first injury I've had this time around." I tugged my hand through my hair. "Mostly they've just been me losing control of my powers and doing myself in."

"So"—Dan waved his hand toward the trash can—"what kind of monster is it this time? Should we be staying here, or are we safe with Russ and Arianna watching us?"

"Yeah, spill." Cody sat on the couch and patted the seat next to him. "Wanna know why you were healed when you woke up." He was wearing jeans and a Phlox Phoenixes sweatshirt.

"You don't know?" Samantha's eyebrows lifted.

I pulled my hand through my wet hair, then fluffed it up so I wouldn't end up with ringlets when it finally dried. "I couldn't talk last night. My fire burned my throat."

"What else?" Cody stretched his legs out in front of him.

I sat next to him and leaned forward, holding my head in my hands. They weren't going to like what I had to say. They would think I was falling for Mavros' lies again, that he had me under some sort of spell.

Looking up, I gazed into each of their eyes for a moment before moving to the next, soft brown eyes, hazel eyes that were mostly green today, and finally, blue eyes that meant everything to me. "I don't want to fight. I don't want a lecture." I squeezed Cody's leg. "Mavros attacked me. Then he healed me. I don't know why, but I believe he didn't want to hurt me in the first place."

Cody's body tensed. His jaw clenched, and I knew he wanted to argue about Mavros' intentions.

"He told me to fight him off." I fiddled with my hoodie's strings, not wanting to see their disbelief, not willing to believe I was falling for Mavros' lies again. "When I tried, my ice turned to fire and then turned on me."

Samantha looked at Dan and Cody, then stared at me. "Don't you see?" She threw her hands up to emphasize the last word. "It's him. He's playing games with you again."

I bit the inside of my cheek to corral the words in my mouth. I needed to think about what to say and how to say it. Impulsiveness would just cause a rift.

"She doesn't." Cody's voice was pain-filled. "With him, can't see reason."

My face felt hot and tingly. I dropped my chin to my chest. "I don't know. Maybe you're right." The words left behind a thickness in my throat that I couldn't swallow. "He toyed with me before." I crumpled against the back of the couch. "Maybe this is a game to him."

Dan blew out a breath. "It could be, but … someone else is involved. Somebody brought him here." He shivered. "Whoever that is, they're the real threat."

"Do you have any ideas?" Samantha seemed to deflate.

I stared at the ceiling. "I don't think it would be the Nephilim. If they're good"—I used air quotes around the word—"it doesn't seem like something they'd do. Nobody else has shown themselves." I pulled my lip into my mouth, trying to think if there had been any clues. "Malcolm said it would have to be somebody pretty powerful."

My muscles relaxed, and a sense of tranquility washed over me. A knock on the door made me realize why I suddenly felt so calm. Aurelia was here. I got up and let her in.

She stood by the door, gazing over my shoulder instead of at me. "I am sorry that you felt I abandoned you. Sometimes I forget that emotions can replace instinct and knowledge." She finally looked into my eyes, and I saw regret in hers. "Even though I live among you, I do not always understand how my actions will be perceived."

"It's okay." I clutched my elbows. "I should've known better." I turned to go back to the couch. When she didn't immediately follow, I glanced at her over my shoulder. "Do you wanna come in and sit down?"

"Yes." She sat in Cookie Monster and nodded at the others. "Malcolm relayed everything that has been going on here. I have to go back to the Nephilim soon, but I talked to him about training with you. I would like him to work with you on regaining your powers when someone else takes control of them."

I nodded. "That'd be good."

"Who's doing it?" Cody asked.

Aurelia didn't miss a beat. "My first impulse is Mavros."

Without meaning to, I rolled my eyes. I hoped nobody noticed. I didn't want to argue, but I didn't agree.

"However, I believe it goes deeper than that." She picked at a string hanging off the chair. "We need to figure out who is controlling him and what they want with Dacia."

Aurelia went with us to Althea. I was sure the other dragons came along, but I didn't see them. We went to The Avalanche. After ordering, Aurelia said, "The Nephilim may be willing to back off. I just have to prove to them that you are incorruptible."

I set my drink down and laughed. "How can you prove that?"

"They have been looking through my memories." She tapped her head.

Rubbing my temples, I took a moment to breathe. "Do they know you're here with me?"

The waitress brought our food. My appetite had been slowly returning, and the smell of my burger made my stomach rumble. I took a big bite of it, and Cody smiled at me.

"Yes, they are aware." She sliced her nearly raw steak and held it in front of her mouth. "When I return, they will sort through my memories and make sure they match up with what they were before. They will also check my new memories."

Samantha stabbed her salad. "How long will you be with them before they decide to leave her alone?"

"I hope it will not take too much longer." She wiped her mouth with her napkin. "I believe I am getting through to them. The Nephilim that have been on campus watching Dacia have reported that she shows no outward signs of corruption. However, they also told them that she refuses to accept their offer of sanctuary." She focused on me. "They do not understand why you feel like they are trying to cage you. They believe they are offering you freedom and a second chance."

Knowing this memory would be shown to the Nephilim, I tried to figure out what to say to convey how I felt. "If they weren't free to come and go as they please, they would probably feel differently about it." I dragged my fries through mustard and shoved them into my mouth. I wanted to tell her how stupid they were for believing that, but I also wanted them to go away soon.

"I will be leaving tomorrow morning." She soaked a piece of bread in the blood on her plate. "While I am gone, let Malcolm know anything you would normally tell me. He will relay it to me." She shoved the bread into her mouth, and I had to look away.

"You can't talk to her"—Dan pointed at me with the onion rings in his hands—"but can't you talk to us?"

"I can project my thoughts to you, but you cannot communicate with me."

Cody put his Philly down and wiped his hands off. "Phones?" He took a drink of his pop.

"Technology does not work inside the Nephilim's safe havens." She smiled at Cody like he should've known that.

"Well, that makes it even worse." I leaned back in my chair. "They want to trap me, keep me away from my friends and family, and there isn't even a way to contact them."

"In their defense, your family and friends would be allowed in to see you," Aurelia said.

I shook my head. "My parents would never understand why I wouldn't visit them." I folded my arms over my chest. "They're in denial about my powers. They'd never believe in dragons, demons, or Nephilim. They wouldn't get it."

"I know, Dacia." Aurelia tossed her napkin onto her plate. "I am doing my best to convince them to back off. The dragons believe you should be free to make your own choices and to live your life however you choose." She placed her hand on mine. "I know that it will be with honor and dignity."

Chapter 11

Malcolm

Malcolm knocked on my door early Sunday morning. Even though I had been awake for quite some time, I wasn't ready to get up. I kissed Cody on the forehead, slipped out of his embrace, and went to the door. "Give me ten minutes."

I pulled my hair into a ponytail, brushed my teeth, and got dressed. As I stepped into the hallway, Cody said, "Be careful."

Malcolm and I walked past Diana and the dark-haired Nephilim. I wondered what her name was, but hopefully, I wouldn't see her for much longer. They followed behind us as we walked to Cacomistle Hall. The morning was brisk. Tiny snowflakes floated through the air, melting as soon as they touched our skin.

"Winter will be here soon." Malcolm lifted his head and sniffed.

I nodded. Already the nearby mountain peaks were more snow-covered than just this time last week. "I hope this is over before it comes."

"As do I," he said. "I would like to be back in the warmth of my cave before winter, but I will stay as long as I am needed."

I touched his forearm. "Thank you for that."

He looked down at my fingers against his skin, and I wondered if he was okay with it. I jerked my hand back and focused anywhere but on him.

The stone building loomed up in front of us surrounded by towering trees and boulder-strewn landscapes. We stepped inside. A fire roared in the massive stone hearth. Alicia's desk sat empty, so we climbed the open staircase to Sarah's office.

Malcolm knocked on the door.

"Come in," Sarah responded.

We entered the room, and she stepped forward, holding her hand out to Malcolm. "I'm Sarah Aspen. Aurelia has told me all about you and your plans to help Dacia." She pulled me into a motherly hug.

"Hello, Sarah," I said as I stepped out of her embrace.

She smiled at me. "It's good to see you. Aurelia stopped by this morning and told me about everything that's going on. Please keep me informed if you can."

"I'm sorry." I lowered my head. "I should've."

Patting my shoulder, she said, "You are free to use one of the rooms downstairs or this space. I will not interfere."

"Thank you." Malcolm bowed his head. "We will stay here this morning."

"Make yourself comfortable. Stay as long as you need." She walked off. "I'll be in my office."

Malcolm waved at the couches. "Have a seat."

"Okay." Butterflies erupted into flight in my stomach. Their wings fluttered against my belly. "Then what?"

He breathed in through his mouth and closed his eyes. "Sometimes your emotions are overwhelming." He rubbed his hand down his face. "You need to trust me for this to have a chance to work."

"I do."

He shook his head. "Not like you trust Aurelia. If you did, you would've told me about your dreams. You would've let me know you suspected Mavros was here."

I looked down at my hands in my lap. Shame flared through me.

"Part of you still fears me, and part of me revels in that."

I jerked my head back, surprised that he'd admit that.

"I told you. I'm a dragon." He leaned forward with his elbows on his knees. "I made a promise to Aurelia to help you, so I will let you read my aura. Hopefully, you will see that I am trustworthy."

I nodded and gazed into his bronze eyes. His dragon stared back at me. His memories flashed through my mind. I saw him guarding Cody and felt his desire to tear him to pieces. I watched as Draconian commanded him and felt Malcolm's hatred toward humans increase with every order. I saw him slash blindly at my back, watched his claws tear through my flesh, and witnessed him hungrily lick each drop of my blood off his talons. Then I saw him flying through the air, fighting Aurelia. He hated himself for each wound he inflicted upon her. I called out his name, and relief flooded through him when I released him from Draconian's clutches.

Leaning back, his gratitude, loyalty, and pride washed over me. I smiled at him. "Those weren't the best memories, but I believe you are trustworthy."

He bowed his head. "Know this. I will do everything in my power to keep you from harm. I swore to protect you, and I will put your life before my own."

I pressed my hand to my chest. "Why?"

"You did not have to free us. You could have taken control of us and used us for yourself." His eyes flashed, and I wondered how any of the dragons could stand to be around me with that fear dangling over their heads. "Even so, it will not be easy for you to sit there and let me take your powers away."

A shiver of dread clawed up my spine. Draconian and Mavros had both taken my powers away, and though Malcolm meant me no harm, it would not be easy to allow it to happen.

"Close your eyes." His voice was softer than I'd ever heard it. "Lean back and think of whatever helps you to relax."

I closed my eyes, but the only thing I could think of was that Malcolm was going to steal my powers. How could I relax, knowing that something so integral to me was about to be taken?

"Trust me, Dacia." The words were soothing, and I wondered if they were laced with magic. "I only want to help you."

Without meaning to, I felt myself relax. I pictured myself sitting on the edge of Falcon Lake with Cody. Our feet dangled in the water. The gentle lapping settled my nerves.

"Good." Malcolm's voice floated in on a breeze. "Now, open your eyes and use ice against me."

I called on my powers. A slight chill raised goosebumps on my arms, but nothing else happened. I pulled harder, willing magic to flow into my fingers.

Malcolm's face tightened. Beads of sweat formed along his temples.

My energy failed to respond to me. I imagined Cody in trouble and called on them again. My hands cooled.

Malcolm clutched his knees. Sweat rolled along his cheekbones. His pupils were slits.

And still, my magic did not respond. I leaned back, and he followed my lead, wiping his hand over his face.

"How am I supposed to regain control?" The desperation in my voice annoyed me. "And, if I'm so damned powerful, why can you take them away to begin with?"

He grinned at me, baring his fangs. "You are powerful, but I am over two thousand years old. I have had a long time to hone my magic, and in spite of that, I had difficulty binding your power. One day you will be undefeatable, but for now, you are still learning." His expression darkened. "The only time my powers have been taken from me, it was done by using my true name. There was no way for me to regain them without first being released from his hold."

I rubbed my jaw, trying to figure out a solution.

"Since you know it is me stealing your magic, you could distract me somehow." As he talked his pupils regained their roundness. Aside from their unusual color, they appeared more human. "However, that tactic will only work if you know who you are dealing with."

I tugged my hand through my hair. How many times had I been in this position over the last year? "So basically, I need to figure this out on my own."

"Yes." He nodded. "Do you wish to try again?"

"No time like the present. I guess."

He leaned forward. "Relax."

Closing my eyes, I pictured my mountain lake again. It didn't take long for Malcolm to restrain my powers. Keeping my eyes closed, I envisioned using them. I remembered the feeling of energy surging through me, responding to my command. I thought about life, about renewal, about love. I took a deep breath and decided I was ready to try.

Malcolm's jaw was tightly clenched. His biceps were flexed. Sweat dripped into his eyes.

I called my magic to me, begging it to take any form. Nothing happened. I tugged on it again, but there didn't even seem to be anything there to answer my call. Every time I reached for it and it didn't respond, I weakened.

I slumped down and yawned, covering my mouth with my hand. "I'm done, Malcolm. I've got nothing left."

He sat beside me and held his hand over mine. "May I?"

"Yes." The word was little more than a whisper.

Gripping my fingers, his energy flooded into my veins, cascading through my body. I sighed in relief. "It's been a long time since I've been so drained from using my powers."

"I felt you pulling on them"—he let go of me—"but it wasn't quite enough to take them back." He stood, lowering his hand to me. "I think you have had enough for today. We can try again tomorrow after your classes."

I allowed him to pull me to my feet. "We're leaving, Sarah."

She stepped out of her office. "Keep me informed, and don't stay away so long."

"I'll try not to." I rubbed the back of my neck and forced a smile.

Malcolm nodded at her. "Thanks for the use of your office."

Chapter 12

Who Should I Trust?

The Nephilim surround me. I spin around, wondering where my dragon bodyguards are. "They're not here," one of the Nephilim from Althea says. "Don't make this difficult. Just come with us."

"No." I step back. "I can't."

"You must." Diana steps beside him. "The dragons have agreed. They no longer feel like this world is safer with you in it."

I stumble, shocked by her words. "But … but I saved them. Without me, they'd still be under Draconian's control."

"Dragons are fickle creatures." The voice comes from behind me this time.

I turn and see another of the Nephilim from the side street.

"Why else wouldn't they be here protecting you? Why would they lead you here then leave?" His voice is filled with disdain.

Several of the Nephilim are bowled over. A panther charges through them, running straight at me. It leaps, knocking me against the rocky ground. The breath whooshes out of my lungs. The beast's teeth graze my neck. It transforms into Mavros, and he rolls off of me. "Take her," he shouts at the Nephilim. "Get her out of here." He clutches his head, fighting whoever controls him.

The Nephilim grab my shoulders and drag me away from him.

"I'm sorry," Mavros says. "I know it's not what you want, but it's the only way to keep you safe from me."

All of the Nephilim gather around me and whisk me away. It's different than when I teleport myself or with the dragons. It's like we step through a bright light. There are no stretching or pulling sensations.

An old church stands in the distance. Its steeple stretches to the heavens. Rolling hills and flowering trees surround me, and I realize I am far from home.

The Nephilim let go of my arms, and I fall to my knees. "Why couldn't you just leave me alone?"

"We saved you." Diana kneels in front of me. "That demon would have killed you."

Rage burns in my stomach. "That demon—" I stand up, getting right in her face "—the one I've already returned to the Abyss once." I have never wanted to punch somebody so badly before. I clench my fists, keeping them at my sides, trying to calm down. I need to convince them to take me back. I need to figure out why the dragons have given up on me. "I can handle Mavros."

"Maybe." She doesn't back down from me at all. "And maybe he would've finally won you over. We know he can control you. We know how you react to his other form. We know you think of him as a friend."

I tug my hand through my hair and turn, pacing away from her. The other Nephilim stand in a ring around us, preventing my escape. I reach inside, searching for my power, but there is an emptiness where it once was. "And what's so wrong with that? That friendship is why he fights against whoever is controlling him." I stop moving and spin around. "Unless of course one of you is holding his leash. Then I played right into your hands."

"We did no such thing." Anger flashes through her eyes. "I told you we are forces of light. We would never align ourselves with darkness." She folds her arms over her chest. "You, however, would. That is why we cannot allow you in the world on your own."

"So, I'm trapped here against my will—" I lower my head in defeat "—but I'm not supposed to think of it as a prison."

"It is not a prison. It is your home." She snaps her fingers, and the dark-haired Nephilim steps forward. "Olivia, show her to her room."

As Olivia leads me to the church, she says, "We'll let your friends know you are with us. There's a pen and paper in your room. Feel free to write to your family, and we'll see to it that your letters get to them."

"After you read them." My voice is despondent.

She presses her hand to my arm and guides me. "Of course."

"Home sweet home," I murmur with as much sarcasm as I can muster.

"Do not try to escape." She sneers at me, and I wonder why I ever thought her eyes were beautiful. There is so much anger and hatred in them now. "The only way in or out of the wards is through our portals. Your magic will not work here. It was stripped from you as soon as you entered our grounds."

I stop, planting my feet firmly. "So not only am I a prisoner, I'm not even myself."

Her lip curls in disgust as she looks at me. "If all you are is your magic, we got to you too late."

"You took away a huge part of me. You brought me here against my will, and you think you're the righteous ones." A humorless laugh escapes my lips as I step away from her. "Tell me where to go. Then leave."

She shakes her head. "I do not take orders from humans, especially not ones who fraternize with demons."

The doors to the church open. A blinding light strikes me.

My eyes fluttered. Cody's arm was thrown over my chest. His breaths were slow and steady. I stared at the ceiling, not moving, not wanting to wake him yet. I wanted to process my dream to figure out which parts might be true, which may come true, and which were warnings.

I thought about Diana telling me that they wouldn't sully themselves with demons. That statement rang with truth. So, if not the Nephilim, who else would have unleashed him on me?

The trees had been blooming, so their fortress must have been in the southern hemisphere. I didn't think they would wait until spring to take me captive.

I slid out of Cody's arms and stood by the window. I stared out at the darkness without really seeing anything. *Malcolm, are you awake?*

Yes. His voice was vigilant. *Are you okay?*

I need to talk. I sent him the memory of my dream. *Will the dragons give me up to the Nephilim?*

He didn't answer right away, and that was answer enough. Fighting back tears of betrayal, I wondered how long I had before they decided I wasn't worth protecting.

I don't know, Dacia. I made a vow to protect you. I will not turn my back on you. He paused before adding. *I know what it is like to be held against my will, and I will vow to you now, that if they take you, even with the dragons' blessings, I will find a way to get you out of there.*

The tension in my body released. I pressed my hand to my chest, feeling a lightness there that took me by surprise. *Thank you, Malcolm.*

I will relay your dream and your concerns to Aurelia. I will tell her nothing of my vow. I felt his loyalty to me. *Though, I believe she feels the same.*

Thank you. I hoped he could sense my gratitude and that he could tell how deeply his words had touched me.

The connection between us broke, and I was on my way back to Cody when I felt Mavros' call. My legs wobbled, and my pulse raced. I looked over my shoulder. I hadn't seen him looking up at me, but had he been there?

I felt a pull on my body, but I kept walking to the couch, intending to ignore him. Just as I was about to sit down, he forced me to teleport.

I shivered as I looked around, trying to figure out where I was and if I was alone. The snow was at least six inches deep here, and my bare feet were freezing.

Mavros landed in front of me. His bat-like wings folded against his back and disappeared. *Leave, Dacia. Teleport away. Tell Malcolm to protect you from my call. They are not—* His voice cut off, and he roared in pain. His face twisted, and he lunged toward me.

I teleported back to my room but not before his claws tore through my arm. I landed flat on my back with a loud thump.

Cody jumped up from the couch. "Dacia? What happened?"

My four guards were in the room before I could answer him. I wrapped the tail of my shirt around my arm, trying to staunch the flow of blood.

Malcolm lifted his nose and inhaled. His pupils turned to slits. Tye stepped around him, but Malcolm snarled. Tension filled the room, and the other dragons froze.

Clenching his jaw, Malcolm strode toward me. He knelt down, carefully lifting my arm. I felt his energy flow into me, healing the wound.

I sat up, looking at my arm, then at Malcolm. "How did you heal it?"

"With magic." The snarky tone of his voice made me wonder if my injury had interrupted something. "How else?"

"Did I do something?" I wrapped my arms around my legs. "Are you mad at me?"

Cash wrinkled his nose. "It's your blood."

"Oh." I rubbed my hand over the nonexistent wound. "But what about the venom?"

Malcolm shook his head. "There wasn't any."

I twisted my arm, not believing what I was seeing. Demon wounds always took a long time to heal from except for when Mavros himself healed me. "That's weird. Mavros never attacked me without venom before. Why now?"

"Mavros attacked you?" Cody sat down and pulled me onto his lap, holding me tightly against him. "How?"

I folded my arms over Cody's. "He made me teleport. I don't know how he does it or how to keep myself from going to him." I went on to tell them what he'd said and what he'd done. Then I looked at Malcolm. "He told me to have you protect me from his call."

Val sat beside Cody and me. He patted me on the head and leaned in closely, sniffing my hair, and the blood on my shirt. Bending down, he licked my arm. I pushed his head away, and Cash growled at him.

I looked each of the dragons in the eyes. "Keep quiet so Marcy doesn't realize Cody's here. If he's found here, after hours again, he'll be expelled."

"If she comes," Tye said, "we can make it look like the room's empty." He tilted his head. "Can't you?"

"I've never tried." I pushed Cody's arms out, loosening his grip on me. "Right now, I wouldn't trust my magic enough to do it anyway."

"So, can you?" Cody looked at Malcolm.

Malcolm's eyebrows pinched together. "Can I what?"

"Keep her from going to him." Cody's arms tightened again.

"Yes." He flipped his cornrows over his shoulder, making the beads clank together. "I will have to stay here with you, though." He walked to the window and opened it, sticking his nose up against the screen.

I took the hint. "All right." I pushed out of Cody's arms. "I need to clean up and change."

Malcolm turned invisible while he walked to the bathroom with me. As soon as we confirmed nobody else was in there, he showed himself. His presence was comforting. He stood with me at the sink while I washed, turning his back when I slipped on a new shirt.

On our way back to my room, I said, "Who's controlling him? I thought it might be the Nephilim, but after my dream, I don't anymore."

"I don't know," he whispered. "There is no end to the creatures who would try to corrupt you."

My chin dropped to my chest. I knew that but hated hearing it said out loud.

When I opened the door, Cody leaned back and mumbled, "Thank God."

Malcolm made himself comfortable in Big Bird, and I lay on the couch with Cody. I gazed into Malcolm's eyes. His pupils practically glowed in the darkness. "I will keep you safe."

"Thank you." I tried to close my eyes and go to sleep, but it felt so weird having somebody watch me. I turned, trying to get comfortable.

"Would you like me to make you sleep?"

I looked over my shoulder at him. "No, I'll figure it out."

"Are you okay?" Mavros sounds broken.

I step toward him. "Yes. You didn't use your venom."

He closes his eyes, covering his mouth with his hand. "I didn't know if it would work. I've never tried to stop it before."

"Are there any clues you can give me?" I step closer still, reaching for his hand. "Can I see in your memories who's doing this?"

He pulls back, keeping me from touching him. "Someone cl—" He bends forward clutching his stomach. His body shudders.

"It's okay," I say. Tears well in my eyes. I hate to see anybody suffer. "Don't try again."

He sits on the ground. "Try." He points to his eyes.

I kneel in front of him, gazing into his obsidian irises. I see the dragons dragging him off. I see the dragons in my room, protecting me. I see the dragons playing basketball with me and my friends. Mavros stands in the hallway watching us. The Nephilim follow behind me, and the dragons surround me.

Leaning back, I tug my hand through my hair. "I don't know what to make of that. None of it seems very helpful."

"Really?" He shakes his head. "Think."

I look at him, wondering if he saw something different than I did. "All you showed me were the dragons."

He nods. "Bingo."

"But … they're protecting me."

"Some are. Some are only pretending to be." His body convulses. He falls to his side, clutching his head.

I snapped my eyes open.

"What is it?" Malcolm asked.

I sat up and held my head in my hands. "Mavros showed me more memories."

"And?" Cody's hand ran along my back.

I focused on Malcolm's eyes and sent him my memory. "He says it's one of you."

Malcolm's pupils turned to slits, and his fangs lengthened. "And, you trust him?" His voice was more of a growl.

"I don't know." I paced across the room. Ten steps. Then ten steps back. I looked out the window, wondering if Mavros was there. Wondering what would become of him. His master would not be forgiving. "I know it's not you or Russ." I paced ten steps, then ten more, trying to gather my thoughts. "I trust Arianna implicitly."

"Why?"

"I've seen your memories and Russ'. I've felt your auras." I stood in front of him. Up close, I could see that black scales covered his arms and neck. "Arianna saved my friends after I freed her from Draconian."

"The others?" His tongue was black and forked.

I knelt in front of him, taking his hands in mine. His fingers were scaled. They were tipped with sharp talons. "I need you to calm down. There isn't room for your dragon here."

"The vow is sacred." Smoke rolled out of his nostrils. "If one of them is breaking it, they deserve death."

I sent calming energy into him, hoping it would work like it had when Aurelia had done it to me. "I know but not here, not now."

Some of the scales on his neck disappeared. "The others?"

"Val is creepy." I shrugged. "He licked my arm earlier."

"Did he taste your blood?"

"I don't know. He might've." I tried to remember, but I didn't know for sure. "I don't really think he'd betray me, though. Cash scares me, but he stood up for me against the Nephilim. Tye seems trustworthy. He's been really nice since he's been here. I don't know anything about the four who chose to remain unseen. It could be one of them. If Mavros showed me one of their faces, I wouldn't have known who it was."

Malcolm's features had returned to normal while I'd been talking. "I don't even know who the four other dragons are." He let go of my hands. "I need to contact Aurelia and see what she knows." He leaned back and closed his eyes.

I sat back down on the couch with Cody.

"You believe him?" he asked.

I rested my head on his shoulder. "I don't know what to think." Aurelia trusted my guards. They had protected me in

Althea. They'd shielded me from the Nephilim and kept me safe when my magic failed. If I couldn't trust them, who could I trust?

Chapter 13

On the way to class, I studied all of the dragons surrounding my friends and me. Malcolm had stationed Val as far from me as possible. I wondered if he'd discovered whether or not Val had tasted my blood. A chill ran down my spine at the thought of it.

I looked away from Val, not wanting to think about it anymore, and focused on the others. All of them seemed to genuinely care about me and my friends. Even Cash had shown less animosity toward me lately. I scanned the skies, wondering if the other dragons flew above us, if they were invisible, or if they walked among us in plain sight but unbeknownst to us.

Tye stepped closer to me. "Are you okay?"

"Yeah." I looked up into his green eyes and saw his concern for me. "Why?"

"You seem a little somber today." He squeezed my shoulder. "I know last night was rough on you."

I snorted and slowly shook my head. "Most of them are. I used to love to sleep, not so much these days."

"Maybe someday you will find peace." He smiled at me, and hope fluttered in my belly.

"Thanks, Tye."

After class ended, we went to Sedum Hall for lunch. Cassandra and Bryce joined us. "So," Cassandra said, "there are more of them again. Are things not going well?"

"I don't know." I shoved a forkful of pasta into my mouth. "I have …" I looked at them, wondering how much I should really say and realizing Samantha and Dan didn't know what had happened last night yet. "I have premonitions."

"Really." Bryce leaned toward me. "That's so cool."

I rolled my eyes. "It might be if I knew which were just regular dreams and which were prophecy." I took a drink and decided I might as well tell them what I knew. The dragons would be able to hear every word I said, but they were always watching, always listening. "If last night's dream was a premonition, they"—I nodded at the dragons' table—"will let them"—I waved at the Nephilim—"take me … soon."

"Why?" Samantha set her fork down and glared at the dragons.

Cody wiped his mouth. "Don't know."

"I don't know if that's why so many of the N—" I caught myself, remembering I hadn't told Cassandra and Bryce what creatures followed me "—of them started following me again or if they forgot they were afraid of Cash."

Cody looked at Dan and Samantha. "Mavros attacked her."

"What?" Samantha asked.

Dan's eyes widened. "When?"

"Last night." I set my fork on my plate and lowered my voice. "He made me go to him."

"So, are you okay?" Samantha fiddled with her bracelet.

Cassandra leaned closer. "What do you mean?"

Cody nodded at Samantha. "No venom."

"He made me teleport out to him when he was here before." I lifted one shoulder and met Cassandra's ice-blue eyes.

"That doesn't make sense." Dan leaned back in his chair. "He must've told the truth about not wanting to hurt you."

Samantha shook her head. "Don't fall for it for a moment, Dacia. You can't trust him."

I leaned as far forward as possible and whispered. "I really can't trust anyone. It seems that he may have been summoned by someone close to me." I sat back. "That's all I can say right now." I picked up my fork and started shoveling in my lunch. I needed to eat to keep my strength up, but I'd lost my appetite. I hated thinking about being kidnapped and caged. I hated thinking that somebody I trusted would betray me.

One of the last things I wanted was to turn into a cynical person who trusted nobody. I would never be naïve and innocent, but I hoped I could look at people and see the best in them and that I could trust them until they proved otherwise.

"So"—Bryce tossed his napkin onto his tray—"you all up for a game of basketball or do you have classes this afternoon?"

"I'm out," I said. "I've got Shakespeare."

Bryce groaned. "What a horrible class."

Dan and Cody laughed and held their hands out to Bryce for high fives.

"I've got class, too," Samantha said.

I looked over at the dragons. "Who wants to stay with Cody and Dan and play basketball?"

Malcolm glanced at his companions and said, "Arianna will go with Samantha. I will go with Dacia. The rest of you can play." *Is that okay with you?*

Yes. That leaves one dragon I know I can trust with each of us. Thank you.

I finished my lunch and stood up to leave. Cody reached for my hand. "Be careful."

"You, too." I looked at the others. "Have fun. I'll see if you're still playing when I'm done." I brushed my lips over Cody's and walked off with Malcolm.

When we were halfway between Sedum Hall and Quartz Building, Malcolm said, "Be careful what you say. Dragons can hear quite well."

"I know." I resituated my bag on my shoulders. "I was trying to word it carefully. The trouble is they're always around."

"You can make an area soundproof if you want." He guided me away from some other students. "I can show you after class. It might not hurt to do it to your room to keep Marcy from overhearing Cody and for times when you want to be intimate."

Heat flooded onto my cheeks, and I looked away from him.

Malcolm chuckled. "It is too easy to embarrass you, and the scent—" he sucked in a deep breath "—is intoxicating."

Feeling exposed, I folded my hands over my stomach. "Does it …" I broke off and tugged my hand through my hair. "Never mind. Do you know if Val tasted my blood?"

"No." Malcolm flashed his fangs at me. "I have enough willpower not to be tempted. If I didn't owe you a great debt … maybe."

"How'd you—" I shook my head. It didn't matter how he knew. Either he could read my mind, or I was an open book. "Never mind. What about Val?"

"He says he did not." His pupils elongated before turning round again. "Do not let him. He has no willpower."

"I didn't realize what he was doing last night until I pushed him away."

He nodded. "What did you do with the bloody shirt?"

"Tossed it in my trash can."

"Burn it when you get back." *Keep your blood away from all of the dragons until we figure out who is controlling Mavros. Trust no one.*

"Yeah, Mavros and Tye have both told me that." I chewed on my lip. "What did Aurelia say?"

He shook his head. "She hasn't yet. I will tell you as soon as I hear from her."

When class ended, we found the others in the gym. Justin Serpent, one of the guys Cody had played basketball with when we first started going to Phlox University, had joined their game. Cassandra sat against the wall reading a book.

I walked up to her. "Not a basketball player?"

"I don't like to sweat." She tossed her hair over her shoulder.

"Want a couple more?" I asked when Tye was throwing the ball in.

He looked at me and said, "You better join my team. They're skins."

Malcolm pulled his shirt over his head, tossed it on the floor, and ran onto the court to join Cody's team. While I took my hoodie off, I let my eyes rove over Cody, Malcolm, Cash, Val, and Justin. The dragons were built like bodybuilders, and Cody and Justin were lean, sculpted muscle.

I shook my head and ran in. As I did, Tye threw me the ball. He ran alongside me when I dribbled down the court. Dan cut through the lane, and I passed to him. He turned and shot. Cash jumped up, swatting the ball out of the air.

I raced down the court after it, but Cody got there first. "All right?" he asked.

I nodded. "You?"

"About to score." He smiled mischievously.

I planted myself in front of him and stretched my hands straight up into the air.

He crashed into me, and I fell back, sliding across the court on my butt. Cody looked like he might break. "Sorry, Dacia."

"Part of the game." I took his hand and let him pull me to my feet.

Dan and Bryce ran up to us. "Definite charging foul on that one." Bryce smiled at me. "Welcome to the team."

Samantha and Arianna came in and sat by Cassandra. I held the ball out. "Want to play?"

"No." Samantha looked at the teams and shook her head. "You're on the wrong team, Dan."

He blushed and pulled his hand through his hair. "You sure?"

"Yeah." She held up her book. "Homework."

I looked at Arianna. "Do you?"

"No." She shook her head. "I'll sit this one out. Make sure nobody's cheating."

Since everybody else in the game was six to twelve inches taller than me, I let Bryce throw the ball in. Even though the dragons had more stamina, the teams seemed fairly well matched.

The physical activity helped release some of my tension. Malcolm kept Val away from me as much as possible, stepping in to guard me or sending Val to block Tye or Russ. When Val neared me, he breathed in deeply and moved as close to me as he could. His eyes widened with pleasure, and one of the other dragons knocked him away.

Sweat must have been an intoxicating smell to dragons, too. I wondered if there was anything that wasn't or if everything I did amplified the scent of my power.

After our game, we all went to Sedum Hall for ice cream. We pulled two tables together and sat compatibly. Bryce, Cassandra, and Justin sat with the dragons laughing and joking, and I wondered how they would feel if they knew what they were. Bryce and Cassandra suspected they were other, but they had no idea that they were the top of the food chain.

When we got back to the dorm room, I walked straight over to the trashcan to burn my shirt. I dug through it twice, not believing it wasn't there.

Malcolm. My thought was frantic, and he appeared in my room within a second of my thinking his name.

Cody, Samantha, and Dan looked at him, then at me. Their eyes were wide, and their mouths hung open. Malcolm held his finger to his mouth. "Are you okay, Dacia?" He looked confused. *You were panicked.*

I pointed at my trashcan. "It's gone."

He walked over and sniffed the air. "Val." He disappeared.

"What's this about?" Dan asked.

"Last night, Val licked me."

Samantha stared at me with a dazed look. "Why would he do that?"

"Okay." Dan chuckled. "That's weird."

"I had blood on my arm, and apparently it's powerful and tempting." I paced away from them. "Malcolm wanted me to burn my shirt when we got back"—I pointed at the trashcan—"but it's gone."

Malcolm reappeared in the middle of the room, holding Val by the back of the neck. "Where is it?"

Val cowered. "It smelled so good. I had to have it."

"What did you do with it?" Malcolm growled.

Val exposed his throat to Malcolm, then rubbed his head against him.

"Where?"

"In my cave." Val's voice was soft. He trembled and kept his gaze on the ground. He rounded his shoulders, making himself appear smaller, submissive.

Malcolm's grip on Val's neck tightened. "Take me there now."

They disappeared and within minutes returned. Malcolm held my shirt out to me. "Burn it. From now on, burn anything that gets your blood on it. No matter how insignificant it seems."

I grabbed my shirt and lit a fire in my palm. Blue flames engulfed the shirt. Both Val and Malcolm sniffed the smoke. Val reached forward, and Malcolm smacked his hand down. "Control yourself, Val."

"I try." Tears pooled in Val's blue eyes. "She smells so good. I want to keep her safe, and I want to be close to her. I don't want to hurt her."

I dumped the ashes into the trashcan and stepped closer to Val. "It's okay."

He put his arm over my shoulder and smelled my hair.

"If you want to protect me, you have to stay away from my blood." I rubbed his head.

He leaned into my hand and nodded. "You smell so good."

"Okay, Val." Malcolm pulled him off of me. "Go back to Aurelia's room now."

Samantha looked at Malcolm. "Aren't you going to go, too?"

"He's with me." I put my hand on Malcolm's arm. "He can keep me from going to Mavros when he calls."

Dan nodded. "Well, welcome to the club." He turned to Cody. "You ready? Russ said he'd head over with us."

Cody pulled me into his arms. "Nothing stupid, okay."

"Never." I brushed my lips over his. "Be careful."

Russ waited in the hallway for them. As soon as they left, Malcolm said, "If you ladies want to shower, I will send Arianna down with you. She should be able to keep Dacia safe from Mavros." He grinned at me, and I knew he was going to try to embarrass me. "If you'd rather, I can turn invisible and guard you."

I swatted at him. "We'll take Arianna."

"You know"—his features blurred—"I could've chosen a female form." A beautiful black woman stood in front of Samantha and me with long hair braided in cornrows. She put her hand on her hip and winked at me with Malcolm's eyes. In a more feminine voice, she said, "You could've called me Melony." She laughed and turned back into Malcolm.

"That's creepy." Samantha shoved clothes into her bathroom bag. "So, what made you choose this form?"

"Nobody's ever asked me that before." He pointed at the chair.

"Sit wherever, whenever." I pointed to the fridge. "There are drinks in there. If you're going to be here, you might as well make yourself comfortable."

"Thank you." He nodded at me as he sat. "This body was the first non-dragon form I ever took. It came to me naturally when I was trying to become something else, so this is the alternate form I am meant to take. It takes less concentration and less magic for me to hold this form than any, other than my own."

I thought of the first time I'd transformed into something else. I'd unintentionally turned into Mavros as his dragon. Aurelia told me that if other dragons knew I'd transformed into one, they'd kill me. She'd wanted to, and she was protecting me. Since they had no qualms about becoming humans, I didn't understand why it would bother them so much, but if the first shape dragons took was their preferred form, what did that mean for me? "Would the same be true for me?"

"I'm not sure." He tilted his head. "But, it seems like it would."

I grabbed my bag and walked to the door. "You'll be here when we get back?"

"Until you don't need me anymore."

Chapter 14

Watching Me Sleep

*M*alcolm's low growl woke me up. "What is it?" I rubbed my eyes. With the campus lights shining in, he was illuminated enough for me to see.

Cody sat up, curling his arm around me, but didn't say anything.

"Mavros has been calling you for over an hour." Malcolm didn't look at me, just stared at the window. His hands clenched the arms of the chair.

The room was chilly. Shivering, I rubbed my hands over my arms as I walked to the window to look outside. Sure enough, a large, black panther paced restlessly, gazing up at my room. "I haven't felt his call. Thank you."

Malcolm grinned at me but said nothing. His straining muscles made me realize that it must take a massive amount of energy or concentration for him to do this for me.

"Do you need anything?" I placed my hand on his arm. "Energy? Water?"

He shook his head. "Go back to sleep. I will keep you safe."

I lay on the couch and snuggled into Cody's embrace. "Wish Aurelia woulda done this," he breathed in my ear.

I remembered all the times Mavros had called me to him, all the times I'd come back and seen the torment on Cody's face, all the times he should've walked out but didn't. "It would've been nice, but she wasn't allowed to interfere."

"Yeah." He sighed. "I know."

Mavros stands in front of me, looking out at the lake. The waning moon is high overhead. His hands are in his pockets with his thumbs sticking out. "Your dragon won't let you come to me."

The wind blows across the lake, and I shiver. Mavros takes his coat off and slips it over my shoulders. I nuzzle into its warmth. "That's the point of having him there."

"Don't you want to see me?" He looks genuinely hurt.

Shaking my head, I say, "Not if you're going to attack me. I imagine you won't get away with not using your venom again."

"No." His lip raises in disgust. "I've already been warned not to let it happen again." He spits on a boulder. "Stupid dr—" He collapses, writhing on the rocky ground.

I kneel beside him and use my magic to take the edge off of his pain.

He looks up at me. His eyebrows are squished together, and his lips are pursed. "Why would you do that?"

"I don't like to see anybody suffer." I stand up and brush the dirt off my knees.

He rolls into a sitting position, wrapping his arms around his legs. "Nobody's ever done anything like that for me before."

"So, your controller—" I take a few steps away in case Mavros is ordered to attack me "—is a dragon?"

He nods almost imperceptibly.

"Malcolm?"

He looks at me like I'm an idiot.

"I knew that." I shake my head and roll my eyes. "I just want to make sure you're not playing me." None of them seem likely, so I decide to throw their names out one by one. "Cash?"

He moves his chin toward his shoulder.

Since I trust her but haven't read her aura yet, I ask, "Arianna?"

His head turns to his other shoulder. "You're running out of time." A muscle ticks in his jaw, and he clenches his hands so tightly that the veins in his arms bulge.

"Val?"

Mavros screams and clutches his head. When he looks up at me again, his eyes are the flaming irises of the panther. Wild and dangerous.

I step back, and his coat slips off of me, falling to the ground.

"Wake up," he snarls.

I jolted awake. Was Val the one controlling Mavros, or did his controller just figure out what was going on when I asked about Val?

"Everything okay?" Malcolm's voice startled me.

I shrugged. "As okay as it ever is." He seemed more relaxed than the last time I'd woken up. "Mavros quit calling?"

He looked at me knowingly. "Probably about the same time you started dreaming about him."

"How'd you know?" I sat up and raked my hand through my hair.

"I looked in your head when he quit calling for you." He leaned forward. "I got out as soon as I saw him there."

I pulled my lip into my mouth to keep from saying something I'd regret. It felt like a violation of my privacy for him to look into my head while I was sleeping, but part of me understood why he'd done it. "So, why'd you get out?"

"If he'd have felt my presence in there, I doubt he would've told you whatever it was that he wanted." He stood and walked to the window. "Also, since you didn't give me permission, I didn't want to linger." He pointed outside. "He's still here."

"I learned it's not you, Arianna, or Cash. When I asked about Val, he told me to wake up."

Cody rubbed my back. "Think it's Val?"

"Not really." I lowered my head into my hands. "It could be, but I think it's more likely that whoever is controlling him realized what was going on."

"Doesn't seem competent enough," Cody said.

I nodded. "Yeah, but it could be an act."

Malcolm laughed, low and deep. "Not with Val. I've known him for a long time. It's not an act, but his incompetence could make it easy for somebody to manipulate him." He turned away from the window. "So, do you ever sleep through the night?"

"No." Cody lay back down, pulling me with him. "She doesn't, so I don't."

I smiled at Malcolm. "Third time's a charm."

Chapter 15

Damon

Malcolm rested his head on the back of the chair. Even so, his eyes were open, and he was vigilant. "Aurelia will not tell me who the other four dragons are." He leaned forward and rested his elbows on his knees. "She is not allowed to."

"So how do we know if we can trust them?" I wandered to the window, wondering if I'd see Mavros in his human form gazing up at me.

Malcolm squeezed my shoulder, and I jumped. His footsteps had been silent on the carpet. When he didn't laugh, I wondered how bad whatever he was about to say would be. "Last night, she called them to meet with her and the elders. They have been cleared. Their intentions are pure."

I turned to him, pulling my hand through my hair. Just as I was about to ask him who he thought it might be, Cody said, "So who?"

"We'll find out." Malcolm shot me a sympathetic smile before looking over his shoulder at Cody. "The six of us are to meet with the elders while you're in class."

"No." Cody shook his head and stood up. His hands were clenched at his side. "They'll take her."

Malcolm held his hands out in front of him. "We will escort Dacia to class before leaving. Then the other four will keep an eye on her. If anything goes wrong, yell for help." He looked into my eyes. "You'll be all right. The elders want to get this over with before whoever it is finds out there's a witch-hunt."

My regular guards walked with me to Creative Writing while the others went to Speech. Gray clouds covered the sun. I pulled my coat together and shivered. The Nephilim flocked behind us. With each passing day, they grew braver. They were more willing to aggravate the dragons. The one with the honey-colored ponytail walked alongside Val, edging closer until Malcolm growled.

"Sebastian." Diana's voice cut through the chilly air, and he backed away after throwing a snide grin my way.

Tye held the door to Stellaria Hall open, allowing me to lead the way into the classroom. As soon as I sat down, the dragons left. The Nephilim looked at each other. A couple of them edged closer to me, but Diana looked over her shoulder and shook her head. I wondered if she could sense my other guardians or if maybe she suspected it was a trap.

Even though they stayed back, I kept an eye on them. I didn't trust them to keep away from me if they noticed my guard was down.

While I watched them, Damon strolled into the classroom like he hadn't missed a day. My breath caught in my throat, and my pen fell to the floor. His brown hair was tousled, his grin was cocky, and his eyes were filled with mischief. He swaggered past the Nephilim and smiled at me.

My heart fluttered. I didn't love him. I didn't want him, but I missed his friendship, his carefree attitude, and his sense of humor. A friend I'd mourned was back from the dead, and my heart reacted differently than my head.

Seeing Damon here could mean nothing but trouble. Cody was already on edge with Mavros around. I didn't need his alter ego screwing things up.

He strutted up to me and leaned against my desk. His cheek nearly touched mine. "Miss me?" His breath caressed my ear.

"Yes." The word came out huskier than I would've liked.

He brushed a strand of hair off my face, letting his fingers linger. Then he sat next to me, throwing his arm over the back of my chair.

"Why are you doing this?" I fought back the tears pricking my eyes.

His fingers tightened on my shoulder. "No choice." His voice was rough, and he ground the words out through clenched teeth.

I wondered what he was or wasn't allowed to say to me.

He sat close to me throughout class, twirling my hair around his finger, brushing his leg against mine. I should've gotten up, switched seats, or pulled away from him, but I figured he'd just follow me. He had orders and no choice but to obey them.

When class ended, I stayed seated, waiting for the other students to clear out. The Nephilim didn't leave, but they also didn't come any closer. They watched us, disgusted by Damon's presence. Or maybe disgusted with me for talking to him.

I turned to him. "Can I read your aura? Can you let me in your head? Or is that against the rules?"

His eyes lit up, and he nodded. "I'll direct you."

I stared into his obsidian irises and hoped he wouldn't try to control me. His memories were dark and hard to decipher. Mavros held my limp body against him. My head rolled back, and his tears ran onto my face. He screamed into the fading light. The memory ended, and I saw him fighting to tell me who controlled him in my dream. I felt the pain that rippled through his body when he defied orders. I tried to veer away from his chosen memories, but he steered me to the ones he wanted me to see. It went against everything in him to permit the dragons to pull him away from me, but he shoved his hands into his pockets and allowed them to manhandle him.

The emotions tied to his next memory stunned me. I saw Damon and me sitting together on "our" bench. His arm was slung over the back of it, and my head was on his shoulder. A wave of contentment crashed over him, threatening to drown him before he realized what it was.

I pulled away from him. "If that's how you felt, why'd you tell me I meant nothing to you? Why'd you threaten my friends?"

There was a sadness in his eyes I'd never seen before. "I'd never experienced that, and at the time, I didn't see it for what it was." He looked down at his feet, and I followed his gaze. He wore black boots just like the ones in my dreams.

Was Samantha right? Even after what I'd just seen in his memories? Was he playing me?

"I was obsessed with staying on Earth. Then when I held your dying body in my arms, I realized what I'd lost." He folded his hands behind his head and leaned back. "It was too late. I couldn't save you."

His story tugged at my heart. I wanted to believe him, but after everything that had happened between us, how could I?

"I need you to leave." His eyes pinched shut, and he winced. "Now!" He practically roared the last word.

I grabbed my bag and sprinted past the Nephilim into the hall, pushing through students on their way to class. "Excuse me. Sorry," I said as I dashed for the doors. Outside, there were four unknown dragons waiting to protect me.

Over the noise in the hall, I heard Damon's voice. "Dacia, don't go."

I slowed, compelled to stop, to turn around and go back to him. I closed my eyes and tried to picture Cody's face. I held the image in my mind for only a moment before his features morphed into Damon's. As I turned, someone bumped into me hard enough to break Damon's hold on me. Before he could regain it, I darted for the doors and thought, *Help!*

Running outside, I was met by a wall of flesh. I bounced back and looked up at the tallest woman I'd ever seen.

"Where is the danger?" Her voice was low and commanding.

I stared into her luminous green eyes and pointed over my shoulder. "Damon … Mavros is trying to control me."

She slipped behind me, protecting my rear. I was instantly surrounded by four people. The dragon to my right pressed his hand against my back, forcing me to move at his pace. The dragon in front of me had blue spiked hair. His shoulders were broad, and his tight shirt clung to his muscles.

We jogged toward the dormitory. Students dodged to the side when they realized the dragons weren't going to move for them.

Dacia, please come back. Damon's desperate voice echoed through my mind.

The dragon to my left growled. "He's in her head."

I need you, Dacia, please.

His voice tugged on me. The urge to go to him began to overwhelm me.

Images of Damon and I flashed through my mind. I saw us walking around campus holding hands, lying together under the stars, and eating picnic lunches by the lake. I stopped running, and the dragon behind me dodged to the side to avoid plowing me over.

I turned, and the woman picked me up, tossing me over her shoulder in a fireman's carry. Then she ran.

My body bounced against her shoulder, snapping me out of Mavros' hold. She sprinted to the wooded area between Quartz Building and Kalmia Hall before teleporting to my room.

My stomach lurched when we came to a halt. She lowered me to the ground, and I looked around the room. Cody and Dan sat on the couch holding their video game controllers, staring at us.

"Thank you," I said to the dragons. "I'm sorry I made you show yourselves."

A dark-skinned man with blond hair bowed his head. "We are here to protect you at all costs. Do not concern yourself with us."

"What happened?" Cody stepped behind me and slid his arm around my back.

I sucked in a deep breath and pinched my eyes shut. Cody wouldn't like the answer, but there was no way to sugarcoat it. "Damon."

His fingers tightened on my waist, but otherwise, he didn't show any emotion.

The doorknob jiggled, and Samantha walked in. She stopped, surveying the room. "Fun day?" She closed the door and stepped up to the dragons, holding her hand out. "I'm Samantha."

The black man took her hand first. "Jax."

"You may call me Mara." The female dragon nodded. She must've been 6'8". Her dark hair was pulled into a fishtail braid.

The next dragon was shorter and stockier than the others. My thoughts instantly turned to the red dragon that had chased me through the forest in one of my nightmares. He rolled his neck. "I suppose Mortimer will do."

"I can't tell you why, but I've always liked the name Seth." The last dragon stepped forward and shook Samantha's hand. His voice was softer than I expected. It didn't match his muscular frame and blue hair.

Dan waved at them from the couch but said nothing. Cody shook each of their hands. "Thanks for getting her away."

"He is not the problem," the female dragon said. "We must figure out who controls him. Once that person is defeated, Mavros will return to the Abyss."

"This is the first time he's tried to control me." I sat down, slumping forward. "He warned me to leave. Told me he couldn't resist much longer."

"Why?" Cody shook his head. "Why do you believe him?"

"He showed me his memories." I looked at him, wondering how I would feel if our positions were reversed.

Cody sat on the couch and held my gaze with his. "Think they were real?"

I nodded almost imperceptibly.

Pain lanced through his eyes. "He lies."

"I know." I dragged my hand through my hair and told them about the memories I'd seen. I didn't tell them about the remorse I'd seen in his eyes.

Samantha sat next to Cody. Her voice was soft. "He's playing you."

"No." Seth shook his head. "I saw him mourn her death. I watched from the mountaintop as Dacia plunged the blade into her chest. His howl was heartbroken." He sat down. "He held her body until the Abyss called him back. I had never seen a demon grieve before that moment."

Cody leaned back and stared at the ceiling. "Don't believe this."

Seth grasped the arms of the chair and growled. The hairs on the back of my neck stood on end. "I would not lie."

"He knows," Dan said. "It's not you he doesn't believe." He tilted his head like he was trying to figure out what to say. "The situation has him baffled."

The dragon relaxed his grip. "I see."

"Is she safe here?" Mortimer asked. "Shall we go back to our posts?"

Mara tilted her head like Aurelia did when she was communicating with Arion or the other dragons. "Yes. We must keep watch."

"Stay safe." Jax turned invisible. "Do not hesitate to ask for help."

The other dragons followed his lead. I felt it when they teleported out of the room. "They're gone." I stood up and walked to the window, half-expecting to see Damon standing outside. "One of my guards must be controlling Mavros."

"Why?" Samantha asked.

I turned and looked at my three closest friends. "As soon as they found out they wouldn't be in class with me today, they must've sent Damon in. It was the opportune time to have him try to control me."

Dan sat beside Samantha and draped his arm over her shoulders. I wanted to go to Cody, but I was afraid he wouldn't want anything to do with me.

Dacia, come back to me.

I spun around and looked down. Damon stood in the shadow of the trees.

Come out here to me.

"Cody." My voice was strained, and he felt the urgency in it.

He jumped up and wrapped his arms around me. "He here?"

"Yes." I felt like a fish on a hook about to be reeled in.

Cody pressed his lips to mine and pulled me against him. The hook slipped, and Damon tugged harder. I slid my hands under Cody's shirt and up his back. He lifted me, and I wrapped my legs around his waist. He pressed me against the wall and deepened the kiss.

Dacia, help me. Damon's voice was strained.

I held Cody as tightly as I could and teleported us to Cougar Lake. Damon's pull on me completely disappeared.

Hazy, afternoon light filtered down through the spruce and pine trees. It danced along the ground casting shadows on the undergrowth. Cody wobbled slightly as he set me on my feet.

"I'm sorry." I pulled my hand through my hair. Guilt tore a hole in my chest. I didn't want to put Cody through this again, but what was I supposed to do? I couldn't ignore Damon's call. I couldn't go with the Nephilim. I needed the dragons to figure out who summoned him. As much as I had missed him, I needed him out of my life. "He wouldn't stop calling me."

Cody walked away from me and leaned against a tree. "Can't do this again, Dacia."

I stared down at my feet. "I know." My heart plummeted, but I couldn't blame him. Things had been hard enough the first time Damon was in my life. "I can take you back."

"No." He held his hand out to me. "Let's walk."

"Are you sure?"

He wiggled his fingers, waiting for me to slip my hand into his.

The trees were thick here. We ducked under branches and around trunks. Chipmunks darted over the path in front of us. We stepped out of the woods, and the ground was covered with rocks. Mountains rose all around Cougar Lake. Their peaks were snow-covered. The air was cool and crisp.

Cody led us to a picnic table. "How do we get rid of him?" He sat down.

"Everyone says I need to find who controls him." I positioned myself across from him.

He stretched his hands across the table, and I slipped mine into them. "Your powers?"

I squeezed his fingers. "That's why I tried to get into his head. I was hoping I'd be able to catch a glimpse of who summoned him here." I looked down at our hands. "I also wanted to see if he was telling the truth."

"Seth thinks so."

"It doesn't matter." I shook my head. "I don't want him here, Cody. I only want you."

"Yeah."

The wind blew across the lake. Goosebumps lifted the hair on my arms. "I'm scared." I rubbed my arms, trying to warm them. "Will he kill me? Take me away? Use me to fulfill the prophecy and destroy the world?"

"You won't let him." Cody stood up and moved next to me, pulling me against his side. I rested my head on his shoulder.

We stayed at Cougar Lake until I heard Malcolm's voice in my head. *We are back.*

I teleported us to my room. Dan and Samantha sat on the couch. He was playing video games, and she had a pen tucked behind her ear and one in her hand, working on homework.

Malcolm stood by the window with his arms crossed over his chest. "It seems your demon lied. The elder council scanned all of our memories, and none of your guards are responsible."

I sat on the edge of the chair with my elbows on my knees and my head in my hands. "So maybe it's a dragon that's not guarding me, or maybe it is the Nephilim."

"Or maybe Mavros is a liar just like I've been telling you all along." Samantha slammed her book shut and shoved everything into her backpack. She snatched her pen from behind her ear and pointed it at me. "He's a demon. He's not to be trusted. Ever!"

Chapter 16

Mavros and I sit on the bench where Damon and I had spent so much time together. He looks perfect. The most beautiful man I've ever seen, not a hair out of place, not a speck of dust on his black clothes. I, however, am here in my pajamas. My hair pokes out in every direction from sleeping, and I'm freezing. The nights are getting colder, and for some reason, when he comes to me in my dreams, the actual weather comes into play.

He hands me his coat. It smells like him, warm summer nights and sulfur. I pull my legs up and drape it over me like a blanket. "Why can you control me when Draconian couldn't?"

Mavros laughs derisively. "Draconian didn't have the power of Hell backing him. I do." He turns on the bench so he's facing me, pulls one of my curls straight, and releases it so it springs back up. "There is so much I could teach you, so much more you could learn if you would just let me. Your power would be unfathomable." He doesn't try to control me, but there is something compelling in his voice.

"But at what cost?" I pull back from him.

He kneels in front of me and stares up into my eyes. "I will pay the cost, Dacia. There will be none for you. I will give you my true name and let you control me." He smiles at me, not his seductive grin or his sardonic smirk, but a genuine smile. "You are incurably moral. You would hold a tight leash."

"I—" for a moment, words are lost to me "—I've seen you resist your master's control."

"For you, Dacia." He holds his hands over mine, and his jacket slides to my lap. His obsidian eyes beg me to believe him. "I only resist to protect you. You took my pain away when I was hurting. You helped me realize I can do good things. You are my shining light in what I believed would be an eternity of darkness, my savior." He lowers his forehead onto my knee. "I've never begged before. Please don't give up on me now."

My heart goes out to him. What would it mean to him to be free from the Abyss? I could do it for him, but Cody would never forgive me. The dragons and Nephilim would never forgive me. They'd probably both try to cage me or kill me for that.

I pull my hands away from him and drag them through my hair, clutching my curls at the back of my head. I don't know what's right or wrong. I don't know what to do. He's been trying to help me, but does he deserve more time on Earth as a reward? Would he manipulate me and somehow cause the prophecy to come true?

"I … I don't know, Mavros." I lift his coat so that it covers my arms and legs again. "The dragons were sent to the elders, and they saw no evidence that one of them summoned you."

"How?" He slumps back.

"I don't know if I can trust you or your memories." Tiny snowflakes land on his coat. Their shapes are visible for just a moment before they melt. "Is it possible it's a different dragon, not one of my guards?"

He pants, and his body convulses. He throws himself back, putting distance between us. Stretching out his neck, he roars.

The sound raises the hairs on my arms and along the back of my neck.

He stares at me, and his eyes are a swirling inferno. His fingers are tipped with claws.

"Wake up," I say out loud. "Come on." I spring to my feet.

The fully-formed panther stalks toward me. His teeth are bared. I hold his jacket in my left fist, and in my right hand, I create a sword out of ice like the one I had used to kill Draconian.

Wake up! Mavros' command slams through my skull.

"I tried that." I flick my wrist, flinging his coat out, hoping to make him back away, but he doesn't even blink.

He prowls closer, and I walk down the bench, wanting to keep the high ground. I slash the blade down, striking his shoulder. His roar is filled with pain. Black blood runs down his leg and sizzles when it hits the cement.

He swipes his paw at me.

I lower the blade to block his attack, but I'm too late. Three deep lacerations in my thigh gush blood. I press my arm against my leg, nearly dropping my sword. He lifts his paw and licks the gore off of it. His eyes widen, and the flames in them leap.

He limps toward me.

"Wake up." Malcolm clamped his hand down on my shoulder hard enough to pull me out of the nightmare.

I sat in Cookie Monster. Water dripped off of my ice sword onto my leg, mixing with the blood. Mavros' coat was clutched in my other hand. I looked at Malcolm with wide eyes. "What the hell?" I threw Mavros' jacket and the sword on the floor. My blood splattered Malcolm.

He stared at me. His pupils transformed into thin slashes, and scales dotted his face. His nose and chin stretched into a snout. Fangs jutted out of his mouth.

I wasn't sure if Cody was awake or not, but I didn't dare take my eyes off Malcolm. "Cody, I need a towel *now*." I lowered my eyes just a little, hoping not to provoke the dragon in front of me. "Malcolm, your vow is sacred. Remember?"

His head jerked back like I'd slapped him, and his features slowly became more human.

Cody walked over with the towel. Malcolm's head snapped toward him. A low growl permeated the room.

I shoved Cody away. Then I wrapped the towel around my leg, hoping to cover the scent as much as possible. *Arianna, Russ, help me.* "Malcolm, you promised to protect me."

Arianna and Russ appeared between the couch and the door. They both lifted their heads and sniffed the air. Russ looked at me, then at Malcolm. He jumped over the couch and slammed his shoulder into Malcolm, knocking him down. They landed on top of Big Bird, smashing the chair into a thousand pieces.

While Russ pinned Malcolm to the floor, Arianna came to my side. She grabbed my hand, and healing energy flowed into me. I closed my eyes, thought about life, and added to her powers. The pain lessened, and I opened my eyes in time to see the last of the gashes disappear.

"The three of you need to leave while I clean up." I wiped at my leg with the towel. "Please, go now."

Russ and Malcolm disappeared first, followed quickly by Arianna.

Cody slumped onto the couch, holding his head in his hands. "You okay?" His voice was shaky.

"Sure, I guess." I stood up, trying to keep the weight off my leg until I knew it would hold. "I don't know how long they'll stay away. I need to get all the blood cleaned up and burned before they come back."

I grabbed new clothes and went to the sink. Stripping down to my underwear, I washed the blood off my body. As soon as I pulled the shirt over my head, I realized it was one of Cody's. It hung to mid-thigh on me.

I piled the clothes and towels in the sink and went to help Cody clean up the blood. His gaze roved over me. "I'll change. I don't want to ruin it."

"No." His voice was husky, and his eyes were bright. "Like seeing you in my shirt." He grazed his fingers along my cheek, then knelt on the floor and scrubbed the carpet. "Think that's all."

He pointed at the melting sword and Mavros' coat. "What's with that?"

I grabbed the rag from Cody and took it to the sink. "I was using them to fight off the panther. Then somehow, I brought them back with me." I lit my bloody shirt on fire and watched the cerulean flames devour the fabric. I took deep breaths, trying to calm the panic rising inside of me. "I don't get it."

"Me either." He stood next to me, waiting for the fire to die down so he could wash his hands. "Mavros' blood on the blade?"

I looked at the black sludge that stained the carpet. "Yeah."

"Wonder how that'll work."

My thoughts seemed to freeze, and I blinked at him several times, trying to figure out what he meant.

He dried his hands off and pointed at the blood. "Seems like he's been invited in."

"Shit."

When the dragons came back, Malcolm stood against the wall by the door, about as far from me as he could. He watched the floor without blinking.

I strolled over to him and put my hand on his arm. "Malcolm, I get it. It was a lot of blood. It splashed onto your face and took you by surprise."

"I'm supposed to be stronger." He refused to meet my gaze.

I strained to hear his low voice, then shook my head. "You didn't hurt me. You could have."

"I wanted to drain every drop of blood from your body." He looked at me, and his eyes were animalistic. "The scent lingers in here, tempting us all."

Cody walked over to the window and threw it open. Chilly mountain air rushed into the room.

I grabbed a blanket and snuggled with Cody in Cookie Monster. "Sit down." I pointed at the couch.

All three of them looked incredibly uncomfortable, but I needed to talk to them tonight before anything worsened.

"That mean he can enter now?" Cody pointed at Mavros' blood.

Arianna's eyes narrowed, and she hissed. "How did it get in here?"

"It was on the sword I brought back with me from my dream." I pulled the blanket up to my chin and shivered. "I also brought his coat back with me."

"How?" Russ looked at the other dragons.

I pressed up against Cody's side, and some of his energy flowed into me. "I hoped one of you could tell me that."

Malcolm wiped his hand down his face. He was beginning to look more like himself. "The only thing I can come up with is an out-of-body experience."

"I don't like it"—Arianna stared at the blood like it might get up and attack her—"but it makes sense."

"Wh—" my voice caught in my throat "—what do you mean?"

Malcolm pointed at the couch. "You were here, sleeping, but you were there, too."

"Your spirit was there." Russ pushed one sleeve up, then the other. "Your physical manifestation was lying on the couch with Cody, but your spiritual being was with Mavros."

"Then"—Malcolm snapped—"you weren't lying on the couch anymore. You were in the chair with the sword, jacket, and bloody leg. You were sound asleep and striking out against something I couldn't see."

I felt the urge to pace but decided it might be better to keep my scent contained under the blanket. "Why?" I raked my fingers through my hair. "Why this time? And if I was there, why didn't his venom affect me like it normally does?"

The dragons looked to each other for answers. Finally, Arianna lifted her shoulders. "I can't answer that. Maybe he's been trying to get your spirit to join him every time he's met with you in your dreams and this is the first time it's worked."

"He might have held back on his venom again," Russ said.

The urge to get up was overwhelming. I tossed the blanket to the side and walked to my closet. Grabbing a pair of sweatpants, I pulled them on. "He said he wouldn't be able to do that again, though."

"Defied orders before." Cody watched every step I took.

I blew a deep breath out of my mouth. "My dreams haven't been safe for a long time, but they've never been this unsafe."

Chapter 17

After classes Wednesday, Malcolm and I went to Sarah's office for a lesson. A fire roared in the hearth, warming the room. We sat opposite each other on the tan couches, but the coffee table wasn't the only thing between us. He'd distanced himself from me all day. He wouldn't meet my eyes, wouldn't talk to me. I didn't know why we'd even bothered coming here.

"If you don't want to do this, I can see if somebody else will help me." I looked at him, wondering if he'd respond. "Malcolm, please, let it go." I huffed.

He glanced at me and then quickly looked away. "I broke your trust. I nearly broke my vow. I am dishonorable and unworthy." He seemed to shrink before my eyes.

I walked over to the fireplace, holding my hands out to warm them. I didn't know how to fix a broken dragon, but I needed to figure it out. He saw the world differently than I did, not only because of his age but also because he was an apex predator. Hoping that turning my back on him would show him I trusted him, I walked to the window and stared outside. The sky was filled with gray clouds. The mountains were covered in a fresh coat of snow.

When he didn't react, I sat next to him. "You didn't break my trust." I took his hand in mine. "You kept Mavros from calling me. You pulled me out of that nightmare—" I dragged my other hand down my face "—or whatever it was. You've protected me, helped me, and been my friend. You listened to my concerns and set my mind at ease."

He squeezed my fingers and smiled at me. His eyes were softer than I'd ever seen them. "Thank you, Dacia."

I nodded and moved back to the other couch. "I wouldn't be here with you if I didn't trust you."

"Yeah—" he smirked "—but you also trust a demon."

I shrugged and closed my eyes. "We all have our faults." I focused on my breathing until I was relaxed. Holding my hand out, I thought about fire. A small ball of flames formed in my palm. My goal was to hold them without letting them diminish or spread.

It didn't take long for Malcolm to gain control of my powers. Flames danced along my fingers and over my hand.

Fear spread along with the fire. My heart raced. I fought to keep my breathing steady. I fought to regain control of my magic. My stomach tightened, and my hand shook. I remembered how the flames had stolen the oxygen from me in my dreams, and my breathing became harsher, shallower.

"Take it, Dacia." Malcolm's voice was strained. "They're yours. Own them."

The flames climbed my arm until Malcolm stopped them. He wiped the sweat off of his forehead and leaned back. "We will try again in a moment."

Picking up the pitcher on the coffee table, I thought about what he'd said. They were my powers, so how could somebody seize control of them from me. What happened with them should have been up to me. I poured myself a glass of water and drained it.

"Ready when you are." Malcolm narrowed his eyes and clenched his fists. "Try to take them from me."

Holding my hand out, I called flames to my palm. A tiny spark flickered, then died. I squeezed my fist, then stretched my fingers out. I focused on that minuscule bit of energy that responded to my call and summoned it again. *You are mine!* The ember shimmered. I concentrated on it. *I claim you. I do not fear you. Come to me.*

Flames erupted in my hand. I focused on them, binding them to me, not allowing Malcolm to take them.

"Good job." He slumped back. "How'd you do it?"

I closed my fist, and the power seemed to settle inside me. "I claimed them." Saying it out loud, I thought it sounded stupid, but that's what I'd done. They were mine, and no one had a right to take them from me, not now, not ever.

Malcolm tried several more times to seize control of my magic. He was never able to snatch it away from me again. When we left Sarah's office, I felt pretty good about myself.

Nephilim surrounded us as soon as we stepped outside. Diana stood in front of us with her feet spread wide and her arms folded over her chest. "We have wasted enough time here. Give us the girl. Let us go home."

"You want to go home?" I couldn't believe she said that. "You want to put me in one of your sanctuaries and never allow me to go home again, and you're complaining because you've been here a coupla weeks."

The dark-haired Nephilim stepped forward. "We are trying to save the world from the choices you will make all too soon."

"You have no idea what I'll do, Olivia." I jabbed my finger toward her, and she flinched.

Her eyes widened. "How do you know my name?"

"I learned it in a dream." I rolled my eyes. "Just like I learned I'll never be happy or complete in one of your sanctuaries."

Several of the Nephilim whispered amongst themselves. "She has the gift of prophecy." "Is she one of us?" "Does she speak the truth?" "What else has she seen?"

"Enough!" Diana yelled, and the other Nephilim quieted.

"So, you aren't allowed to speak your minds?" I spun around, looking at as many of them as I could. "Are you trapped, too?" *I think we can teleport out of here without anybody but the Nephilim noticing.*

Not yet. Malcolm stepped closer to me, reaching for my hand. "My people and your people are negotiating Dacia's status. Are you going to take her and widen the rift between our species?"

Diana laughed. "Have you spoken with Aurelia? The negotiations ended. Your people decided my people were right." She stepped closer. "Hand her over, dragon."

He angled his body between us. "I made a vow to protect Dacia. That vow is sacred, and until I hear from my own kind that I am released from it, I will protect her with my life."

"You have until tomorrow morning." Diana stepped back and smirked at me. "We will take her by any means necessary after that."

The Nephilim opened up a pathway between them. Malcolm wrapped his arm around my waist and positioned me slightly ahead of him. We walked through the leering crowd.

Once we were beyond them, Malcolm pressed his hand to my back, and we jogged to the dormitory. Instead of going to my room, Malcolm took me to Aurelia's. Her room had fewer plants in it than before, but with six dragons staying here, it probably got a little crowded.

All seven of the dragons stood in the room with me. Aurelia's skin shimmered more than normal, and when I stepped closer to her, I realized why. Gold scales glistened along her arms, neck, and face. Tears dampened her eyes. "They have decided not to protect you any longer."

"Why?" I sank onto her couch. "I've done everything that's been asked of me."

She sat beside me, wrapping her arm around my shoulders. "They fear the Nephilim will go to war if you remain free." *I believe one of the elders has been compromised.*

Who? Malcolm's thought was filled with rage.

The image of a silver dragon flashed through my mind. It was nearly twice as big as Aurelia with broken horns and rheumy eyes.

Malcolm growled. *Whose memories did he scan?*

I do not know. Aurelia sucked in a quick breath.

The other dragons stared at us like they knew we were having a silent conversation. "What am I supposed to do? I can't go with them."

"For now, you must." Aurelia's eyes flashed with rage, though she tried to control it. "We are not allowed to protect you. If we do, the elders will renounce us. The only way we can help you is to work with them to change their minds."

Malcolm stared into my eyes. *I will fight by your side if that is what you wish. I will take whatever punishment the elders decide to dole out.*

Thank you. I pulled my hand through my hair. "I'll pack a bag tonight." *But, I don't know if I'll go with them.*

Malcolm and I went to my room. Cody, Dan, and Samantha were already there. They no longer paused their activities when one of the dragons came in with me. They'd accepted them into our group. I had no doubt they would still fear them in dragon form, but they no longer thought of them as blood-thirsty beasts. They saw them as people.

"How'd it go?" Cody stood up and came over to me. "Not good?"

Samantha was curled against Dan's side on the couch. They both looked up at me over the back of it.

Malcolm held his finger over his mouth. He tilted his head. After a moment, he said, "Aurelia has soundproofed her room, and I did this one. You may talk freely now."

I shook my head and walked over to the window. "I can't." I stared outside at nothing. "I can't believe they would do that to me."

Malcolm told my friends about the Nephilim and the dragons. I tried to tune him out. I didn't want to hear about their betrayal. I didn't want to believe it could be true. I had no idea if I should stay and fight for my freedom or if I should go peacefully.

Cody stood next to me, and I buried my head in his chest. Tears came unbidden to my eyes. My shoulders shook, and he held me tighter, kissing the top of my head, rubbing my back.

Malcolm growled. The sound made me shiver. I jerked away from Cody and saw Mavros standing behind the couch.

"The hell do you want?" Cody's fingers tightened into a fist.

Mavros didn't pay any attention to Cody. "You brought my blood in here." He strode toward me. "You gave me an invitation. My *master* isn't aware of it yet, but I can't keep the knowledge hidden for long. You must go with the Nephilim. If you don't—" his chin dropped to his chest "—I can't guarantee your safety. Please go." He disappeared.

Nobody said anything for quite a while. We just stared at the last spot we'd seen Mavros, waiting for him to reappear.

Malcolm was the first to look away. "Your demon's words rang with truth. Maybe you were right to trust him."

Cody stepped away from me. "I'll go with you."

Samantha sat up and covered her face with her hands. "I'm sorry."

"For what?" I sat down in Cookie Monster and looked at the place Big Bird used to be. It was so weird having one without the other.

"He was the reason we've been staying away." She stared down at the ground. "I thought he was manipulating you. I didn't want to suffer for your mistakes. I—" her voice broke "—I was being selfish."

I leaned back and stared at the ceiling. "I thought you and Dan just wanted some privacy. I should've asked what was going on, but I've been so wrapped up in my stuff, I didn't. I'm sorry." I got up and sat beside her, bumping her shoulder with mine. "I don't blame you for trying to stay out of my crazy." I tugged my hand through my hair while I searched for the right words. "He's the only one who can tell me who summoned him. I don't trust him blindly, but I have to find out who it is."

She looked up at me. Her eyes were red-rimmed. "I get it now." She grabbed my hand and squeezed it. "I'm sorry."

"No harm done." I got up and walked over to Malcolm. *Can you have the dragons watch my friends? I'd like to talk to you in private.*

He bowed his head ever so slightly.

I slipped my hand into Malcolm's and felt like a tiny kid. "You guys'll be safe. We'll be back." I didn't give them a chance to respond. I closed my eyes and felt the stretching sensation of being teleported. When I opened them, we were in the clearing where I'd killed myself to return Mavros to the Abyss. The mountains surrounding us stretched to the heavens. The ground was covered with snow. The heat from some of the larger boulders had melted them off. I found one of those and sat.

Malcolm looked around. "Is this where you disappear to with Cody?"

"Nope." The p popped out of my mouth. "That's going to remain a secret."

He positioned himself beside me. "What do you need from me?"

I focused on my flames, not igniting them, but bringing them to the surface to see if they'd warm me. "I need to know what you'd do. Would you go with them? Or should I just disappear?"

"They will expect you to disappear." He held his hand over his mouth, slowly dragging it down. "If they catch you, they'll punish you."

I huffed out a humorless laugh. "I thought they were creatures of light."

"You will find that sometimes there isn't much difference between darkness and light." He paused for a moment. "Both sides believe in punishment. Light punishes in the hopes that you will repent. Darkness punishes for pleasure, for retribution, to feel strong."

I lowered my head and nodded. "Okay."

"The forces of light don't recognize that there are shades of gray. I believe it is better to see the varying colors and to try to bring them closer together." He squeezed my shoulder.

"There is no one right answer for everything. You were kind to Mavros, and because of that, he is fighting his master. Actions and not beliefs are what are important."

It was hard to believe that I was sitting here with a dragon who had once shredded my back with his claws. It was hard to believe that I now counted him among my friends, but he was right. If I'd only believed the worst in him and not given him a chance, my world would be much different.

"So, what would you do?" I leaned into him, needing to not feel quite so alone.

He casually slung his arm over my shoulders. "I will never be held captive again."

My stomach plummeted, and I pinched the bridge of my nose. "So, will you run with me?"

"For eternity if you need me to."

"Why?"

He stared off into the distance, not answering for a long time. When he finally did, he didn't look at me. "I have not always done the right thing … even before Draconian. I am not proud of what I did and how I acted. You showed me that one person with a desire to do good can change the world. Even after all he did to you and your friends, you tried to spare him." He lowered his gaze to me. "How many people do you think would do that? Then you sacrificed yourself to save your friends"—he waved his hand in front of him—"to save the world."

My face felt hot. I chewed on my lip to keep a stupid grin off my face.

"You befriended your enemies." He lifted his arm off my shoulders and patted my back. "You've shown me what we can do to make this world better."

I wiped my hands over my face. "So where do we go, and how do we make it seem like you're hunting me, not helping me?"

His head snapped back. "I don't care if they know."

"If they think you're after me, if they think I evaded you, we might be able to keep informed about what's going on." I massaged the back of my neck. "We might know when it's safe to go home."

Chapter 18

When we got back, Cody was sitting in Cookie Monster, holding his head. I stepped toward him, and he looked up. He'd been pressing his fingers so hard against his face that they left red marks behind. "What's the plan?"

I lifted a finger. "Malcolm, I'd like to talk to my friends in private." I intentionally hardened my voice.

He narrowed his eyes at me and walked out into the hall. As soon as he was gone, I soundproofed the room. "I'm leaving tonight." I knelt down in front of Cody. "You can come with me, but it won't be easy, and I have no idea when or if I'll be able to come back."

Dan leaned forward. "Would it be so bad to go with them?"

"Yes." I sat on the floor, running my hand over the carpet. "They will never let me leave. They will strip me of my powers. I will be imprisoned for saving the world twice, for saving the dragons." I pulled my legs up and wrapped my arms around them. "I need to be free to figure out who's controlling Mavros and what it is they want."

Dan nodded. "That's what we thought." He waved his finger between himself and Samantha. "I just wanted to be sure we were on the same page."

"Will you be okay?" Samantha seemed to shrink a little. "Do you need anything? I have some money, not much."

I held my hand up. "I don't need money." I let out a deep breath. "I could use your prayers, though."

"We can do that." Her lips turned up in a sad smile. She tapped her temple. "Let me know that you're safe."

I got up and hugged her and then Dan. "I will." Wiping under my eyes, I said, "Stay safe."

"Get a jacket," I said to Cody. He grabbed his and tossed me mine. Mavros' coat had been thrown in the corner, and it still sat there. I wondered if I should give it back to him or if one would just materialize next time he needed one.

Wrapping my arms around Cody's waist, I teleported us to Cougar Lake. He pinched his eyes shut as soon as we stopped moving. His body swayed, and he stuck his arm out to steady himself. "Wasn't expecting that."

"Sorry." I kept my arms around him until he opened his eyes. "You good?"

"Yeah."

We walked through the trees. It was becoming a familiar trek. I knew where roots jutted out of the ground far enough to trip us, when to duck under branches, when to step over boulders, and which rocks I could step on to cross the small snow-melt streams.

I held onto Cody's hand pulling him with me to the rocky shore of Cougar Lake. We made our way to a bench and sat. Cody slumped down, staring out at the water with vacant eyes. "What's the problem?" His voice was thick.

"Malcolm is going with me." I folded my hands behind my neck and leaned into them, hoping to relieve some of the tension there. "He's going to pretend like I slipped away from him and he's chasing after me so that we can keep informed about what's happening here." I bit my lip, pulling it into my mouth. "I understand if you don't want to come with me. It won't be fun."

Cody's fingers slid along my chin, angling my face toward his. "I'd follow you to Hell."

The tightness in my chest loosened. "You might be."

"Malcolm." I sat on the floor in front of my closet, an open duffle bag in front of me. "What do I need to pack? What's the sanctuary like?"

He tilted his head and tapped his finger against his chin. *Pack warm clothes, boots, more socks than you think you'll need, gloves, a hat, a couple of blankets, that sort of thing. I'll create an illusion of you packing for warm weather.* "Shorts, T-shirts, whatever girls need."

Can you do the same for Cody? "So … books and chocolate?"

"Ha." His smile was genuine. "Funny."

Even with Malcolm watching over me, Mavros' call was irresistible. I pulled Cody's arms around me and snuggled against him. I pressed my lips to his, tangling my hands in his hair, pulling him on top of me. Still, I felt Mavros tugging on the line, reeling me closer.

Realizing it wasn't going to end, I slid off the couch, pulled my coat and boots on, and stretched my hand out to Malcolm. "Will you come with me?"

He closed his eyes and slumped forward. The tension released from his body, and he grasped my hand.

"You sure?" Cody asked.

I nodded. "I can't keep resisting him. It's better to have it on my terms."

"Come back. Okay?" He sat on the edge of the couch.

"Always."

Malcolm released whatever magic he was using to keep me from being called out, and we were immediately pulled to Mavros' side. He stood by the lake we'd picnicked at, staring at the night-darkened water.

Mavros lowered his head. "Dragon."

"Demon." Malcolm kept hold of my hand.

Mavros turned to me. His eyes looked pained. "I hate that you can't trust me, but I understand. You never know when I'll turn on you." He kicked a rock into the lake. "Are you leaving?"

"Who's asking?" Malcolm positioned himself between us while still holding my hand. "You or your puppeteer?"

Mavros narrowed his eyes at Malcolm. "Me." He bent down and picked up several stones, tossing them one at a time into the lake. "I want her to leave."

"Why?" I asked.

He crossed his arms and threw his shoulders back. "Because I don't want to torture you into madness or kill you or whatever else the bastard decides I need to do."

"Thank you." I stepped toward Mavros and put my hand on his arm.

His head jerked back, and he looked at me like he didn't know what to think. "So"—his voice lost its edge—"are you going to the sanctuary?"

"I'm leaving in the morning."

"Good." He turned and strode off, melting into the darkness.

I need to leave before whoever controls him finds out, I thought to Malcolm.

He teleported us back to my room. *I agree.*

Chapter 19

$\mathcal{P}$retending to be asleep with Cody's arms wrapped around my waist, I let my hand fall limply to the side of the couch. I slowly worked the straps of the duffle bags around my wrist, hoping that any prying eyes wouldn't notice my actions. I laced my fingers through Cody's and thought of the cave where I'd defeated Nefarious.

Just as we disappeared, I heard Malcolm roar.

The cave was pitch black. I summoned fire to my palm and set it on the ground, willing the flames to grow to give us heat and light. Stalactites and stalagmites filled the cave. The firelight flicked its shadows throughout the cavern, making it even eerier.

Like I'd asked him earlier, Cody had clutched the pillow and blanket so they teleported with us. I had no idea how long we'd be on our own, but I didn't think a little comfort was too much to ask.

I set the bags on the floor and dug the other blankets out, spreading the heaviest one over the ground, hoping to ward off some of the chill. Then I turned to Cody. "Well, what do you think?"

He looked around, nodding. "Home is where the heart is, and you're here."

In all the time I'd known him, Cody had always been a man of few words, but when he said things like that, I felt like the luckiest person in the world. "Hopefully, not for too long." I wrapped my arms around him and tilted my head up. He brushed his lips over mine. "I don't know if the fire will last after I fall asleep. It might get cold."

We lay down on the ground and covered up with the two remaining blankets. I planned to fight sleep to keep the fire going for as long as I could.

Picturing Samantha's face, I thought to her, *We are safe for now.* There was no way for me to know if she heard me. I hoped the Nephilim would leave her and Dan alone, that whoever summoned Mavros wouldn't harm them, and that the dragons would keep them safe.

I stared at the ceiling, trying to hold the ghosts of this place at bay. I didn't want to be here, but it was the only place I could think of besides Draconian's castle, and since the dragons knew it better than I did, I figured I should avoid going there.

Hundreds of lights dotted the ceiling. As I gazed at them, they seemed to move closer, growing larger until I saw them for what they were. The silver-haired fairies that healed me when I fought Nefarious hovered all around me. Their presence filled me with peace.

"Hello." I stood up and held my hand out.

One landed on my palm. She was about two inches tall. Her bare feet left tracks on my hand as she stepped closer. "Welcome," she said in a high, squeaky voice.

I bowed my head. "Thank you. Without your help, I wouldn't be alive."

"Evil must not prevail." Her iridescent wings fluttered even though she was standing still. "You were demon-marked, and with his taint still on you, he can track you."

I slumped forward. "Is there anything I can do to remove it?"

"No, but we can." The fairies surrounded me, landing on me and then flitting off, over and over again. Their wings shimmered and hummed as they zipped through the air.

When they stopped, a silver glow emanated from my body, lighting up the cavern. "Did it work?" I looked into her purple eyes.

"Yes. His stain has been removed." She flapped her wings, lifting into the air.

A lightness filled me. "Thank you."

They flew up, making the cave ceiling twinkle like the night sky. Then all at once, their lights disappeared.

I lay back on the hard ground with Cody.

"That was cool." He sounded awestruck.

"Beautiful actually." I rolled over so I was facing him. "They're the fairies that healed me when I fought Nefarious. I didn't think I'd have the privilege of seeing them again."

"Might be a lotta grief with your powers, but also a lotta good." He brushed my hair back, tucking it behind my ear. "They should go to the Nephilim and vouch for you."

I fell asleep with my head on Cody's shoulder. When I woke up, my fire still blazed, holding the darkness at bay.

Malcolm leaned against a stalagmite. "You're glowing."

"Fairies removed Mavros' taint from me." I stood up and lowered my hand to Cody. He shook his head and sat up, combing his hands through his hair.

"Interesting." Malcolm rubbed his chin. "I didn't realize it was still there."

"Me either"—I shrugged—"but they sensed it."

He stepped closer to the flames, and the light made the shadows on his face look creepy. "I wonder if the Nephilim could sense it but didn't realize what it was."

"Yeah." I pulled my hands through my hair, wondering how bad it looked. "Cody thinks the fairies should talk to the Nephilim."

"So, what's your story?" Cody knelt in front of the fire, warming his hands.

Malcolm handed me a bag. "There's no meat in there, but you humans eat strange food."

The sack was filled with donuts and bottles of milk. "Thank you." I took one of each and passed it to Cody.

He pulled a glazed one out, took a big bite of it, and nodded at Malcolm. "Much obliged."

"They believed you fooled me." Malcolm waved his hand through the flames. "How did you keep the fire going while you slept?"

I held my finger up until I swallowed the food in my mouth. "I don't know. I didn't think I'd be able to, but it worked." I licked the icing off of my lips. "Do they think you're searching for me?"

"Everybody is searching for you." He flashed me a smile that showed more fang than normal.

"Everybody?" Cody popped the last of his donut into his mouth.

Malcolm nodded. "The dragons and the Nephilim. The Nephilim won't stop looking until they find you. The dragons haven't committed yet."

"Great." My legs wobbled, so I leaned against a stalagmite for support.

"Nobody has seen Mavros since you disappeared." Malcolm's bronze eyes reflected the firelight, reminding me of a cat's. "They believe you went with him."

"And brought Cody along?" I shook my head and tugged my hand through my hair. "Right."

Malcolm didn't say anything. He just stared at me over the flames.

"They think I turned to darkness. Don't they?" My stomach churned, and I regretted eating breakfast.

He nodded. "We'll find a way to prove your innocence."

"How?" Cody walked over to me and leaned against the stalagmite, not touching me but there if I needed him. "Didn't believe when it was obvious."

"They never will." I clutched my stomach and bent over.

Chapter 20

ody, Malcolm, and I spent the day exploring the cave. We searched for more secluded places to hide, places where I could soundproof the area and create the illusion of a rock wall, places we could escape if the need arose. The cave we had spent the night in was too open, too vulnerable.

We discovered several water sources, and Malcolm showed me how to purify them for drinking. He leaned close to me, guiding my hands over the water. I worried Cody would be jealous of Malcolm's proximity to me, but he didn't seem bothered by it at all.

When Cody's stomach growled, Malcolm teleported away. He came back about twenty minutes later with burgers from the student center.

Cody's eyes lit up as the aroma filled the cavern. "Thanks." He smiled when Malcolm handed him two of them. "Wondered what we'd do for food."

"After we figure out where we'll be, I'll teleport out to get supplies." I took a bite of my burger and winced. As grateful as I was for food, I could've done without the ketchup on it.

Malcolm shook his head at me, and the beads on his corn-rows clanked together. "You will be spotted. Tell me what you need, and I'll bring it back for you."

"I was planning to go somewhere secluded, somewhere they wouldn't suspect." I took a drink of the freshly purified water.

Malcolm sat on the ground next to me. "There are eyes everywhere, Dacia."

"Won't they wonder why you're getting supplies?" Cody had already downed one burger and was starting on another.

Still eating his food, Malcolm transformed into an older man with a shaved head and silver goatee. "I will be careful." He morphed back into the version of himself we'd come to know.

"I can do that, too, you know?" I stared into Malcolm's eyes as I took his features as my own.

He shook his head. "They aren't just looking for your physical manifestation. They're also searching for your aura. Now, we need to discuss Aurelia."

My stomach dropped, and I set my burger down on its wrapper.

"You're gonna eat that." Cody pointed at it.

I couldn't think about food right now. I felt horrible for leaving without letting Aurelia know what was happening, but if she went to the dragon council or met with the Nephilim, I didn't know if she'd be able to hide the memory from them. "What about her?"

"She is worried about you, but she told us that if any of us knew where you were, we should tell you that you did the right thing."

"She suspect you?" Cody leaned back, bracing himself with his arms and stretching his legs out in front of himself.

Malcolm tilted his head and raised one shoulder. "She looked right at me when she said it."

I thought about Arion and wondered if he had been keeping an eye on me for her. Not knowing how much Malcolm knew about Aurelia's pegasus companion, I didn't bring him up. "She tends to know more about what's happening than she lets on."

"She is on your side and will continue fighting for you for as long as it takes." Malcolm stood. "Shall we continue searching?"

Cody shook his head. "Dacia needs to eat."

Malcolm nodded. "You have to keep your strength up. We have no idea how long this will last or how easily I will be able to continue slipping away from the others." He sat back down. "It wouldn't surprise me if to placate the Nephilim, they start having us split up into groups to search for you. If they are with me, I won't be able to continue to bring you supplies."

I ate my burger as quickly as I could and washed it down with water. "Satisfied?"

Both the dragon and the human nodded at me. We continued on our trek through the cave system. A crack partially hidden behind stalagmites opened up into a decent-sized chamber. "This looks like a good place to hide your stuff." Malcolm squeezed through the crevice. "There's plenty of room for a makeshift bed, and there's another way out back here."

I didn't like the idea of guarding two doors but understood why Malcolm wanted us to have more than one exit. We explored a little more before going back for our things. While I packed stuff up, Cody and Malcolm tried to figure out what we might need for an extended stay in the cavern.

Malcolm helped us bring our stuff to the other chamber. Then he disappeared. I laid the blankets on the floor, sat down, pulled my knees up to my chest, and wrapped my arms around them. I felt like I should be doing something more than just sitting around. I didn't want to be here forever, and unless I did something to change my situation, I would be.

Cody sat beside me. "Not the enda the world."

"It seems like it." I rested my chin on my knees. Aurelia might have believed I made the right choice, but I wasn't sure I had, and worst of all, this choice affected Cody, too. "How can I ever get the Nephilim to believe that I'm innocent if I just hide away?"

"Come up with something." He threw his arm over my shoulder and pulled me into his side. "Don't do anything rash."

"Dacia." Mavros strides toward me. A thick fog rolls in with him, filling the night, muffling everything but his low growl. "You lied to me."

I fold my arms over my chest. "Not technically."

"You told me you were going to their sanctuary." We stand toe to toe. He glares down at me, and his black eyes are hard. Sometimes I forget how much bigger he is than me, but looking up at him, I feel intimidated.

I want to step back, but I fight the urge and hold my ground. "No, I told you I was leaving. You assumed I was leaving for the sanctuary."

"Why couldn't you just go with them?" He steps away. His shoulders droop. "I was trying to keep you safe, but now the moron is sending me to find you and do whatever's necessary to keep you from going to the sanctuary."

I smile at him, fully aware that he's a demon but still hoping he's on my side. "Thanks for the warning."

Chapter 21

Caged

By the middle of the second day, living in a cave was wearing on both Cody and me. Not knowing if it was day or night, not being able to smell the fresh air, and not being able to step outside all took their toll on us. The constant sound of water dripping put me on edge. I paced the cavern like a tiger in a cage.

"Dacia, stop." Cody's voice startled me. It sounded harsh in the stillness of the cave, but his eyes were compassionate, understanding. He stood and walked toward me. "Let's go for a run."

We both changed into shorts and T-shirts. Then I created a ball of fire and made it hover in the air in front of us. We jogged side by side through the chambers and single file in most of the passages. The steady thumping of our feet on the rock covered up the sound of dripping water.

The flames lit up all of the different formations. In the dry areas of the cavern, some of the ceilings were covered in box-work. Crystal formations glistened in the firelight. The cave system was fascinating, beautiful in its own way, but the outside world called to me.

I pushed myself, running faster and harder until sweat soaked my shirt. I needed the physical activity to clear my mind and help me come up with a way out of this situation.

The ground rose, and I slowed my pace. My calves burned from the exertion. The passage leveled off and opened into a chamber filled with a lake. I ran to the water's edge. With the fire's light, I was able to see the bottom of it for a couple of feet.

Cody stopped beside me and looked out. "Kinda creepy."

"Why?" I pulled my shoes and socks off and stepped into the lake. I gasped and stepped back.

He chuckled. "Don't know what's in it."

"There's probably nothing in here that's worse than what's already hunting me." I stepped forward again. The shock wasn't too bad this time. The water was cold. I would love to warm it up and go for a swim, but I didn't want to hurt any of the creatures who called it home. I trod a little further into the lake and slid on the slick rock. Cody reached out for my hand, but I caught myself before falling in.

His shoulders slumped. "Careful. You get hurt, I got no light, no way to contact Malcolm."

I stepped out of the water. "Maybe we should have him bring us some flashlights … just in case something happens to me." I chewed on my lip. "I could have one of my lovely nightmares, and you'd be screwed." I sent a wave of heat to my feet to dry them, then put my socks and shoes back on. "Better yet, we could go get them."

"We can't." Cody closed his eyes and massaged his forehead.

I walked up beside him and set my hand on his bicep. "We might have to leave. They've sent Mavros to look for me."

His muscle tightened beneath my fingers. "This why you're wound up?"

I shrugged. "I hate feeling trapped." I stepped back toward the water. The blue flames followed my lead. Cody was right. I needed to be careful, to be here, to keep him safe. I lifted my hair off my neck and splashed cold water on it. "To avoid a cage, I put myself in one."

The run back was more subdued. I was stuck in my head, trying to figure a way out of this mess but not seeing even an inkling of how to do it. When we were almost back, something spooked me. I turned to Cody and lifted my finger to my lips. Then I snuffed out the flame. The cave was pitch black.

A light moved in front of the passage in the next chamber. Low voices drifted up to me. I leaned close to Cody and whispered, "Don't move. I'll be right back."

I turned invisible and teleported right outside the chamber.

Cash stalked through the cavern, tossing balls of flame against the walls, lighting up the vast space. "I can smell both of you all over this place. You can't tell me you don't know where she is."

"I caught her scent here, too." Malcolm leaned against the stalagmite blocking entry into our new shelter. "I've come back here several times to try to track her, but so far the only thing I've found is her aroma."

"You know more than you're letting on." Cash turned toward me for just an instant, and I fought to hold in my gasp. Purple horns ringed his head. He had more scales on his face than skin, and his hands ended in wicked talons. "I promised to protect her, too. Don't take that from me."

Malcolm lifted his head and inhaled. Then he looked directly at me and shook his head slightly. "You've never acted like you cared, so why now?"

"Because now she's gone, and I can't keep her safe!" His eyes were wild.

Do you trust him? Malcolm's voice in my head surprised me almost as much as seeing Cash partially transformed had.

I don't know. I wanted to trust him, but if Mavros was right, one of the dragons had betrayed me. *He's always scared me a little.*

Malcolm strode toward him. "Look at me, Cash."

Cash locked eyes with Malcolm, and Malcolm opened his thoughts to me. I saw Cash being beaten by Draconian. I saw myself setting him free and heard his vow to never be controlled again. I saw his animosity toward mankind. I felt his fear at me knowing his name and his determination to keep me from using it against him. Then I felt his concern at my disappearance, his failure in not keeping me safe, and his desire to help me.

I stepped forward, making myself visible to him. Cash looked from Malcolm to me. "I swear to you, Acacia"—I hoped he would understand why I said his true name and not his human one—"I will never use your name to control you. However, I will use your name to help you if I can."

He bowed to me, and his features became human once again. "I am pleased to see that you're safe."

"Thanks." I looked toward the passage. "I need to get Cody." I ignited my flames and followed them to where I'd left him.

He stood and brushed the dirt off his shorts. "What's going on?"

"It looks like we have another protector."

"Who?" He motioned for me to go in front of him.

"Believe it or not … Cash."

"Hmph."

Cody and I led the way into our chamber. Malcolm had stocked it with a bunch of necessities, and most of the floor was covered by black and dark gray cushions. We sat away from the sleeping area, and after I soundproofed the grotto and set up the illusions, I waved my hand at the room. "Thank you for getting all of this for us."

He shrugged. "If I hadn't, you would've."

"Yeah." I played with the tassels of the black cushion I was sitting on.

Cash crinkled his nose and breathed through his mouth.

"What?" Cody asked.

His lip curled. "The two of you need to bathe."

"I found a lake, but the water is freezing." I hoped my cheeks weren't as red as they felt. "I thought about warming it up, but I don't want to hurt the creatures that live in it."

"Where?" Cash asked.

Cody told him where it was, and Cash ducked out of the crack.

"This isn't easy for him." Malcolm leaned back against the cushions he'd piled around himself. "He didn't want to like you—" he smiled at me, showing his fangs "—but with your honorable intentions, it's hard not to. Ever since the day you told the Nephilim they should have helped us, he's been thawing."

The floor of the cavern shook. "What in the world?" I pressed my hands down, bracing myself.

"I'd say he's building you a bathtub." Malcolm laughed. Then he sobered. "It is good that he knows about you. We can trade off bringing you supplies. The Nephilim might think I'd harbor you, but Cash is the last dragon they'd expect."

"You shouldn't talk about me when I'm not here," Cash said from the shadows.

Malcolm sat up. "Do you really think I didn't hear you squeeze through that tiny hole?"

Cash flashed him a smile. "You can bathe now. I didn't warm the water for you, though. I don't know how much heat your fragile bodies can handle."

I thought about flames until my hand became them. "Mine can handle as much as yours." I stood up. "Cody's ... not so much." I gathered spare clothes and toiletries and turned toward Cody. "You coming?"

His cheeks turned bright red. "Uh …"

"You need the water heated and fire so you can see, and I'll need to soundproof the area in case somebody else comes wandering in here." I turned toward Cash. "How did you find this place anyway?"

He shrugged. "Luck. I was flying overhead and caught your scent."

"Some way to remove it?" Cody searched through his duffle bag for clothes.

"It's already been done." Cash looked at Malcolm. "Didn't think I noticed, did you?"

The firelight was reflected in Malcolm's eyes. "I thought I was being sneaky enough."

"Maybe with anybody else's scent, but not with hers." Cash pointed at me.

I tugged my hand through my hair. Near my scalp, it was still wet with sweat. "Why? What do I smell like?"

Malcolm and Cash looked at each other. Malcolm said, "Like a lightning storm but more powerful."

Cash nodded. "Like strength, desire, and power."

"Just to dragons?" Cody shoved his stuff into my duffle bag and took it out of my hand.

"I doubt it." Cash sat on the cushions. "We just have a better sense of smell than most creatures you've come across thus far."

Malcolm said, "Ask your demon?"

"He's not *my* demon." The dragons' laughter followed us out of the room. I created a ball of fire in the air in front of Cody and me. It was a silent trek to the underground lake.

Cash had created a pool behind several stalagmites. It was nearly big enough for him to bathe in while in his dragon form. I soundproofed the area and created an illusion so my fire couldn't be seen by anyone passing by. Then I stuck my fingers in it to gauge the water.

Cody stood off to the side, watching me. "So, uh"—his voice was husky and sent a pang of desire through me—"what's your plan?"

"For you to get in and tell me if the water's warm enough."

He kicked his shoes off, wiggling his toes as he pulled off his socks. I watched him tug his shirt over his head and admired his physique. When he reached for his shorts, I turned away.

"You can look, Dacia." His voice was soft. "I'm not shy."

I shook my head. "Now's not the time." My heart beat faster than I could ever remember. I felt it in my chest, my throat, and my temples. Warmth flooded through my body, and I pressed my eyes shut to avoid the temptation.

I heard the water splash as he stepped into it. "Hotter, please."

Knowing I could hurt him, I slowly warmed the water. "Thanks."

Ripples lapped at my arm. I pulled it out and dried it off, keeping my back to him.

"Dacia"—he sounded like he was talking to a frightened animal—"it's dark. I'm underwater. You can turn around."

I walked to a boulder that I assumed came from Cash's excavation and sat down, facing him. The fire lit up his face and nothing more. I leaned my head back, and my eyes drifted shut.

"Dacia." Cody sounded alarmed.

I opened my eyes, and the room was black. I ignited a ball of flames in my palm, growing it until it lit the chamber. "I'm sorry, Cody. I guess I fell asleep."

He rinsed the shampoo out of his hair, then scrubbed the rest of himself. "Getting out."

I turned away. Part of me wanted to peek, but like I'd said earlier, now wasn't the time.

"Okay." Cody stood with a towel wrapped around his waist, combing his hair.

For a moment, I saw him standing in a real bathroom. The walls were pale yellow, and the woodwork looked like oak. Light from two big windows illuminated him. Then the cave returned.

The air rushed from my lungs, and my heart clenched. I wanted that future more than anything, but would it be like other visions and not come true? I steadied my breathing, then walked to the water, and purified it like Malcolm had shown me.

Standing at the edge of the pool, I stripped down to my underclothes. Cody watched me until I motioned for him to turn around.

The pool had a lip around the edge. I stepped onto it, and the water came to mid-thigh. There was no way I'd be able to sit and keep my head above the surface. Deciding I'd have to stand, I stretched my toes down, trying to find the floor. Jumping off the ledge, I sank to the bottom. The water was over my head.

When I surfaced, Cody said, "Shallower on the other side."

I swam to the other side, settling myself on the lip. Realizing I'd left my bag where I'd initially gotten in, Cody brought it over to me. "Need help?" His eyes sparkled in the darkness. "I can wash your back." He put his feet in the water, one on either side of me.

It would be so easy to yes. So much easier than it would be to say no. I bit my lip, trying to stick to my guns. I remembered the day we'd spent in the pool by ourselves. The feel of his wet body against mine.

Cody yanked his feet back. "Ow!"

I turned to look at him. "Are you okay?" I touched his foot, and he jerked it back.

"Water's practically boiling." Steam rose off the water, filling the cavern.

"Oh, God, Cody, I'm sorry." I stretched my hand out, waiting until he moved his foot toward me. Then I sent cool, healing energy through him.

He sighed.

"Better?" I asked.

He smiled. "All good." He stood up and walked back to the other side.

I used my powers to keep the steam from dissipating, blocking it in the same area that was soundproofed.

By the time I finished washing, the steam was so thick in the room that Cody couldn't have seen me if he was standing right beside me. I climbed out and wrapped one towel around my hair and one around my body.

The cold stone floor felt good against my feet. I let the air cool me off before getting dressed. As soon as I finished, I allowed the steam to dissipate.

Cody sat with his shirt off, leaning against a stalagmite. He stood and finished dressing. "You okay?"

I flipped the towel off my head and dried my hair as much as possible. "A little warm. You?"

"Same." He stuffed our things into the duffle bag.

I walked to the edge of the pool and purified it again. If somebody or something came looking for me, I didn't want them to find evidence that we'd bathed here. I needed to re-member to ask Cash or Malcolm if they could remove my scent from the area or if they could teach me how.

When I stood, a wave of dizziness crashed over me. The flames dimmed. Cody rushed to my side. "What happened?"

"Used too much." My words sounded slurred to me, but he seemed to understand.

He hung the duffle bag off his shoulder and lifted me into his arms. I leaned my head against his chest.

"Don't sleep yet." He jogged toward the cavern we'd set-tled in. "Need the light."

I fought to keep my eyes open. "Sorry, Cody." *Malcolm*, I thought right before I passed out.

Chapter 22

$\mathcal{I}$ woke up on a pile of cushions with three sets of eyes staring at me. The flames lighting the room were red, not blue. Sitting up, I pulled my hands through my hair. It was still wet, so I hadn't been out that long.

"Sorry." I looked down at my hands. "I haven't used too much power for so long. I guess I wasn't paying attention to the warning signs."

"What were you doing that used so much?" Cash backed away from me.

I closed my eyes and lowered my chin to my chest. "I was soundproofing this room and that one. Creating illusions for this one and that. I had fires lit in both rooms. I was heating the water and keeping the steam from leaving the room." I looked into his eyes. He was staring at me with a dazed expression. "Oh, I purified the water twice and had to heal Cody."

Malcolm and Cash both turned toward him. He lifted his hands. "I'm good."

Cash pulled his hand down his face. "You ever heard of a human who could do all that at once?"

"Nope." Malcolm shook his head. "It might even make one of us tired." He stood up. "Since you exhausted yourself, Cash is going to stay here tonight. I will try to return tomorrow."

"Before you go, can one of you show me how to clear my stench from the pool area?" I let out a deep breath. "I don't want to get ambushed there next time I go to bathe."

"I'll show her later," Cash said. "Could you do it when you leave?"

"No problem." Malcolm focused on me. "Don't exert yourself. Cody or Cash can get you whatever you need tonight." He disappeared.

I combed my fingers through my hair, and since I wouldn't be able to stay awake until it dried, I braided it. Both Cody and Cash watched me. Neither one of them made it obvious, but even though their heads were turned away, their eyes tracked every movement I made. I pressed my hands down to stand, and Cash said, "Sit. What do you need?"

I slumped down. "Water."

Cody started to get up, and Cash motioned for him to stay. Then he rummaged through the supplies Malcolm had brought until he found a bottle of water. "Want it cold?" he asked as he delivered it to me.

"Yes, please." I smiled at him. "Almost frozen."

He cooled it off and handed it to me. As he turned away, he said, "I am sorry for the way I treated you. I thought any human with access to my name would use it like Draconian had."

"I understand." I unscrewed the lid. "Once bitten, twice shy." I took a drink, then lay down.

Cody stretched out beside me. "Take some of my strength."

Cash's eyebrows pinched together, and he tilted his head.

"It helps me regain my energy, but sometimes I take too much from him. Then he has to sleep it off." I shook my head at Cody. "I can't risk it. If we have to make a quick getaway, I need you cognizant."

Cash knelt beside me. His purple eyes were inquisitive. "Can you take mine?"

"Yes." I set my hand on his forearm. "Aurelia says that dragon power runs so deep that I only take a sip of it."

His fingers brushed mine, and I was surprised by their softness. "Take whatever you need."

I siphoned his energy into me. Like Aurelia's, it was instantly revitalizing. The pure strength of it made adrenaline surge through me. I closed my eyes and savored the feeling.

"Are Russ and Arianna with Samantha and Dan?" I asked after letting go of his arm.

Cash moved back to the other side of the room, opening and closing his hand.

"I didn't hurt you, did I?"

"No." He looked down. "It feels weird."

"How?" Cody asked.

"Like a part of her flowed back into me." He shook his hand, then looked at us. "Your friends are being guarded by them. They are safe."

I rolled onto my side and propped myself up on my elbow. "Do they know you're here?"

"No. The fewer who know, the safer you'll be." He looked like he wanted to say more but didn't.

"I don't know if Malcolm told you, but Russ let me look into his head. I know I can trust him."

Cody slid his hand around my waist and rested his head on my shoulder.

A sudden rush of desire flared through my body.

Cash sniffed the air, and his pupils turned to slits. "I'm going to stand outside for a while. Go to sleep." His voice was gruff, and I remembered Malcolm telling me that desire made me smell even better to the dragons.

"I'm sorry, Cash."

He smiled back at me. "I was young once. I understand."

Heat flared in my body, rushing up my neck, and spilling onto my cheeks.

Cash laughed as he stepped through the crack.

I turned in Cody's arms and slid my hands under his shirt, tugging it off. I pulled his body closer to mine and trailed kisses from the base of his neck, up over his chin, and onto his lips.

He moaned in response, clutching my butt. "What's this?"

"I have all this energy—" I laughed "—and since I can't even stand up to get a bottle of water, no way to use it." My hands roved over his chest, and he leaned back, stretching his neck up.

I kissed the bottom of his chin, then pressed my mouth to his. He wrapped his arms around me and flipped me over.

I pulled my head back. "He's probably watching. He vowed to guard me."

His eyes shone. "Won't let him see anything." Cody's voice was husky.

I nodded, and his head descended. His lips claimed mine, pressing harder, opening them, trapping the moan in my mouth.

Our bodies were pressed together. I rubbed my leg along his and slowed the kiss, savoring every touch.

He moved his kisses from my lips to my neck and up to my ear. "I love you." His tongue traced along my ear, making me suck in a breath and stealing my reply. I dug my fingernails into his skin. Clutching his body, I closed my eyes and rolled my head back.

His lips brushed mine, and I yawned. Cash's energy had been like adding lighter fluid to a fire. It burned bright and quick.

Cody rolled onto his back, and I laid my head on his chest. His arms were wrapped around me, strong, comforting. "I'm sorry," I said.

"Just rest, Dacia." He traced his fingers along my arm in a soothing motion, raising goosebumps on my skin.

"Thank you for coming with me." My words were thick and slurred together.

"Wouldn't miss it."

Closing my eyes, my breathing evened out. I trailed my fingers over his chest. I was vaguely aware of Cash coming back into the room.

Chapter 23

When I woke up, Cash and Cody were huddled together in the corner whispering. Cody glanced over when I stretched. "Morning, Sleeping Beauty."

"Morning." Standing up, I pulled the blanket with me, draping it over my shoulders. The cave seemed chillier than it had been last night. They watched me carefully as I walked over to them.

"How're you feeling?" Cash scrutinized every move I made.

"Much better." I wrapped the blanket tighter around me, feeling extremely self-conscious. "So, what's in store for today? A whole lotta nothing?"

"Well, I could stand outside the room while you two make out—" Cash flashed his teeth "—or we could figure out a way to prove to the Nephilim that you're a good person."

Propping my elbow up on my hand, I tapped a finger against my chin and kept my face as serious as I could. "Wanna go stand out in the hall then?"

Cash threw his head back and laughed a full-belly laugh that made Cody and I giggle.

When he stopped, I said, "What do you have in mind?"

"I think we should try to find the fairies that removed Mavros' taint." He knelt on the pillows and dug through the bag of food, pulled out a couple of protein bars, and handed them to me. "You need to eat before we leave."

"One's good." I handed the other one to Cody and peeled the wrapper back on mine. "I don't know how to find them. Both times, they've found me."

"Let's hope they find you again then." Cash pushed himself to his feet, and I noticed that his features seemed to be softer.

Trying to figure out what it was, I gawked at him. His chin and nose weren't as sharp as they'd been, and his eyes didn't have the same hardness to them.

"What?" He folded his arms over his chest.

I waved my hand at him. "You look different this morning."

"Yeah." He brushed his purple-streaked hair back and looked down. "I was a jackass. I wanted to intimidate you."

I waved my protein bar at him. "It worked."

"I could smell it on you"—he tapped his nose—"but you did a good job of not showing it."

"Eat." Cody crumbled up his wrapper and grabbed another bar.

I could barely choke mine down. It was dry and tasteless. As soon as I swallowed the last bite, I cooled off a couple bottles of water for Cody and me. "What are you going to eat? And when do you have to show yourself again?" I asked Cash.

"I'll hunt for something later." He pointed at the last of Cody's breakfast. "I'm not sure that should be considered food."

I wrinkled my nose. "Not so much, but I appreciate you guys bringing us supplies and keeping us fed."

"So … when?" Cody prodded.

"They're not going to watch me as closely as Malcolm. I should be good for two or three days." Cash rubbed his hand along his jaw. "I can tell them I was following your scent."

"So … am I going to have to lay a false trail? Teleport somewhere, wander aimlessly, and then teleport back here."

Cash tilted his head, and I realized he hadn't considered the consequences. "The Nephilim can't smell you, but the other dragons can." He spun around, taking a few steps away from Cody and me, then turning back. "They'll want me to lead them to your scent so they can try to track it. I'll discuss it with Malcolm."

I grabbed a change of clothes and stood behind a stalagmite. I would've traded a suitcase full of dragon loot for a bathroom, but at least I was safe for now. "How do you plan to find the fairies?"

"I don't know." He let out a hefty sigh and dragged his hand down his face. "I don't even know if they'll come around if I'm with you. I haven't always followed the light."

"Malcolm said the same thing." I folded up my pajamas and set them by our make-shift bed. Both Cash and Cody followed every movement I made. Their attention was a bit unsettling. "What?!"

They shared a conspiratorial look. Then Cash waved his hand for Cody to explain. "Slept for fifteen hours."

"Holy crap." I tugged my hairbands out and pulled my fingers through my braids. "I guess I really overdid it." I lit a fire in my palm.

Cash closed my hand. "Not today."

"But"—my chest tightened, and I rubbed the heal of my other hand over my breastbone—"if I don't use them, I can't get stronger."

He patted my shoulder. "Not today. Today you need to rest and recharge."

We filled a backpack with food and drinks. Then we left the cavern. My first instinct was to create an illusion to keep it hidden from anybody who might be searching for me. I rubbed my forehead. "Cash, can you hide the fissure?"

"Yes." He waited off to the side while Cody and I walked past him.

We wandered through the passages, following Cash's red flames. The steady sound of dripping water was our constant companion. "Both times I've seen the fairies, they were in the chamber where I defeated Nefarious, but I've been in there several times without seeing them."

"Good a place as any." Cody entwined his fingers with mine.

Long shadows spilled across the floor, collecting outside of the flame's reach. I wanted to add my fire to Cash's to dispel the darkness, to prove that no demon lingered beyond the light's reach. Too many of the passages and chambers triggered memories of me nearly dying at Nefarious' hands.

"Dacia"—Cody spread his fingers out—"too tight."

I loosened my grip on his hand. "I'm sorry." I pointed to a stalagmite. "I ran through that when I battled Nefarious."

He brushed his thumb over mine. "He's gone."

"Yeah." I blew out a hefty sigh. "So was Mavros. What if somebody decides to summon him next? What if they bring worse to try to lure me out?"

A low growl rumbled through the cavern. My knees locked, and I stifled a scream. Cody darted a glance over his shoulder.

Cash inhaled deeply and groaned. "Sorry."

I turned to look at him, and he flashed his teeth and held his hands up, palms out. "Didn't mean to scare you."

"Why'd you growl?" Cody asked.

"Because Dacia's right." He folded his arms over his chest. "The longer she's hidden away, the more desperate Mavros' puppeteer will become."

I knelt on the cold ground, holding my head in my hands. More enemies were not what I needed. I needed to figure out how to get rid of the Nephilim so I could deal with whoever summoned Mavros.

"Dacia"—Cash's voice was strained—"these passage-ways are too enclosed for so many emotions."

Standing up, I pushed the sleeves of my hoodie up and narrowed my eyes at him. "What do you want me to do? I can't turn them off."

He laughed. "Anger is good. Hold onto that. It doesn't make you smell like prey."

As he walked past me, I flipped him off. Cody and I followed behind him. My anger simmered. It was too easy for me to embrace it. Everything about the Nephilim annoyed me.

When we walked into the chamber where I'd seen the fairies, I held onto Cody's hand, hoping he would guide me while I watched the ceiling for any trace of them. I saw no flashes of silver light. I climbed over and around stalagmites, searching every corner for them.

There was no sign that they'd ever been here, no footprints in the dust, no treasure hoards, no food stores, no messes.

I sat down and bowed my head. The Nephilim would never believe anything I said. They wouldn't trust the dragons. As far as I could tell, the fairies were my only hope. "If you don't want evil to prevail, I need you," I whispered.

Cash turned his head, looking at me from about twenty feet away. "What did you say?"

"Just talking to myself." I shrugged, then shoved my hands into my pouch. "They're not here."

"We'll search the next chamber and the next until we find them." He walked toward me, and tiny pinpricks of light illuminated the darkness behind him.

The ball of anger in the pit of my stomach loosened, and I breathed easier. "No need." I pointed behind Cash's back.

He looked over his shoulder, and his posture relaxed. They landed on the stalagmites and stalactites. In a shrill voice, one asked, "Why do you despair?"

I traipsed toward them. "The Nephilim believe I have fallen to darkness. They are hunting me with the help of the dragons and the demon, Mavros."

As one, they turned to stare at Cash. "Where does your loyalty lie?"

"With Dacia." He bowed to them. "She saved me from Draconian and has proven to be honorable."

My heart tingled and warmth spread through my chest. I couldn't stop the stupid grin from lifting my lips. I walked back to him and squeezed his forearm. "At least one other dragon is on my side."

"Two." Cody held up two fingers. "Malcolm and Aurelia."

I bit my lip. "I don't know for sure where Aurelia stands."

"By your side, with me." Cash smiled down at me.

"Arianna and Russ are on my side, too—" I dragged my hand through my hair "—but I don't know if they'll fight by my side. The elder dragons threatened to renounce any dragons that stand with me."

One of the fairies flew toward me. I held my hand up so she could land on it. "What is it that you need from us?"

"You are undoubtedly creatures of light." Cash leaned closer, and the fairy backed away from him, pinching her lips together. "If you could vouch for Dacia, maybe they would believe you. We cannot allow Dacia to be imprisoned or killed."

The fairy flew away to join the others. They gathered together. Hundreds of tiny shrill voices filled the cavern with a language I couldn't understand. Their iridescent wings fluttered like hummingbirds', sending a breeze through the chamber.

The tiny fairy flew back over to me. Her silver hair was windblown. Her purple eyes sparkled. "We have never left the cave."

"Maybe …" I walked toward a stalagmite, then turned around and walked back. "What is your name?" Realizing she could be offended by that, I quickly said, "Not your true name. I didn't mean that."

"You may call me Rayne." She bowed slightly.

"I'm Dacia. This is Cody, and that is Cash." They both nodded at her. "Your help has been invaluable. I would not have defeated Nefarious without being healed by you, and I couldn't have removed Mavros' taint on my own. If you don't want to leave the cave, maybe we could lure the Nephilim here and you could confront them for me."

She tilted her head and looked up at me. "What is it that you fear?"

I laughed, and the sound bounced through the cavern, echoing back to me, sounding more humorless with each reverberation. "Everything." I pulled my hand through my hair. "I fear everything these days. Being caged, being captured, being killed, having my powers controlled by somebody else, having my powers stripped. I fear for Cody and my other friends. I fear that someone close to me has betrayed me. I fear sending Mavros back to the Abyss again and losing another piece of my soul. I fear what will happen if I don't. I fear hurting people close to me either through my actions or inactions." I swallowed over a lump in my throat. "Most of all, I fear I'm losing myself."

Rayne flew off my hand and hovered by my face, staring into my eyes. Then she placed her palm on my cheek.

Strength and peace flowed through me, staunching my fears.

She pulled her hand back. "Those fears are what keep you true to yourself. They will keep you from turning to darkness. They will make you strive to be better." She flew back to the other fairies. "We will help you. Bring them to this cavern, and we will watch for them. If you need us, just ask for help. We hear everything that happens in this cave system."

"Thank you." Cody stepped up to my side.

"Do you want us to let you know when we have a plan?" Cash asked her.

All at once, the fairies lifted into the air. "We will know."

Chapter 24

Stepping outside the cave, I look up, hoping to see the stars. I've been stuck inside for too long, but it's nearly as dark outside as it is inside. I inhale the fresh air, filling my lungs greedily. My breath puffs out in front of me, and I shiver.

I turn around to go back to the chamber and smack into Mavros. He pulls me against him. "Finally—" he sucks in a relieved breath "—you finally came to me. I've been calling you for days."

"Why?" I try to step away from him, but he clutches me tighter.

He wraps one arm around my waist and brushes his other hand over my hair. "I think I've finally figured it out." His voice is filled with excitement.

"What?" I can't stop the smile that tugs at my lips.

He leans down and closes his eyes. "I think I know how to get you out of here."

My body feels like a rubber band about to be shot at an unsuspecting passerby. Suddenly, I'm flung through the night sky. The air whips my hair around my face. My stomach drops, and I pinch my eyes shut.

When I opened them, I stood next to Mavros outside the cave. I'd been dreaming, but this was real.

He gazed into my eyes, and I felt my inhibitions disappear. He wrapped his arms around me, clutching me against him. I looked at his soft, supple lips, and desire flared in my body. I snuggled against him, not remembering why it was wrong or why I should be scared.

Wings sprouted from his back, and he shot into the sky. "I'm sorry about this, Dacia." His voice was low and agonized.

"Why?" I couldn't imagine any reason he would have for apologizing to me. "I love flying with you … being near you."

"I'm trying to break his commands, but I can't find a loophole this time." The light in his eyes dimmed.

Nuzzling my face into his neck, I snuggled closer to him and kissed just below his earlobe. "You're not making any sense."

He growled, and a chill tiptoed along my spine. My mind cleared long enough for me to realize I needed to get away from him. The thought fluttered away too quickly for me to cling to it, and once again, I was no better than a starstruck fan meeting her favorite actor. Mavros was the only thing I could focus on, my entire world.

His arms tightened, and a muscle in his jaw ticked. Images flashed through my mind. Blond hair. Blue eyes. My breath hitched. The love I saw in those sapphire depths tugged me out of Mavros' sway.

Focusing on the snow-covered mountains, I willed my body to turn to ice. Frost coated my fingertips, climbing up my arms. Mavros jerked his arms away, and I plummeted.

My body was a solid block of ice, dropping through the air without feeling anything. I sped toward the ground, unsure of whether or not I should teleport or fly off. I didn't know if Mavros could trail me, but I couldn't risk leading him to the cave.

Before crashing to the ground, I teleported to a mountain in the distance. Standing on its rocky slope, under the cover of pine trees, I watched Mavros circle just below the clouds.

Leave, he spoke into my mind. *Leave before I take you. I won't be able to show you Cody again. He'll stop me next time.*

The flashes of Cody had come from him? Mavros had freed me again. The wrath of his controller would be unbearable.

Thank you. Making myself invisible, I teleported to the clearing where I'd died. When Mavros didn't show up or speak inside my mind, I went to the cavern.

Cody paced through the chamber. Malcolm and Cash faced off in the corner. They were both a strange combination of dragon and human. Malcolm lifted his head and sniffed the air. Then he turned and looked directly at me. "She's back." His words were a low, ominous growl.

I stepped forward, turning visible as I did. "He—"

"Where've you been?" Cody spun around. Anger, fear, and relief mixed together on his face. "Can't just wander off."

"I was right there." I pointed at the cushions I'd been using for a bed. "And, he snatched me. Right out of my dream." Turning toward the dragons, I pulled my hand through my hair. Tears threatened to spill from my eyes. "How could he do that?"

"He?" Cash stepped toward me. His purple scales shimmered as they slowly morphed into skin. "Mavros?"

Unsure if I'd be able to talk over the lump in my throat, I nodded.

All three of them surrounded me, looking me over, making sure I was safe, uninjured. Cody's hands framed my face, but he didn't touch me. "Wha'd he do?"

"He pulled me out of my dream and told me he couldn't find a loophole to free me." I tugged my hands through my hair, gripping it at the back of my head. "Whoever's pulling the strings made him control me, but then he sent me images of Cody." I looked up into his eyes, and he ran his thumbs along my cheeks, wiping my tears away. "Seeing your face made me come to my senses. I froze myself and got away."

Cody opened his arms to me, and I stepped into them. He brushed his hand down my back. "How's she stop it?"

Malcolm's answering growl was so low that I couldn't hear it, but I felt it rumble through my body. "I don't know." His fangs seemed to be longer than normal still.

"She should try to sleep during the day." Cash ran his hand down his face, and I realized the scent my emotions were tossing into the air must be driving them nuts. "That might throw them off for a couple of days anyway."

"For now, we'll train." Malcolm's voice left no room for argument, and with the look on his face, I wouldn't have even if I had wanted to. His dragon was too close, too riled up.

I sat down on the cushions and created a cyan ball of fire. It hovered above my palm. For the next few hours, Malcolm tried to gain control of the flames.

My eyes became leaden, and my command over the fire slipped. Flames licked at my skin, climbing my arm, spreading along my body. My breath hitched, then sped up until the air barely touched my lungs before being spewed back into the chamber.

Light danced in front of my eyes. *You are mine.* The thought finally settled in my panicked mind, and I tried to grasp onto the power, to leash the flames, but still, they spread. *You are mine!* The fire seemed to respond to my call, retreating back to the sphere in my palm. My hand trembled, and my vision wobbled.

"Enough." I snuffed out the flames. "I need rest."

He shook his head. "It is not yet morning."

My shoulders slumped. "What now, then?"

"Do it again."

I stared at him, and he motioned me to get going. "If your powers are stolen from you, it won't be when you're well-rested and raring to go. It'll be when you're near exhaustion."

There was sympathy in his bronze eyes, but mixed with it was resolve.

Once again, I created a fireball. I stared into the green and blue blaze. The flames undulated and writhed. Their beauty equal to their power of destruction.

The fire danced along my wall. I sat on my bed with Glacier as the flames devoured my room. Dad stood in the hallway, trying to figure out how to get to me, but then he left. He left me with no way out. The smoke burned my eyes and my lungs. It crawled over the floor, clung to the walls, and hung from the ceiling. I screamed as they leaped toward the bed.

Arms wrapped around me, holding me close. "Shhhh. You're okay. It's okay," Cody whispered in my ear, and I snapped back to the present.

Malcolm and Cash kept my fire contained, and as soon as I quit screaming, Cody stepped away from me, rubbing his arms. I called the flames back to me.

"She's done," Cody said. His skin was red, and blisters dotted his hands and arms.

I pulled my hands through my hair. "Oh, God, what did I do?"

"You warned him." Cody glared at Malcolm.

I reached out to Cody, not sure if he would touch me again. He placed his hands in mine, palms up. Closing my eyes, I focused on life and healing. He sighed as my energy flowed into him.

As soon as Cody's burns were healed, Malcolm said, "What happened?"

"The flames pulled me into my memories … the night I killed my brother." My heart clenched. I stood up, turning my back on them, not wanting to see their sympathy. I didn't deserve it. My brother had deserved a life, but that night I'd ended his to save mine. One more death at my hands and I'd be a serial killer … or did taking my life count? Was I already one?

Soft footsteps padded up to me. Cody stopped in my peripheral vision. "You were six. It was an accident."

"It doesn't matter." I wiped underneath my eyes. "Accident or not, I killed Jonathan. I took him away from my parents."

"There was a demon in your house." Cash's voice was softer than I'd ever heard it. "I wouldn't be surprised if it caused his death." He squeezed my shoulder. "You have saved more lives than you've taken."

I knew he meant well, but how many other people my age had taken a life, let alone two or three? And, how many more would I have to take before mine was taken?

Chapter 25

Building My Stamina

Malcolm came back the next two nights and trained me harder than he had before. When I asked him why, he said that if we were going to lure the Nephilim here, he wanted to make sure my stamina had improved.

We jogged through the passageways using my fire for light. Malcolm fought to wrest my powers from me as we ran over the uneven ground. I stumbled, and he reached out to steady me. "Careful."

"I'll heal."

He nodded. "But you'll bleed."

By the time we got back to the chamber, my clothes were drenched with sweat. Cash shot me a look that let me know I needed to bathe.

I grabbed up my bathroom bag and stomped out of the room with Malcolm on my heels. "You're not going to watch me bathe."

"No"—he shook his head—"but I will stand guard and make sure you're safe."

"I'll be fine on my own."

He grabbed hold of my arm, and I looked up into his concerned face. "You are nearing exhaustion."

I yawned in response.

"You will have your privacy."

Heating the bath to lukewarm took more energy than it should have. I sunk beneath the water and rested my head against the ledge. Malcolm's red fires illuminated the room. I looked up at the ceiling and wondered how my friends were doing. I hoped the Nephilim and other dragons were leaving them alone. I hoped Aurelia was figuring out a way for me to get out of this if my plan didn't work.

Even though I was scraping the dregs of my power, I willed my eyes to see through the ground to the outside world. There was only darkness above me. I couldn't even see the stars or moon. My heart seemed to drop further.

Being inside a cave with only fires for light, it was easy to adopt a new sleep schedule. As I lay down the next morning, I prayed that Mavros wouldn't be able to pull me from my dreams and that nobody would stumble upon my hiding place. Then I fell into the deep sleep of extreme exhaustion.

When I woke up, Cash was gone. I sat up and shot Malcolm a curious look.

"He figured he should check in." He tossed me a protein bar, and I let it drop on top of the blanket. "Eat."

I picked it up but couldn't bring myself to open it. "Couldn't you teleport out and bring back bacon and eggs?"

He shook his head. "Not today. Not with Cash gone."

I grimaced at my breakfast.

"Eat it, and I'll get some different food when I go out again."

"Thanks. There's only so many of these I can eat." I smiled at him. "Will he be back?" I peeled the wrapper off and nibbled on the bar. It was dry and tasteless.

Cody sat up, and Malcolm threw him a couple of the bars. "He's going to lead them to where you teleported to yesterday."

"Won't they be able to tell Mavros was there, too?" I pulled my legs up and wrapped my arms around them. My stomach seemed to roll over itself. "Won't that just reinforce their beliefs that I'm with him?"

"He'll cover up Mavros' scent." He stared pointedly at the bar until I bit into it. "It could be a day or two before he makes it back here. After that, we'll lure the Nephilim in and hopefully put an end to this."

"Toss me a water, please." I caught it, unscrewed the lid, and gulped down half of the bottle. "Do you think it'll work? Will the Nephilim believe them?"

He nodded. "They'll believe them, but I don't know if they'll care. They seem to have their own agenda." He pointed at Cody. "You're with us today. Get dressed and put your running shoes on."

I groaned but did as ordered. When I stood up, my muscles protested, but running through the cave was better than sitting around, wondering when we'd be found.

Malcolm pushed me harder, made me run faster, and keep multiple fireballs under my control. By lunchtime, I was ready to collapse, but he pressed me more stringently.

Cody kept up easily, occasionally whispering words of encouragement. His belief in me kept me moving, kept me in control of my powers, and kept me from losing focus.

When Malcolm allowed us to stop, I collapsed onto the ground and slipped my shoes off, rubbing my aching feet. Malcolm pulled water bottles out of his backpack and tossed them to me. "Cool those off. Then you can rest for a minute."

I did as he said and handed a bottle to Cody. He pressed the cold plastic to his forehead and neck before drinking it.

Malcolm looked between the two of us. "Will you be okay for fifteen minutes while I get food?"

"If I can't keep the two of us safe, why are they concerned that I'm such a threat?"

He flashed his fangs at me and disappeared.

I sipped my water, then lay down, not caring that rocks jutted out, poking into my back.

"How you doin'?" Cody's voice was soft and filled with concern.

I opened an eye and peeked at him. "I'm ready to get out of here and to figure out who's controlling Mavros. I'm worried about Samantha and Dan, and I feel bad that you're missing all of your classes."

"Don't worry." He brushed my hair back. "Drop 'em if I need to."

"You know I don't deserve you."

"Funny." He smiled, and it was stunning. "Think the same about you."

Malcolm returned, and the smell of pizza filled the chamber. My stomach growled in response. He handed each of us a bottle of pop and napkins, then set the pizza down between us.

"Thank you, Malcolm." I put my hand on top of his. "I'll never be able to repay you for all you've done for me."

He shook his head. "I have a long way to go to settle my debt."

After stuffing ourselves with pepperoni and all meat slices, the jog back to our cavern was much slower. Malcolm had me light the way back while levitating him, turning Cody invisible, straightening my hair, and changing my eye color.

Slowly, my stamina improved. Besides exercising my abilities, getting eight hours of uninterrupted sleep probably helped.

Malcolm went inside the chamber first. When he decided it remained safe, he motioned for Cody and me to enter. "Cash hasn't been back. His scent lingers here but not strong."

My chest tightened, and my shoulders dropped. Even a few days ago, I would've been glad to hear that Cash was nowhere to be seen, but now, I worried. "Should I try to contact him?" I pulled my hand through my sweaty hair and wiped it on my leggings. "Make sure everything's okay?"

"No." Malcolm tilted his head. "They may have a way to tell if you're contacting him. I'll check in with him. That shouldn't seem suspicious."

He sat on top of a pile of cushions and closed his eyes. I walked up to Cody and slid my hand into his. I was more nervous than I would like to admit. Even though the game plan was to lure the Nephilim here, I wanted it to be on our terms, and if they didn't believe the fairies, I didn't want the dragons to suffer for helping me. They had been under Draconian's control for a long time, and they deserved freedom.

"He is leading them on a wild goose chase." Malcolm's voice was reassuring. "He took them to a few places you've been. Some of the other dragons are with him, so he can't just say he smells you there."

Cody rubbed his thumb along the back of my hand. "Maybe she should teleport a few places. Could go invisible, leave her smell, and get out."

"Not yet." Malcolm stroked his jaw. "Her scent is in a few places thanks to Mavros. We'll wait, and if we need to in a couple of days, I can lead them to new spots. It would seem odd if Cash discovered them all. Besides, it might lend me a little credibility."

"They still don't trust you?" I asked as I gathered up a change of clothes.

He shook his head. "I believe the Nephilim can sense where my loyalty lies. They have ways of discerning the truth."

"Why wouldn't they be able to tell with Cash then?" I shoved my stuff into my duffle bag.

"Nobody expects him to have loyalty." Malcolm smiled. "He hates everyone equally."

Chapter 26

"Dacia?" Mavros' voice is so forlorn. I want to answer him, but I'm afraid that if I do, he'll be able to call me to him.

I hide in the trees, hoping if I stand perfectly still, he won't be able to see me. The sun is high overhead, and the air carries the bite of winter. I wonder how many days I've been hidden away in that cave. Not for the first time, I wonder if I traded one prison for another.

"Please, Dacia, I need to see you … to know you're okay." His desperation nearly undoes me. *I can feel you, Dacia. You need to wake up. Go back to sleeping at night. Maybe I can give you a few days' rest that way. He's getting impatient.*

Why are you trying to help me?

Wake up!

His scream jarred me awake. Malcolm stared at me, his eyes knowing. "He found you?"

"Yes." I sat up and pulled my hand through my tangled mass of hair. "He told me to start sleeping at night again. Said he might be able to buy me a couple days."

"Why?" Cody's voice was groggy.

I shook my head. "I don't know. I have no idea why he's trying to help me. Maybe he does want to help. Maybe he's just playing a game. Either way, I think I should listen."

"Well—" Malcolm walked over and handed us a box of donuts "—let's wear you out so you can sleep tonight then."

We ran through the cave. Malcolm told me to keep the illusions up on the chamber we were calling home. He also had me light our way, teleport the three of us ten to twenty feet along the passageway, cool the tunnels with a breeze, and transform my features. One time, just because I could, I turned myself into a wolf and shot him a toothy smile.

By the time we got back to the cavern, I had to have Malcolm come along to keep me protected while I bathed. I still heated the water for both Cody and me and kept the cavern lit, but I figured it would be better to have him along in case I'd worn myself out more than I thought.

That night, I laid my head down on the pillows, and Cody wrapped his arms around my waist. Peacefulness and exhaustion washed over me, and I was asleep within minutes.

"He made me, Dacia." Mavros stands above me. His hand is transformed into claws, and silver lines his eyes. "My powers are stronger at night. I couldn't pull you out of your dreams during the day."

I scoot back. The pine needles and rocks bite into my back. "I trusted you." My voice shakes, and anger swells inside of me. *How could I have been so stupid?* I wonder as I prepare myself to fight him.

"I know you did. I am so sorry." He sounds so sincere, but I don't know if it's real or an act.

The muscles in his arms go taut, and the tendons in his neck bulge. I think about glaciers, wintertime, and snow-covered mountains. Frost spreads over my hands, coating my arms, and climbs my neck. My entire body turns to ice, but the frost continues spreading into my mouth. It coats my throat, freezing my breath.

No! I scream inside my head. *You are mine. I control you, nobody else.* I look up into Mavros' eyes. His are panicked as he watches me struggle with my powers.

My breath hitches. Tiny shards pierce my lungs, and the ice slowly fades from my limbs.

Mavros watches as the ice recedes, then he grabs hold of me.

Cold air struck my body, and I shivered in response. A million stars lit up the night sky. The Milky Way was a bright streak illuminating the darkness.

Freeze, Mavros shouted in my head. He held his hand back. His claws were extended. The tips of them glinted.

I willed my body to turn to ice, but my powers were not mine to control. Mavros swiped his claws across my chest. They tore through my skin, ripping into my lungs, shattering my ribcage. Pain sliced through my body. I sucked in a startled breath, and the blood pouring from my wounds bubbled.

Mavros' eyebrows pinched together, and his mouth turned down. He stretched his hand toward me, fighting some invisible force.

Great wings beat against the air. My vision darkened. Blood spewed out of my mouth when I tried to breathe.

The ground beneath me shook, and a gust of air blew across my body. Mavros reached down. His hand brushed across my arm. A breath filled my lungs, and I disappeared.

The massive silver dragon with rheumy eyes stepped up beside Mavros. His voice was ancient and angry. "Where is she?"

Mavros knelt in front of him. "I did as you said. I attacked her. She couldn't breathe, yet somehow, she disappeared."

The beast lowered its head and licked my blood from the ground. His eyes rolled back as if it was the best thing he'd ever tasted. "Find her, and bring her to me. No more excuses, Chaódis Skotádi."

Mavros' eyes flicked to me, but the dragon didn't notice. *Go.* His power shot through me, and I clung to it, using it to teleport me away from them. My body stretched and pulled, and agony shot through me. Lights flashed in my vision, pulsating with the pain.

I landed flat on my back in the snow visible once again. I looked at my chest. My shirt was shredded. My chest was torn open, but I could breathe. Blood seeped from my wounds. *Malcolm* —I sent him a vision of where I was—*help me.*

I thought about life until darkness took hold of me.

Chapter 27

*V*oices.

They were so far away. I couldn't make out what they were saying, but I felt compelled to answer them. It seemed like they were searching for something. Frantic. Terrified. They drifted away, and I was left alone.

"Dacia, I know you heard him." Mavros' voice fills the darkness, but I can't see him, can't respond to him. "You can use my name. You can free me from his control before I hurt you again. It won't take me long to find you with my venom in your veins. Don't make me hurt you please."

"Dacia, you have to wake up." Malcolm sounded frazzled. "We have to leave here. This place has been compromised."

I tried to pull my eyelids apart, but they felt like they weighed a ton. They barely fluttered.

"Come on, Dacia." Cash growled, and his energy flowed into me. I tugged on it, drawing it into me. He groaned, but he didn't stop me from siphoning his power.

I opened my eyes, and relief flashed through his amethyst ones. "She's awake." He lifted me into his arms and teleported away.

My insides spun, and my stomach heaved.

"Don't throw up on me." Laughter filled his voice as he set me down. We were inside a different cavern. Treasure was heaped all around, reminding me of Aurelia's den, but this was different. It was easily twice the size of the chamber with the underground lake. The ceiling was at least a football field or more above my head. The air was dry, and the cave was free of stalactites and stalagmites.

Cash knelt down next to me, and Cody and Malcolm stood behind him. "You took a lot of my strength. So, how are you doing?"

I tried to sit up, but my arms gave out. "Not great." I sank back down, and the coins shifted beneath me. Bloody bandages wrapped my torso. "How long?"

Dark bags circled Cody's eyes, and I knew the answer. Far too long.

"Two days," Cash answered. "It would've been longer if you wouldn't have leached onto me."

My mouth felt like it was stuffed full of cotton. "Drink?"

Malcolm slid a backpack off his shoulders and rummaged through it, handing a bottle of water to Cash. "Slowly," he said.

Cody started to walk toward me, but Malcolm stretched his arm in front of him and shook his head.

"Why?" Cody's voice was a plea.

Malcolm's eyes were sympathetic when he said, "You know why."

Cash lifted my head and held the water up to my lips. I took small sips of it. "What'd I do to him?"

"Same thing you did to me." Cash looked over his shoulder at Malcolm and Cody. "You pulled too much from both of them. When I got to the cavern, all three of you were zombies."

My heart clenched, and I felt the urge to throw up again. "I'm a menace. You should let the Nephilim take me."

Cody fell to his knees. "What happened?"

"Mavros and a silver dragon."

Cash's pupils turned to slits, and fangs jutted from his mouth.

As I explained what had happened, both dragons fought to keep their human form. When I finished, Malcolm said, "We promised to protect Dacia. How could one of the elders have broken his vow?"

"The elders make the vow?" Cody asked. "Or they just make you?"

Cash and Malcolm looked at each other. Anger flashed through their eyes. "Aurelia needs to know," Malcolm said, and Cash nodded his agreement.

"They'll know we've been with her." Cash held the water out to me, and I propped myself up on my elbows to have another drink.

As I sipped at the water, I remembered the silver dragon lowering its head to lick up my blood. My heart plummeted.

"What?" Cash clenched the bottle, and water squirted all over me. "Sorry." He wiped it off of me with his sleeve.

"The dragon tasted my blood. It was on the ground beside me when Mavros turned me invisible."

Malcolm and Cash shared a knowing glance. "That's how they knew where to find her." Cash's voice barely held any of its humanity.

Malcolm nodded. "We can only hope the fairies can convince them of her innocence."

"In a dream, Mavros told me he could track me." My voice was faint, but they heard.

Cash's head whipped toward me. "How?"

"His venom."

Malcolm and Cash leaned in, talking to each other. I couldn't make out their words and didn't have the energy to try.

While they talked, Cody darted around them, coming to my side. He sat next to me, stretching his hand forward but stopping before his skin met mine. "Worried me."

"I'm so sorry, Cody. I tried to stop him, but I couldn't control my powers." I tried to smile up at him, but my pain and my guilt wouldn't allow me to.

"Not your fault." He brushed my hair back from my face, and Malcolm growled at him. "I'm fine. She's conscious now."

I closed my eyes. "I probably could kill you if I take too much. You can't let me, Cody." I looked up at him and saw pain flicker across his face.

"Can't let you suffer."

"You can." I took his hand in mine, twining our fingers together. "You can't let me kill you. I'll heal eventually. I couldn't live with your death on my hands."

The dragons watched us. Their features were caught somewhere between human and dragon. Cash said, "I'll go back, say I stumbled on her scent. They'll never believe you weren't helping her, but there's a chance they'll believe me. If not, I owe her."

He disappeared before any of us had a chance to argue with him.

Malcolm sat next to me. His face appeared more human, but anger lingered in his eyes. "Argentum betrayed us all. He was once wise and just, but he's outlived his usefulness."

"He probably fears me like Cash did." I tried to sit up, but pain sucked the air from my lungs.

He dipped his head, then flashed his fangs. "Yes, but fear is not reason enough to betray an ally. I must warn Aurelia of his deceit."

Within minutes, Aurelia and Arion stood in the lair with us. Aurelia knelt beside me and took my hand. "Show me," she said as she sent healing energy flowing through me.

Closing my eyes, I remembered my encounter with Mavros. When Argentum licked my blood off the ground, she squeezed my hand hard enough that I whimpered.

"I am sorry, Dacia." She unclenched my fingers. "He has betrayed not only you but all dragons."

Arion bowed his head. His white coat shimmered. "I tried to speak to the Nephilim on your behalf, but because of my connection to Aurelia, they would not listen to me."

"Thanks." My tongue felt thick and heavy. I glanced at the bottle of water Cash had been helping me drink from before he disappeared.

Cody noticed, picked it up, and held it out as if asking if I wanted a drink. I nodded, and he supported my head, helping me drink. When he lowered the water, I asked, "Will they listen to the fairies?"

"Only time will tell." Arion backed away. "We should know soon."

Aurelia stood beside Arion. "We must take your memory to the elder council. Argentum cannot be allowed to get away with his betrayal. Any other dragons who helped him must also be punished."

They disappeared, and the cavern seemed huge without them in it.

"Dacia needs to rest." Malcolm's voice startled me.

Cody started to stretch out beside me, but Malcolm said, "Not tonight, Cody. We can't have her accidentally taking more of your strength."

Cody narrowed his blue eyes at Malcolm. "If she needs it—"

"No, Cody." My voice was softened by exhaustion, but he still heard me. "I don't want to hurt you."

He kissed my forehead, then walked away from me.

I thought it would take me a while to fall asleep. I was worried about Cash, Aurelia, and Arion, but when I closed my eyes, sleep embraced me.

Chapter 28

Names Have Power

"He's angry, Dacia." Mavros prowls toward me. Each step is slow and deliberate. "You've backed him into a corner, and now he's desperate."

Gentle flurries drift to the ground. The snowflakes catch on my eyelashes, melting a second later. Lights from the campus shine on the bottom of the clouds.

I bite my lip, wondering what a desperate elder dragon is capable of. "Well, that makes two of us." My chest still aches from Mavros' last attack, and I don't know how well my body will be able to cope with another one. "The Nephilim drove me out of my home."

Mavros rolls his obsidian eyes at me. The action is so human it's hard to remember he's a demon. "That cave wasn't your home."

"It was the closest thing I had to a home." My voice rises, I fold my arms over my chest, and glare at him. "Your blood and the Nephilim drove me out of my real one."

He tips his head to the side still stalking closer to me. "I am sorry about that, but the Nephilim would've driven you out without my blood there."

"What are you waiting for, Mavros?" I watch every step he takes, waiting for a sign of attack, hoping I can force myself to wake up before he takes me out of my dream.

He stops moving and lifts his hands in the air as if surrendering. "He did not send me here tonight."

"You can say his name now. You know I know it."

"He hasn't given me permission to speak it yet."

I shake my head, sending snowflakes flying through the air again. "Then why are you here?"

He lowers himself to one knee and folds his hands together. "Use my name. You heard him say it. Use it and free me from his command."

"How?" I lift my hands in front of me. "Won't he just use your name and take you back?"

He shakes his head. "He might, but you are stronger than him. That is why he fears you, why he wants you stopped."

"If I'm so strong, why do I keep losing control of my powers?" Nervous energy moves my feet across the snow-covered ground. I pace twelve steps away but only ten steps back, wanting to increase the distance between Mavros and myself.

"Remember what Aurelia told you about Draconian." He says each word cautiously as if waiting to be stopped or punished.

I continue pacing more steps away from him than back toward him. "She told me a ton of things."

"What could you have done with fifteen dragons that he never considered?" He clutches his head, dropping to the ground. "Think!"

I press my eyes closed and pinch the bridge of my nose. "He's using your power to increase his?"

"What do I do?" I asked Malcolm. "If I use Mavros' real name to gain control of him, will the Nephilim think I've been in cahoots with him all along?"

He was curled up in dragon form on top of a stack of treasure. His ebony, horned head rested on top of his massive paws. Even though his dragon form was intimidating, his bronze eyes were those of my friend. "The dragons, Arion, and the fairies have all vouched for your character. I don't see how they can deny you freedom without undermining their authority on other issues." His deep voice made the treasure rattle and the ground beneath me vibrate.

Cody sat up and stretched his arms over his head, arching his back. "So, is she free?"

"I will know more when Aurelia arrives." He opened his massive jaws and yawned. Flames curled in the back of his throat, begging to be released. "As far as his name, part of me thinks you should use it, and part of me believes nobody should ever use somebody else's name that way."

"Even if I free him?"

He lifted his head off his paws and stared down at me. "You mean to free him from his bonds?"

"I don't know." I tried to push myself to a seated position, but my chest resisted the move. I fell backward, gasping for breath. "He needs to be released from Argentum, but should I free him? What will he do if he can roam the Earth without being called back to the Abyss? Will he become my enemy again, or will he repay me by being honorable?"

A black fog filled the cave. I lit a fire in my palm, but it did little to dispel the dark. The ebony mist pulsed, then receded until Malcolm the person stood in front of me. "Mavros' only experiences had been deceitful, vengeful, and evil until he met you. You were the first person to treat him with honor or respect."

I tilted my head, staring at Malcolm, trying to figure out what looked different about him. He sat down beside me, pulling his legs up to his chest. Dragon earrings sparkled against his earlobes.

"Because of that, he may choose to repay your kindness, but if you allow him to stay on Earth, how will you know if he's under Argentum's control or yours?" He grabbed my hand and sent energy streaming into me. I fought the urge to increase the flow between us. "If you return him to the Abyss and he comes back, you'll know who is pulling the strings."

Cody came over and lifted my head onto his lap. He traced his fingers along my jaw. "Know how long it took her to cope with sending him back last time?"

Malcolm nodded. "The choice is hers. I'm just letting her know what's at stake."

Chapter 29

$\mathcal{C}$ash, Aurelia, and Arion teleported into the cavern. Malcolm stood next to me and said, "Dacia has a decision to make, and she would like to hear what everyone has to say first."

Aurelia nodded. "The Nephilim have taken the fairies' message back and are deliberating. We will know soon enough if they will leave Dacia alone." She knelt down and held her hand out to me, offering her strength. "Argentum has disappeared. He is most likely in his lair, but none of us know where it is."

I shuddered at the thought of him being out there, of knowing what my blood tasted like, and being able to track me for fifty miles. "I know Mavros' true name." I clutched Aurelia's hand, and a burst of energy stormed through me. "I don't know what I should do with it, though."

"Send him back to the Abyss." Arion stamped his hoof on the ground to emphasize his opinion.

Cash rubbed his chin. "He's been helpful. Should she really send him back?"

"Yeah." I sat up, and the scabs on my chest pulled tight. Cody wrapped his arm around me, supporting me.

Malcolm waved his arm, indicating that they could make themselves comfortable. Everyone but Arion sat. I tugged a shaky hand through my hair, feeling self-conscious. "Those are the choices. I just don't know which one is right."

"Demons are evil." Aurelia pulled her hand away.

I yanked mine back, wondering if I'd taken too much, but she didn't seem to be suffering. I wanted to get up and move around. It helped me think, but I knew if I did, I'd have three dragons, a pegasus, and a human telling me to sit down and rest. "He warned me that he could enter my room. He attacked me without using his venom. He let me see his memories and told me it was a dragon that summoned him. He's warned me so many times and helped me get away from him, so I don't know what to think." I dropped my chin to my chest. "I trusted him before, and I was wrong, but I just don't know."

Cody ran his hand along my arm. "Hate the bastard, but he helped."

I looked up toward the ceiling of the cavern. "Take me somewhere where I can summon him." I stood up, and everyone watched me like I was a fragile China doll. "I don't imagine you want him here. I'll take control of him, then figure out where to go from there."

"She strong enough?" Cody stood next to me.

The dragons all stared at me. Finally, Malcolm said, "I think she should wait one more day."

"No." I fisted my hands on my hips and glared at them. "He came to me in my dream and told me I need to use it. I can't wait. If I do, he'll end up pulling me out of my dream and killing me."

Cash stood up. "So, we all go with you and keep you safe."

"We can lend you our power if you need us to," Aurelia said.

Arion stepped forward. "I will stay here with Cody. Neither of us needs to be there."

"Please," I said before Cody could object.

He sighed and lowered his head. "It's what you want?"

I nodded, unwilling to give up on this. "If things go wrong, I don't want him to be able to use you against me."

Cash held his hand out. "Before we go, take strength from me."

"Me, too." Malcolm stepped forward.

Aurelia nodded. "I have plenty to give to you."

They each took turns holding my hand, and by the time they were done funneling their energy into me, I felt like I could move mountains. Pure energy flowed through my veins and made me feel bullet-proof.

Aurelia held her hand out. "Ready?"

"No." I walked up to Cody and wrapped my arms around his neck. "I'll come back."

"Better." He brought his mouth down on mine, kissing me like he might not ever see me again. His hands moved to my back, pressing our bodies together. Pain surged through my wounds, but I tried not to let it show.

Cash groaned, and I pulled away from Cody. I never looked away from him as I joined the dragons. Aurelia and Malcolm each grabbed one of my hands and teleported the four of us.

Darkness surrounded us. "I got it," Cash said. A ball of fire lit up across from me in the circle we'd made. Cash's amethyst eyes widened. "Didn't think I'd ever see this place again."

"No." Malcolm's voice was a growl.

We stood in the treasure room of Draconian's castle. Only a handful of riches remained. Gouges marred the gray stone walls. It took me a minute to realize they'd most likely been made by dragon talons.

"Why here?" I asked Aurelia.

Her lip was curled with disgust. "I do not think the Nephilim or Argentum will come here."

"No." Cash lit the torches that hung from the walls. "He wouldn't come to this place, not with what happened here."

"Mavros has already been summoned to this plane." Aurelia kicked a goblet across the room. "You will not need to bind him. You just need to command him to appear and to serve you."

The dragons backed away, and I closed my eyes, sucking in a deep breath. *Please let this work, Lord. Let me do the right thing and not hate myself in the end.* "Chaódis Skotádi, I summon thee to stand in my presence and serve me."

I expected the result to be instantaneous. When it wasn't, I looked at each dragon, trying to understand why nothing had happened. Mavros should have appeared. The threat from him should have ended.

Malcolm stepped toward me. His brows were furrowed. His gaze darted around the room.

Electricity sizzled through the air. Followed by a loud boom. Cash slammed into me, knocking me to the ground, shielding me with his body. Pain lanced through my chest as the wound reopened. Blood seeped through my shirt.

"My liege." Mavros practically purred.

I wrapped my arm around my wound and pressed my other hand against Cash's chest. He pulled me to my feet.

Mavros stood in the middle of the room. His hands were tucked into his pockets, and his obsidian eyes sparkled with delight.

Gold, ebony, and amethyst hazes blended together, blocking my vision temporarily. When they cleared, the three dragons had transformed into their true selves. The room no longer seemed empty.

Mavros dropped to his knees in front of me. "What do you command of me?"

"I need to know what to do." For the first time in a long time, I felt like a little kid asking their parents for help. "If I leave you on this plane, will Argentum be able to regain control of you? Would I be better off sending you to the Abyss so I know whose control you're under?"

He slowly stood. "Send me back. You won't know if he regains control of me if you leave me here. He will use it against you, make you think you are my master, and then make me kill you."

"But—" I pulled my bottom lip into my mouth "—how can I do that to you? You've helped me. You've protected me. How can I send you back to that Hell?"

He stepped forward and took my hands in his. "I won't stay there long before I wind up on another plane. I was actually sunning myself on a beautiful beach when Argentum called me here."

"Really?' I wiped my eyes on my sleeve, my fingers still held in his.

"Send me back."

"Can you heal me first?" Knowing I was about to return him to the Abyss, I hated to ask him for anything, but I needed to be healthy to stand a chance against Argentum.

He pressed his hand to my wound and drew the venom out. I felt like I could breathe for the first time in days. "Thank you."

He took a step away and dropped his hands. "It has been a pleasure knowing you, Dacia Wolf." He smiled a real smile that lit up his perfect face.

"Chaódis Skotádi, I command you to return to the Abyss." I watched as he turned into a mist and disappeared. Then I fell to my knees, held my head in my hands, and cried.

Chapter 30

Aurelia and Arion left as soon as we returned to Malcolm's cave. She was supposed to meet with the Nephilim council when they decided my fate.

I pulled the bandages from my wound and burned them. My shirt was blood-stained from when Cash had knocked me down to protect me, but I didn't have anything else to change into. We'd left everything in the other cave when the Nephilim had shown up.

"So, what happens if they decide to take away my freedom anyway?" I sat on the treasure and pulled my knees to my chest. There was enough wealth in this room to feed a small country for decades, maybe centuries. Torchlight reflected off the gems and coins. Priceless works of art lined the cave walls.

Cash rummaged through a sack, pulled out a package of mixed nuts, and threw them to me. "We won't give you up."

"We're here for you," Malcolm said.

I dumped a handful of the nuts out. "I can't run forever. I can't do that to you guys or to Cody." I stared at the cashews, feeling like I'd throw up if I put them in my mouth. If I went with the Nephilim, I'd never be able to live life my own way, but Cody had brothers and a sister who cared about him. He had parents who would never understand why he'd disappeared. I'd live in a cage if it meant he could be with those he loved.

Cody sat next to me. "I'm with you."

"I know—" I smiled a sad smile at him "—but I still can't do that to you and your family."

"Hopefully, they won't debate for too long." Malcolm cooled a bottle of water and handed it to me. The beads in his cornrows clanked together as he sat beside me. "This"— he waved his arm, encompassing the entire cave—"isn't very comfortable. I'm sorry about that, but it was the only place that I knew for sure would be safe. I've never let another being into my lair before."

Cash nodded at him. "I will take you to mine when this is done, but for now, I need them to believe I am hunting Dacia, not helping her."

"Since Mavros is gone—" Malcolm squeezed my shoulder when I winced "—you can go back to sleeping at night. Then, when you go back to school, you will be accustomed to it."

I plucked one cashew out of my hand and held it in front of my mouth. "Do you really think I'll be going back?"

"I can't see how they can deny you and remain honorable." Cash strode across the treasure, admiring certain pieces. Malcolm watched him like a starved hawk eying a mouse. "I'll see if I can get something to make Dacia and Cody more comfortable. If nothing else, I'll bring them more food." He disappeared.

"I haven't done anything for a few days." I stood up. "I should exercise my powers and my body."

Malcolm assessed me. "You only just healed. Are you sure you don't need to rest more?"

"And lose all the stamina you've been helping me build?" I folded my arms over my chest and tapped my foot. Coins toppled over each other, clinging as they fell.

"Fine." He stood. "Make a fireball. We'll run that way." He pointed at a narrow opening on the other side of the chamber.

"Coming?" I asked Cody.

He stood beside me. "Where you go, I go."

Malcolm led the way. His pace was slower than it had been for the days leading up to Mavros' attack on me. Cody stayed right beside me, watching me from the corner of his eye, making sure I was doing okay. I ran faster, passing Malcolm. The passage we ran through looked like it had been carved, not formed by nature. It was wide enough for Malcolm to fly through in his dragon form. There were no flowstone formations, and I couldn't hear the constant sound of water dripping.

The passage turned, and a pungent aroma filled the cavern. I looked up to see hundreds of bats hanging from the ceiling. I dimmed my fire, keeping it closer to me. Some of the bats flapped their wings and some crawled along the ceiling, but none of them took flight.

I was relieved when we left that chamber and the smell behind. We ran for a while longer. My legs shook, but I didn't want Malcolm or Cody to know. I didn't want them to think I was weak.

"We should turn back." Malcolm's voice startled me, and the flames flickered. "I don't want you to overdo it."

I turned around, hoping they didn't see me wobble as I did. "Okay." I ran past them, setting the pace for the way back. Once again, I lowered the flames when we ran through the chamber with bats in it, hoping not to startle them.

As we left that cavern behind, my leg buckled under me, and I fell forward. Malcolm wrapped his arm around my waist, righting me. "Let's walk." He lit the chamber around us, and I closed my hand, suffocating my flames.

Cody walked on my other side. "Shouldn't push so hard."

"I know." I pulled my hand through my hair. "But I never know when something's going to happen. I've got to stay strong."

"You need to rest, too." Malcolm let go of me. "Get it while you can."

By the time we returned to Malcolm's treasure horde, Cash was back. Cushions were piled on the coins, and it looked like I might get a comfortable night's sleep. I started walking toward the purple and black cushions, but Cody grabbed my arm. I looked at him in question, and he nodded his head toward the dragons.

Malcolm's pupils were slitted. A low rumble filled the cavern, rattling the coins. Cash lowered his eyes and lifted his neck while making himself seem smaller.

Malcolm strode toward him. He pressed his fangs to Cash's neck. Cash stood absolutely still. After several tension-filled moments, Malcolm stepped away.

Cash kept his eyes lowered to the floor. "I touched nothing. I didn't know you'd be gone."

"Dacia wanted exercise." Malcolm's voice was like the deep rumbling of thunder.

Since they'd both pledged their loyalty to me, I hoped I'd be able to diffuse the situation. "And now I need food and a bath, so quit trying to assert your dominance."

Cash shot an uneasy grin at Malcolm. "I kind of miss the days when she was terrified of us. Don't you?"

"Every day." Malcolm reached his hand toward Cash. "Thank you for restocking their supplies."

Cody let out a deep breath. "That was tense."

"Sorry." Malcolm's pupils and voice had returned to normal. "Two thousand years of instincts are hard to overcome."

"It doesn't help that dragons are greedy bastards." Cash shrugged, then dug to go boxes out of several sacks. "I wasn't sure what you'd want, so I grabbed a few things." He handed two containers to Malcolm. "Rare steaks."

I chose chicken Alfredo, and Cody took a steak and baked potato. We all sat down and ate in silence. After we finished,

Malcolm walked over and took our containers from us. "This cave system is dry. The baths will have to wait."

Unintentionally, my chin dropped to my chest. I was sweaty and gross, and I didn't even have any other clothes to change into.

"If it was warmer outside, I'd take you to a waterfall to wash off, but you'd freeze." He pointed at the cushions. "Get some rest. Maybe tomorrow will bring good news."

Cody looked at Cash. "Sticking around?"

"No." He shook his head. "I'm supposed to be hunting Dacia." He tossed a bag at us. "Might be better than nothing."

Two T-shirts and two pairs of sweatpants were in the bag. I took the smaller ones and handed the others to Cody. "Thanks," I said. "Be safe."

Chapter 31

Reprieve

I woke up to hushed voices. Aurelia, Cash, and Malcolm stood together across the vast cavern from me. I sat up, and Cody put his hand on my arm. "Leave 'em."

"But you know it's about me." My voice was loud enough that they all looked at me.

Aurelia strode toward me. Her gray slacks were tailored to fit her. Her blue silk shirt was perfectly pressed. Compared to her, I looked like a hoodlum in my baggie sweatpants. "We wanted you to rest."

"That's pretty much all I do these days." I stood up, striding across the cavern toward them. Treasure jingled under my feet. "So, am I to be caged?"

"No." She shook her head, and a smile spread across her face. "They have decided you are not the threat they feared."

The wave of relief that washed over me nearly knocked me down. I held one hand out to catch my balance, lifted the other to my chest, and held back a sob. "I really thought they'd come up with a reason to take me."

Her smile faded, and she looked at me like I might not like what she had to say next. "They plan to keep some representatives on campus to make sure Argentum does not abduct you."

"What about Malcolm?" I didn't want to dwell on the Nephilim right now. I didn't want to worry about whether or not they would change their minds. I wanted to smell fresh air and see the mountains and sky and trees and my friends.

He grinned at me from behind her. "They don't know for sure that I was helping you, so no repercussions."

I smiled at him. "Thank God." Nobody should have to suffer for helping me.

"When do we go back?" Cody had walked up beside me without me noticing.

Cash shrugged. "As soon as you want."

Aurelia held her hand up. "You will be under our surveillance still. Until Argentum is found and we determine if anybody else was helping him, we will escort you to classes and watch over your rooms."

"Okay." Cody looked down at me. "Let's go."

Malcolm's expression darkened. "My lair's not good enough for you?"

"I'd like a shower and clothes that fit." Cody visibly swallowed and backed up a step.

"And a comfortable bed." Malcolm grinned. "I couldn't resist. I love the smell of fear."

"Funny, real funny." I walked over and slugged his arm. "I'm taking Cody." I grabbed his hand and teleported us to my dorm room. It was empty, and it was early enough that the hallway was still quiet.

Within seconds, all three dragons appeared. "Will one of you take Cody to his room so he can shower and change?"

Cash stepped forward and put his hand on Cody's shoulder. "Ready?"

"Be careful, Dacia." He nodded at Cash, and they disappeared.

I gathered up clothes and stuffed them into my bag. "Thanks for everything you guys have done for me. I really thought I'd have to spend the rest of my life in one of their sanctuaries. I didn't think they'd give up."

"Keep following the light, and we should be able to keep them from threatening you again." Aurelia gave me a quick hug that took me by surprise.

I squeezed her back, then asked, "What day is it? What's the weather like?"

"It is Tuesday." She stepped away. "It is cold and snowy. I talked to Sarah when you left. She told your teachers that you had a family emergency and had to leave in the middle of the night. They will give you a copy of the notes you missed and let you make up your assignments and tests."

I hadn't been too worried about college for myself, but it was a relief to know Cody would be able to catch up. "I'll go see her after classes and thank her."

"I will not be here when you return." Sadness filled her voice. "The elders are sending me to hunt Argentum."

"Be careful."

"You, too."

Malcolm and I stepped out into the hall. He didn't bother turning invisible this morning. I hoped Marcy wouldn't come out of her room and find him here. I didn't feel like dealing with it today. Diana and Olivia stood with their backs against the wall, watching me. I waved at them as I walked past. Diana lifted her lips in an attempt at a smile, but Olivia just glared at me. *We're back,* I thought to Samantha, hoping she was awake already. *The Nephilim are supposed to leave me alone.*

I took a longer shower than I normally would, savoring the feel of the water pulsing against my skin, letting it work out some of my stress. When I stepped into my room, Samantha threw her arms around me. "I was so worried about you. Arianna said Mavros attacked you and one of the dragons betrayed you and the Nephilim and dragons were hunting you and you sent him to the Abyss again."

The last statement was like a punch in the gut. It must have shown on my face because Samantha took my hands in hers. "I'm sorry you had to do that. I thought he was playing you, but then that day, he came in here and warned you, and I thought maybe, just maybe he'd actually changed. You changed a demon. How many people can say that?" Excitement rushed her words.

I tried to smile at her, but I still felt like there should have been another way. He deserved my gratitude, not punishment.

Before I could sink too deeply into those thoughts, Cash and Malcolm knocked on the door. "Hello, Samantha." Malcolm nodded at her. "Ready for class?"

Hoping Professor Fisher would be there, we got to my creative writing class early. Professor Fisher looked up from his desk and smiled at me when I entered. "Hello. I hope everything is okay."

I nodded. "Yes, things turned out all right. Thank you for asking. I'm sorry I had to leave without saying anything."

"These things happen." He rummaged around in his briefcase. "This is everything we covered. I'll give you a week to get the assignments turned in to me. If you need more time, let me know. We'll see if we can work something out."

As I sat down with my bodyguards, I wondered what the teachers thought had happened to drag me away, which rumor they believed was true.

After class, I met my friends at Sedum Hall for lunch. Cash and Malcolm sat at the table next to us, and my heart dropped a little. I'd gotten so used to being with them. It felt weird for them to sit away from me, but there wasn't enough room at one table for all the humans and dragons to sit together.

Russ nodded at me as he joined the other dragons. "Glad you're back."

Val gave me a hug and sniffed my hair. Arianna waved, and Tye shot me with his finger gun. "Good to see you back."

I was just taking a bite of my burger when Cassandra and Bryce set their trays down. "Where have you been?" Cassandra's voice was accusing. She waved her arm at Dan and Samantha. "They wouldn't tell me."

"They didn't know." I set my food down. "I had to leave quickly, and only Cody knew where I was because he was with me." I didn't want anybody to know Malcolm and Cash had helped me. There was always the chance the wrong people would overhear, and they would have to face the consequences of their actions. I'd protect them as long as I could.

Bryce pulled out a chair for Cassandra, then sat next to her.

"Why'd you have to leave?" She pointed at the Nephilim. "Them?"

"Yeah. They decided it was time for me to go with them, but we got it worked out."

She lifted one narrow eyebrow at me. "If it's worked out"—she did air quotes around the last two words—"why are they still here?"

"They're just keeping an eye on me to make sure I stay safe."

"Or so they say." Cody shoveled food into his mouth like he'd been starved since we'd been gone. "Don't trust them."

"Me either." I looked at them and wondered if, like the dragons, they could hear what we were saying.

"Where did you go?" Dan asked.

I pressed my lips together, debating what to say.

"Can't say." Cody saved me from making the decision. "Might have to disappear again."

"I can tell you that I'd've rather been here." I took a drink of my water. "I felt just as trapped as I would've been in their sanctuary. I had to stay hidden at all times, so they couldn't track me. It wasn't a vacation."

"And now you've got so much homework to catch up on." Samantha fiddled with her bracelet. "That's not going to be easy."

I shrugged. "If it gets done, it gets done. All we can do is our best."

"I'd be so stressed." Samantha's face paled at the thought. Grades were more important to her than they were to me these days. In high school, I would've gone crazy at the thought of getting less than an A on any assignment, but now, I was more concerned about surviving, keeping my friends safe, and saving the world. Grades had slipped several notches on my list of priorities.

Cassandra flipped her hair over her shoulder. "Don't give her more to worry about. She's got enough."

"Oh." Samantha's cheeks reddened. "I don't mean it like that."

"It's okay." Dan grinned at her. "I'm sure Dacia understands."

As soon as I swallowed the bite in my mouth, I said, "I do. I used to obsess about grades, too. Now, I've got dragons, demons, and Nephilim to worry about."

"Dragons?" Bryce stopped with his sandwich halfway to his mouth.

"Yeah." Mentally, I slapped my forehead. "I forgot you didn't know."

"There are dragons here, and you weren't going to tell us?" Cassandra practically yelled.

Samantha held her finger up to her lips, but Cassandra wasn't paying any attention to her.

I pushed my plate forward, doubting I'd have a chance to eat any more. "They were more of a concern last year when they were under Draconian's control. Now—" I shrugged. I didn't know what I should say.

Malcolm stood up, came to our table, and held his hand out to Cassandra. "We won't even eat you." He flashed his fangs at her and allowed his pupils to turn to slits.

She leaned away but placed her hand in his. "All of you."

"All of us." Cash turned in his seat and smiled at her, and the others waved. "Dacia freed us. Now we're here to protect her."

"So, what are Nephilim?" Bryce asked.

I nodded toward Diana and Olivia. "Half angel and half human."

Cash growled, and Samantha, Dan, Bryce, and Cassandra all backed away from him. The last Samantha and Dan knew I'd been terrified of Cash. They didn't know that he'd been one of my protectors, and I couldn't really tell them in case I had to leave again. I couldn't risk one of the other creatures reading their minds and finding out. As far as I knew, only Cody, Malcolm, and Aurelia knew the truth.

"Sorry." He breathed in deeply and grinned at me. "They get under my skin."

I shook my head, but I couldn't blame him, and after what he'd done for me, I couldn't be mad at him for having a little fun.

"So, your bodyguards are dragons in human form?" Amazement filled Bryce's voice. "Will we ever see you as dragons?"

"We have." Dan pointed his fork at Samantha, Cody, and me. "We were even dragged off by them. I'd say we had the scars to prove it, but Dacia and Aurelia healed them."

Cassandra's mouth hung open slightly as she looked at each of our faces. "You're kidding, right?"

"They are not." Malcolm lowered his head. "We were under the control of a madman and had no choice but to do his bidding. Unlike the demon, we weren't strong enough to rebel."

I grabbed hold of his hand. "You were under his control much longer than Mavros was. You also didn't care about me."

"You're right." Malcolm pulled away and wiped his hands over his face. "But we should have. We knew Draconian was evil. We just didn't care. We thought all humans with magic would be like him."

"Live and learn." Cody shrugged. "We survived."

Samantha drank the last of her tea, stood, and picked up her tray. "And now we have new friends." She turned toward Cody and me. "You want to get to class early. Don't you?"

"I suppose we better." I grabbed my tray and stood. "See you in class," I said to Bryce and Cassandra.

The dragons walked amongst us, not surrounding us like they had in the past. Olivia and Diana followed us, keeping further away, not watching us quite so closely.

Dr. Cedar wasn't in the classroom when we got there. We took our usual seats in the back and waited for class to begin. As soon as he entered the room, he started talking about Psyche and Eros. For once, I actually managed to listen and take notes.

When class was over, Russ and Val left with Samantha and Dan. The other dragons stood back and watched Cody and me while we talked to Dr. Cedar. "Dacia, Cody," he said. "I hope everything is all right."

"Yeah, it worked out." I hefted my backpack up, resituating it on my shoulders.

He rubbed his jaw. "Good, good, good. I trust you can get a copy of the notes from Samantha?"

"Yeah, that shouldn't be a problem," I said.

His eyes darted toward the dragons. "Her notes are probably more detailed than mine, and the two of you probably know as much about creatures of myth as I do."

My eyebrows drew together, and I turned toward Cody. His expression looked as confused as mine felt. At the same time, we both turned back toward Dr. Cedar.

"Oh, I know your guards are more than they seem, and your watchers are, too." He waved his hand. "No need to confirm or deny. Just look at your syllabus and turn in the assignments you missed by a week from Thursday. Be careful out there." He picked up a pen and started jotting notes down for himself.

"Well, that was weird," I said to Cody when we walked out into the hall.

He slid his hand into mine. "Figured he'd be one to know."

We walked to Sarah's office with the dragons and Nephilim trailing us. The sidewalks were covered in a fresh layer of snow. I pulled the collar of my coat up to help protect my face from the stinging wind.

When we got to Sarah's office, I stomped my feet on the rug, getting as much snow off of them as possible before walking to her receptionist. Alicia sat behind the desk. Her spiky hair was dyed hot pink. She drummed her manicured fingernails on the desk as she took in me and my entourage. "All of you going up?"

"I don't know about them." I pointed to Diana and Olivia. "The rest of us need to see Dean Aspen if she's available."

She lifted a slender eyebrow and pointed to the chairs. "Have a seat."

Cody and I sat in front of the fireplace, stretching our hands out to warm them. I stared out the window. The distant mountains were hidden behind blowing snow.

A few minutes after we sat down, Alicia said, "Go on up. She'll see you now."

The six of us strode up the staircase while Diana and Olivia watched us. Sarah's door was open, and she waved at us. "Come in. Come in. I'm so glad to see you." She rushed over and hugged both Cody and me. "I've been worried about you. Next time, you should let me know before you disappear."

"I'm sorry." I tugged my hand through my hair. "I really couldn't. I couldn't let the dragons or Nephilim in on our plan."

She looked at my bodyguards with disapproval. "I understand."

"We have orders that we have to follow." Malcolm lowered his eyes to the ground. "We have no choice, unless we want to face the elder council."

"Aurelia explained that to me." She waved at the couches, and we sat. "Where is Aurelia?"

"She is searching for Argentum." I didn't know what her role with the elder council was, but she seemed to play a significant part. She was always off somewhere doing something for them anymore. I understood, but I also missed having her around.

Sarah sat on the coffee table in front of me. Her eyes softened. "I am sorry for all you've been through."

"Thanks." I pictured Mavros' smile just before I returned him to the Abyss. Maybe he was okay. Maybe he'd get to go back to that realm and sit on the beach. Maybe it really was what he'd wanted. "Hopefully, they find Argentum before he comes after me again."

All of the dragons growled. The sound would spark fear in anyone with a pulse, but none of the dragons took the time to enjoy the scent.

Sarah looked at them. Her eyebrows drew together. "Do you not want him caught?"

"He broke a solemn vow." Cash's irises expanded until the scleras were barely visible. "He needs to be punished."

"Did he make the same vow as you?" Sarah asked.

"We don't know what he said for sure, but Dacia freed us." Arianna's soft, lyrical voice was hardened. "She is our ally, and he should've stood by her no matter what."

Chapter 32

Never Saw It Coming

$\mathcal{M}$avros stands in front of me. His eyes are soft. A genuine smile spreads over his lips. "Send me back, Dacia."

"I can't. I can't do that to you after you helped me." I look down at my hands. "What kind of person would that make me?"

"One who wants to live."

I woke up with tears in my eyes and Cody staring at me. He didn't say anything, just held me while I cried.

Wednesday's classes were much the same. The teachers all asked if everything was okay. They gave me assignments and notes, giving me a week to get everything done.

The walk back from Shakespeare was a tense one. Malcolm strode behind me, keeping my pace from dawdling. The dragons' apprehension rubbed off on me, making me jerk at every noise and snap my head toward every movement.

Tye slowed, lifting his head to the sky, scenting the air. "He's here." Without hesitation, he grabbed hold of my shoulder and teleported away with me.

Before my body solidified, the smell of death and decay assaulted my nostrils. Darkness surrounded me. I lifted my hand to light a fire in my palm, but he pressed it down. *Not yet.* He spoke into my mind. *Let me make sure it's safe.*

I transformed my eyes, making them dragon-like. He spH

I was in a cave. Bones and animal carcasses lay scattered over the floor. Water ran down one wall, filling a vast underground lake. Waves rippled along the surface, moving quickly toward us.

A sense of foreboding crept over me. A haze clouded my vision. Then darkness swallowed me up. Unable to see, I tried to teleport out.

Nothing happened.

Reaching for my powers, I found a vast chasm in their place.

Several torches flared to life.

"What's going on?" I held my hand over my eyes, blocking the unexpected light. I turned toward Tye to find him in his dragon form. He was about half the size of the others with brown and green scales.

He nodded his horned head toward the water. "My massster is coming. We mussst wait for him."

"Why?" Every kind word Tye had said, every time he'd been nice to me played through my memories. *How could he betray me?*

"Draconian never controlled me." He stalked toward me. His finned tail swished through the air. "He gave me a home, a purpose, power. I couldn't let the othersss know, so I had to pretend like you'd freed me, too. Then thisss opportunity arose. It wasss too good to be true."

I stepped back from him, but that put me closer to the water's edge and whatever sped through it. "Why not just kill me?"

"Where'sss the fun in that?" He laughed. "Thisss time it wasss my turn to be the tricksssster."

I tried again to call on my power, to bind it to me, and make it mine, but nothing answered.

His head snaked along the floor as he prowled toward me. "It wasss much better ssseeing you fall apart and debate becoming a caged beassst."

I needed to keep him talking while I figured out how to get away. "Why'd you pretend to like me?"

He chuckled. "That was a niccce touch. Wasn't it? You're so easssy to fool. You never once thought to look at my memoriesss, to sssee if I would betray you. Acting like your friend kept me off your radar. If I'd have acted hateful like Cash, you would've sussspected me all along." He stepped closer to me.

"No, I just needed to bide my time. I knew I'd get the chance to bring you here eventually."

"Did you?" I took another step away from him.

"I wasss a little worried when you disssappeared with the boy." He grinned at me, showing his fangs. "I planned to kidnap your friendsss if necccessary."

Something lifted out of the water behind me. If the splash was any indication, it was massive. The ground trembled, and I nearly fell over. I turned to the side so I could keep one eye on Tye and one on whatever emerged from the water.

A colossal silver dragon stepped out, and water sluiced off its body. Tye lowered his front legs to the ground, bowing to the ancient beast.

I staggered back. "Taipan, return my powers to me."

He turned toward me, and for a moment, I thought it had worked. "You think you can control me when Draconian couldn't?" He stepped closer to me. His finned tail swished angrily behind him. "I'm smaller than the othersss but ssstronger in different ways. Unlike them, I've been able to shield my true name."

My heart plummeted. I couldn't see a way out of this. I stumbled and stretched my arm out behind me to catch myself. A rock sliced through my hand, and both of the dragons lifted their snouts, breathing in the scent of my blood.

"Well done." Argentum's voice was like the rumble of boulders sliding against each other. "Her power will sustain me for centuries."

"What?!" Surprise made my voice high-pitched.

He lowered his head, looking at me with one rheumy eye. "You are far too powerful to live, so instead of sending you with the Nephilim as I'd originally planned, I am going to consume your flesh. It will strengthen me for centuries, maybe millennia."

Tye's eyes widened, and he stared at Argentum. "That wasssn't our agreement."

"The terms changed." Argentum pulled his other foot out of the water, sending waves crashing against the rocks. "You fulfilled your end of the bargain. Now be gone."

As Tye disappeared, my powers settled back into place.

Argentum roared. The sound was deafening as it bounced around the cave. I slammed my hands over my ears. Blood dripped from the palm of my hand down the side of my face.

My powers slipped out of reach again. "You are mine!"

Argentum's lip lifted into a snarl, and flames rolled through his fangs. "No dragon will ever be yours. I will not let another human control us."

"I don't want to control another creature." I scooted away from him, trying to get my feet under me.

Two massive steps shook the earth, and then he stood over me. "Then why did you say I was yours?" His forked tongue shot out, sliding up my neck and along the side of my face. His hot breath blasted my face.

My stomach heaved, and I turned away in disgust. I willed my pinky to turn invisible and thought I might sob in relief when it worked. "I didn't claim you." I wiped my injured palm across the ground, spreading my blood over the rocks, spilling it into the cracks. "I claimed my powers," I said as I teleported to my room.

Five dragons and three humans stared at me when I arrived.

"What happened?" Malcolm's voice was barely human.

I walked to the sink and washed my face and neck. I cringed when soap seeped into my cut, but I washed that, too. The dragons were too agitated to deal with my blood. Wrapping a towel around my hand, I turned toward them. "Tye was never under Draconian's control, and he was working with Argentum."

"I'm gonna kill him." Russ' amber eyes flashed with anger, and low growls filled my room.

Pulling the towel off my hand, I held my palm up. "I fell. Before I left, I wiped it on the cave floor." I covered the wound back up. "I thought maybe Malcolm could track my blood."

"Why can't you just take them there?" Samantha tilted her head, studying me.

"I don't know if I should go back." I chewed on my bottom lip. Nobody in the room was going to take what I had to say very well.

Malcolm strode toward me. "Why?"

I lowered my eyes to the floor. My shoes were filthy, and the smell of Argentum's lair lingered on me. "Argentum wants to eat me."

"What?!" White scales covered Arianna's arms. Her face elongated, and smoke rolled out of her nostrils.

"He believes my power will sustain him forever." My legs wobbled like a newborn foal's. I staggered to the couch and sat next to Samantha.

Cody stared at me from Cookie Monster. His unreadable mask was in place. If it wasn't for the bulging tendons in his neck, I wouldn't be able to tell how angry he was. "I liked Tye." His voice was dull.

One side of my mouth pulled up. "So did I. He said he acted like my friend because if he'd acted like Cash, I would've been leery of him."

Cash dropped his chin to his chest.

"He said that since he was nice to me, it never occurred to me to read his memories, and Taipan is not his true name." I leaned forward, dropping my head into my hands.

Val knelt in front of me and nuzzled his head against my uninjured hand. "Read my aura, Dacia. Trust me."

I looked into his azure eyes. Images of Val as a juvenile dragon being beaten by Draconian flashed through my mind. Then I saw him whipped as an adult. I felt his desire to be wanted and loved and his devotion to me. If Draconian would have shown him just one ounce of tenderness, Val would've been loyal to him forever. I blinked, and the images of his torture disappeared. "Thank you, Val."

He petted the back of my hand as he stood up. "Thank you for being kind."

Swallowing over the lump in my throat, I nodded at him. Arianna looked at the others, then took her place in front of me. "You saved my friends," I said. "I trusted you before any of the others."

She bowed her head slightly. "I appreciate your faith in me, but I want you to know for sure."

Looking into her lilac eyes, I saw a mother's joy when her egg hatched. Horrified, I watched as she was captured by Draconian. I felt her fear for her son and her relief when he wasn't taken. When I freed her, I felt her desire to flee, to find her son, but her need to repay me overrode that urge. I felt her strength, her gratitude, and her devotion.

"Thank you for staying and helping my friends." I leaned back. "Did you find your son?"

She stepped away. "Yes, he remained safe. He is grateful to you for freeing all of us. Val was the same age as my son when he was taken. If Draconian would've taken him, I might have been able to resist orders as Mavros did for you." She stepped away from me and looked at Cash.

He held his hands up. "Been there. Done that. She knows she can trust me."

Arianna lifted her brows and looked at me. I nodded. "I've read all of your auras and Aurelia's. I don't know anything about the unseen dragons, but they helped me when I needed it."

"Did anybody ever find out who Argentum screened?" Samantha seemed so small in a room full of dragons. "Obviously, Tye must've been one, but did he check anybody else?"

Russ rubbed his chin. "I don't know if Aurelia found out, but I'll ask her." He closed his eyes and lowered his head.

We all watched him, wondering what the answer would be or if he would even be given one. While we waited, I walked behind Cookie Monster and rubbed Cody's shoulders. "When

Tye found out what Argentum wanted, he quit helping him. They'd been working together to take my powers from me. Without Tye, Argentum would've eaten me."

"Still betrayed you." Cody clenched the arms of the chair.

I shrugged. "He did, but I think he just wanted me to be taken by the Nephilim so that I couldn't control him. It seems to be something most of the dragons fear."

Chapter 33

Searching

"Tye was the only dragon that Argentum screened." Russ shook his head. "I still can't believe one of the elders would do something like this. All our lives, we're told that they are the best of us, the wisest, the strongest, the bravest. We all endeavor to be like them. How could he do this?"

Arianna rubbed his arm. "Maybe the elders should be scrutinized after this."

"They should've been after Dacia freed us." Cash clenched his jaw. "They never lifted a finger to help."

"They were scared." Arianna's voice was soft and soothing.

Cash stood rigid; his hands fisted at his sides. "If they would've all gone in at once, they could've overcome him, but they were safe. As long as they stayed hidden, they had nothing to fear."

"At least the others know about his deception." I pulled my hand through my hair, forgetting about the cut on my palm. A strand caught on the scab, ripping it off. Blood pooled.

The dragons all turned toward me, and Cody stood up. "Out. Now!"

They all disappeared, and Cody dug out the first aid kit Nancy had stocked for me after learning about my nightmares. He rubbed antiseptic cream on the cut, then carefully wrapped it with a bandage. "Need to be more careful." He taped the end. "They're friends, but your blood does something to them."

"Yeah." I flexed my hand to see how bad the bandage impaired it. "Why didn't it affect Aurelia like that?"

"That's a good question." Dan stood up and stretched his arms straight up in the air.

Cody sat down in Cookie Monster and held his head in his hands. "Malcolm was the only one with a problem last time. He's tasted her blood."

"So has Argentum." Samantha curled her legs under her, pressing herself into the corner of the red couch.

"Val liked the smell of it, but luckily, he didn't taste it." I walked over to the window and looked outside. The sun had set, but the campus was illuminated all the time. Snow blew into huge drifts. "It looks nasty out there. Is anybody hungry? We should go before it gets much worse."

We bundled up to go to Sedum Hall for supper. The dragons met us in the hall and escorted us. As soon as we stepped outside, the wind seemed to tear through my clothes and bite into my skin. Cash moved in front of me, taking the brunt of it.

"Thank you," I said as we trudged through the drifts.

His voice was muffled by the wind. "It doesn't bother me."

I don't think Tye will be a problem anymore, but he threatened to kidnap my friends to get me to come out of hiding, I thought to the dragons. They all perked up, seeming more alert. *I don't want them to have to worry about it, but I'm afraid Argentum might try something.*

We will be extra vigilant, Arianna responded.

When we were all seated, Samantha asked, "So, should Dan and I stick closer to you so all five dragons can keep an eye on you?"

Malcolm leaned back in his chair. "Three of us will do. Either Cash or I will stay in her room. She'll be safe."

I pushed my pasta around, occasionally taking a bite. Nefarious was the only monster I'd faced that wanted me dead, but at least he hadn't wanted to eat me.

Looking around the room, I saw Diana and Olivia sitting at a table with a couple other students. I wondered if they would follow me forever to make sure I didn't fall to darkness. According to Aurelia, I would spend the majority of my life fighting monsters. Maybe their sanctuary would appeal to me sometime in the future. I nodded at them and ran my breadstick through my sauce, taking a bite. Now that they weren't actively trying to capture me, I should try to make them my allies.

Thursday and Friday passed by uneventfully. Cody and I spent most of our free time working on homework. Cash and Val sat in my room with us while Malcolm searched for the cave Tye had taken me to. Either I'd been too deep underground or the cave was far from here. It seemed more and more likely that I would have to return there and face the silver beast. Even though the dragons would be there with me, I had the feeling that it would be up to me to bring Argentum down. I didn't think I'd be able to win him over with my good looks and charm either.

When Malcolm returned to my room Friday night, his posture was rigid, and his hands were clenched. He stared out the window, slowly rolling his head from one shoulder to the other, over and over again. Time seemed to slow while I waited for him to tell us what had happened. Finally, he turned toward me. "I'm sorry, Dacia, but I can't smell even a trace of your blood out there."

My shoulders slumped, but I really wasn't surprised. What were the odds that an elder dragon's lair would be within fifty miles of Phlox University? "So … I've been thinking. Is Argentum his true name?"

"No." Cash huffed a laugh. "That would be too easy. Wouldn't it?"

Malcolm narrowed his eyes at me. "You can't do that. If you control one of us using our true name, you'll show all the other dragons you're no better than Draconian."

"That's not what I wanted to do." I set my pen down on top of my notebook. Even though most of my assignments had to be turned in electronically, writing things down helped me remember them. "I wanted to show him that even though I know it, I wouldn't use it. Kind of like I did with Cash."

"I should've known better." Malcolm sat on the couch between Cash and Val.

Cody set his book on the floor. "Aurelia having any luck?"

"No." Malcolm shook his head. His hair bounced from shoulder to shoulder. "I'm beginning to wonder if all this secrecy is worth it?"

Cash snorted. "And who would we trust? The elders? I think not."

"I'll take you there." Knowing Cody wouldn't be happy with that decision, I looked anywhere but at him.

"You crazy?" Anger and desperation filled his voice. "He wants to eat you."

I yanked my hand through my hair. "I know, but I can't just wait for him to come after me. He needs found."

"Give me a couple more days," Malcolm said. "If I can't find him by Sunday night, we'll get everybody together, including Aurelia, and figure out what to do. Until then, let's train."

Argentum emerges from the underground lake. The water falls off of him, and his sterling scales shimmer in the firelight. Six dragons stand with me, but compared to him, they're tiny.

"You brought her to me." His voice rumbles through the cave.

I step over a pile of bones. "These dragons are my friends. They know I won't hurt them."

"If they believe that, you must be controlling them." He lifts his front leg. Water pours off his talons into the lake. "No dragon in its right mind would befriend a human."

Malcolm steps forward. "She freed us, and we vowed to protect her."

Argentum swings his neck around and clamps his jaws down on Malcolm's neck. Black blood puddles on the ground. Bones snap, and Malcolm's aura blinks out.

"Stop!" I press my hands out in front of me. "Why'd you kill him?" I fall to my knees. "He was my friend."

"He was a miscreant before Draconian took control of him—" he looks down at Malcolm's body "—and it doesn't appear that he changed."

Aurelia steps toward him. Her gilded scales twinkle. "Argentum, the elder council wishes for you to stand before them and be judged for your crimes."

"Crimes?" He scoffs. "I've committed no crime. If I rid the world of Dacia Wolf, she will only be missed by a few insignificant humans, and the world will be better off."

"No." She shakes her crested head. "She is a friend to dragons. Fairies have vouched for her to the Nephilim. They have accepted her. She has even made a demon change his ways."

"Lies." He swats his paw and knocks Aurelia to the ground. "Give her to me, and go in peace."

"We cannot." Russ fans his wings. "Dragon vows are sacred, or have you forgotten?"

"Do not insult me, boy." Argentum drags his other leg out of the lake. "I helped make the laws that we live by."

"So, why do you think you can break them?" I yell at him to draw his attention from the dragons.

"In times of danger, the elders have always had the right to do whatever was necessary." He narrows his eyes at me. "Tell them to back away, or they will all die for you."

"No one else is going to die." The last word catches in my throat. I clap my hands, and all of the dragons but Argentum disappear.

He growls, and a shiver sprints up my spine. "It is time for you to give your life for the greater good." He swipes a massive, taloned paw at me.

His claws slice through my back. I fall to my hands and knees. My vision darkens.

Cody stood above me. I couldn't make out his words, but I could hear the anger in his voice. It took a few tries, but I finally opened my eyes.

"She's awake." Cash sounded relieved. He knelt down at eye level with me. "Are you okay?"

I tried to shake my head, but it sent a spasm through my back.

"Let us heal her," Malcolm said to Cody.

He stood firmly in front of me. "Can't trust you around her blood."

"Please." My voice was so soft I didn't know if he'd hear it.

He looked down at me. "You sure."

"Please."

Cash and Malcolm each took one of my hands. Malcolm held on tighter than he normally would, and I wondered how much longer his self-control would last.

Their energy flowed into me, lessening the pain. The tension in my body released, and I looked into Malcolm's bronze eyes. "He killed you."

"Not going to happen." He shook his head and smiled at me. "I won't let him."

"How do you know?"

He smiled at me. "Because you're going to tell me exactly what happened. If it was a premonition, I'll see it coming."

Chapter 34

Hanging Out

Cody and I waited until he was allowed to be in the women's dorm before we stepped into the hall with my dragon guards. Marcy grinned shyly at Val as we walked past, and I hoped he didn't see it for what it was. With his instincts, I wasn't sure how he'd react.

"Dacia," Cassandra shouted from behind me when we stepped outside.

Huge snowflakes fell to the ground, blanketing everything. They caught on my eyelashes. Reaching up to wipe them off my face, I turned around and smiled at her. "Hello."

"What are you doing today?" She trotted to catch up to us.

Pulling the collar of my coat up to block the wind, I pointed toward Sedum. "We're meeting Samantha and Dan for breakfast. Then I thought about going to Althea."

"Oh." She looked down.

"Wanna come?" Cody asked.

She lifted her head, and a smile lit up her face. "That'd be great. Bryce, too?"

"Sure." I shrugged. "If Samantha and Dan come, we'll have to take a coupla cars. Cody's is out. Too much snow."

She walked with us to Sedum Hall. Bryce stood just inside the door, waiting for her. "Hey." He nodded at us.

"Want to go to Althea with them?" Cassandra sounded excited, and I couldn't help but smile at how things changed if you let them.

He shrugged. "Sure. It's nice to get off campus every once in a while."

I got pancakes with strawberries and whipped cream and a few strips of bacon. Then sat down with my back to the wall. Diana tossed a smile my way as she sat at a table between me and the door. I smiled back and made a mental note to try to talk to her.

When I was about halfway through breakfast, Dan and Samantha showed up. "Sorry we're late." Samantha took her coat off and hung it on the back of her chair.

"Althea?" Cody asked before shoving his toast into his mouth.

Dan nodded and sat beside Samantha. "Sounds fun. We haven't been there together in a while."

"Bryce and Cassandra"—I pointed my fork at them when I said their names—"are coming, so someone else will have to drive. My truck only fits two."

Dan shrugged. "I can fit five in mine."

"We don't need a ride." Cash leaned closer. "It'll be nice to spread our wings."

Both Bryce's and Cassandra's eyes widened.

"You won't see them." I sopped up as much syrup as I could with my pancakes. "Unless they want you to."

"Cool." Bryce put scrambled eggs on his toast.

Malcolm picked up his tray. "Do you want me with you? Say the word, and I'll go."

I looked at Cash, Val, Russ, and Arianna and pulled my hand through my hair. It was still damp from walking in the snow. I shook my head. "Unless you want to, I think you should keep looking."

"Stay safe." He nodded.

"You, too."

We met in the commons at two o'clock to go to Althea. Before we left, I said, "I don't feel right going anywhere with you—"

Cassandra's face fell. "Then—"

"Let me finish." I held my hand up. "I don't feel right going anywhere with you, without warning you that there is an elder dragon hunting me."

Bryce tilted his head. "So, what does that mean?"

"Not much since you haven't seen a dragon before." I tucked my hands into my coat pockets. "He's about twice their size, and he's one of their leaders."

"I thought you helped them"—Cassandra moved closer to Bryce—"so why's he after you?"

I looked around the room, hoping nobody else was listening to our conversation. "He's afraid."

"Dacia's really powerful." Samantha rolled her eyes at my answer. "He's scared she'll try to control him, and he thinks if he eats her, he'll gain her powers."

"He wants to eat you?" Cassandra's mouth hung open. "And you sent one of your guards away?"

I toed the ground. "Yeah, I'll be okay. I just wanted to warn you that if you hang out with me, things can get kinda weird."

"Okay." Bryce rubbed his hands together. "Consider us warned."

When we got done brushing the snow off my truck, Cody said, "Why don't I drive?"

"Your car doesn't get around in this, Cody."

He held his hand out. "Your truck."

"Oh." I reached into my pocket and gave him my keys. "Why?"

He unlocked the doors and held the passenger one open for me. "Mavros pulled you away twice. What if Argentum can?"

"Okay." I nodded. "Good point."

He shut the door and walked to the driver's side. Dan followed us out of the parking lot and into Althea.

Snowflakes drifted lazily from the sky, making Cody take the curves slower than normal. He kept both hands on the wheel the entire drive. Normally, our fingers would've been entwined, the music would've been louder, and the tension wouldn't have been so thick.

There was more to his apprehension than the weather. He had driven faster on worse roads. I opened my mouth to ask him about it but decided not to. Instead, I rubbed his shoulder. Then I traced my finger along his ear. His grip on the steering wheel loosened slightly.

He turned off the main road in Althea, driving through the less touristy areas. The bowling alley was on the far edge of town. Trees lined one side of the parking lot and continued behind the building. Snow clung to their branches and mounded at their bases.

Cody pulled into the lot, and the dragons made it look like they got out of a car a few down from us. They stopped by my truck. "Is bowling as easy as basketball?"

"Something tells me it will be for you." I laughed.

When we got our lanes, Dan said, "So what are teams? I was thinking The Mere Mortals and The Fire Breathers. Dacia can be one of The Fire Breathers."

Samantha laughed, and the teams were set. Cody, Dan, and Bryce explained the rules to the dragons while Cassandra, Samantha, and I searched for the perfect ball.

The first few frames were interesting. My teammates had to check their strength. Their bowling balls were being launched about halfway down the lane. After they figured out the subtlety of the release, they did much better. I'd never witnessed so many turkeys in my life.

We talked and laughed, and I got my mind off everything. After three games, we left to go to The Avalanche. The snow hadn't let up, and at least eight inches covered the ground.

"Maybe we should just go back to campus before we end up stranded here." Cassandra pulled her gloves on.

Cash threw his arms over Bryce's and Cassandra's shoulders. "You won't get stranded." He grinned at them. "We can even get your vehicles back."

"Really?" I tilted my head and looked at him.

Russ put his hand on my back and led me to my truck. "We can teleport them back to campus if we need to, but right now, you should get off the street."

"Problem?" I asked.

Russ shook his head. "No sense in making one." He melted the snow off my truck while Cash melted the snow off Dan's. "We'll follow you."

It took a while to get a table for ten ready. We stood in the waiting area and shivered every time the door opened. When we were all seated, Abigail came over and took our drink orders. "You've got extras today." She smiled at the newcomers. "Do you need more time?"

"Yeah." I nodded at the dragons. "They've never been here before."

"Okay. I'll be back in a few minutes."

When she walked away, I looked at Cash. "I bet you never thought you'd be eating out with six humans. Did you?"

"No." He shook his head. "Fifteen hundred years and I've never done anything like this before."

Bryce set his menu down and stared at Cash. "You're fifteen hundred years old?"

"Give or take." Cash shrugged. "Time is irrelevant, and it's hard to keep track."

"What about the rest of you?" Cassandra asked.

Val counted on his fingers, then looked at Arianna. She answered for him. "You're three hundred seventy-six."

"Wait." I looked up in surprise and noticed Abigail bringing our drinks. "In a minute." I nodded toward our waitress so they'd know not to say anything else.

She handed us our drinks, then stood across from Dan to take our orders. She nearly melted when he smiled at her, but I couldn't blame her. It was a great smile.

When everyone had placed their orders and she walked off, I said, "How long were you under Draconian's control?"

"Three hundred seventy-one years." Arianna picked up her glass and stared at the contents.

"Oh, wow." Samantha held her hand up in front of her mouth. "I had no idea it had been so long."

I unwrapped my silverware and smoothed out my napkin. "I didn't either."

"I spent nearly half of my life in captivity." Russ stared at the table. "I'm seven hundred forty-four."

Arianna looked around. "Like Cash, I'm not quite sure, but I believe I'm somewhere between fifteen hundred and seventeen hundred. Aurelia and Malcolm are the oldest of us."

"That is so cool." Bryce took a roll out of the basket and buttered it. "We've got maybe seventy to a hundred years to make our mark. Wouldn't it be awesome to have a thousand or more?"

I tugged my hand through my hair and looked down. This wasn't something I wanted to start thinking about again. Death said I would meet him again, but Draconian had lived for centuries. I didn't want to watch my friends and family die. I couldn't imagine the anguish.

Cody reached over and squeezed my hand.

"Dacia may have that chance." Cash looked directly into my eyes before bowing his head. "I would be honored to serve you for eternity."

"Thank you, Cash." I tried to smile at him, but I wasn't sure if it worked. "Hopefully, that won't be the case."

Everyone but Samantha, Dan, and Cody looked at me in confusion. "Why?" Val asked.

"It's unnatural." I couldn't give them more of an answer without breaking down, and I didn't want to do that in a crowded restaurant.

"To live forever"—Cassandra flipped her hair over her shoulder—"might be unnatural, but it would be awesome."

Cody set his roll on his plate. "Drop it." His voice was hard. He wiped his hand over his mouth. "Please."

They looked at me with pinched eyebrows and tilted heads but said no more.

By the time we finished eating and went outside, at least another four inches of snow had fallen. The wind picked it up and flung it across the parking lot, spinning it up into snow devils. They whirled into the trees, then dropped to the ground.

"This isn't good." I clasped my hood around my face, trying to keep the snow and wind from pelting it.

Cash looked out at the road and rubbed his chin. "Drive to the edge of town. We'll take it from there."

"Sure." Cody unlocked my truck and opened the door for me. He climbed in behind the wheel and waited while Cash evaporated the snow.

The roads were covered, and few cars had made tracks through it. Cody drove slowly with Dan following behind him. As soon as we reached the edge of town, I felt something land in my truck's bed. Then we were stretched out and pushed in. When I felt like myself again, the truck was on the road right outside of campus. Cody drove it into the lots between the dorms, and Cash and Val jumped out.

Cody opened the door. "Thanks. Woulda been a long drive."

"That was wicked!" Bryce held his hand out to Cassandra.

She was grinning like the Cheshire Cat. "Yeah, it was."

"Can you do that?" Bryce helped Cassandra across the parking lot.

"I've never tried with a truck"—I yanked my hood up—"but I do it a lot."

Cassandra shuffled her feet. "That would be wicked. I'd never walk outside in this."

"I have to be careful about using my powers." It was tempting to teleport to my room right now, but I didn't know how many people might be looking out their windows. "I can't let people see me use them."

"It'd still be sweet," Bryce said.

When we got inside, Cassandra turned to me. "Thanks for letting us hang out with you. Things haven't been the same with Vanessa and Alvin since everything that happened in our first semester. We've just been drifting further apart."

"I'm sorry to hear that." I'd enjoyed hanging out with them today, but I meant it. I'd lost friends when they decided I was weird.

Bryce unzipped his coat. "They seemed to enjoy the cruelty. It's become part of them."

"Oh." Samantha stuffed her gloves into her pockets. "That's not good."

Cassandra stared straight ahead, not looking at anyone. "No, it's not. Sometimes I wonder why he chose us."

"I wonder the same about myself."

Chapter 35

Making Plans

$\mathcal{I}$ flipped the lights on, and my heart jumped like a scared cat. Malcolm sat on the couch. He leaned forward with his elbows on his knees, staring at nothing. Lines etched his forehead.

"Nothing?" I pulled my gloves off and shoved them in my pockets. My friends followed me into the room.

He shook his head. "Not even a whiff."

I hung up my coat. With my back turned to Malcolm, I said, "I might as well take you there. That's what's going to happen in the end."

"I have one more day." Malcolm's voice was a low growl. "I won't put you in danger unless there's no other choice."

I took my boots off and set them on a rug beside the door. "I know you won't, but it wouldn't be my life if I wasn't in danger."

"Have a little faith." Cody hung his coat beside mine and took my hand, leading me to Cookie Monster. He sat down and pulled me onto his lap.

I snuggled against him. "I actually have a lot of faith, but I also know how this will play out. I've done it a few times."

"I'm not the only one looking for him," Malcolm said. "The elders and Aurelia are also searching."

Samantha offered the couch to the other dragons. When they all shook their heads, she and Dan sat down. "So how many elder dragons are there?"

"Thirteen sit on the council." Arianna sat on the floor and brushed the snow out of her cropped hair. Her eyes were just slightly darker than the carpet. "So, twelve now. They will have to find a replacement for Argentum." She patted the ground next to her, and Val sat down. He put his head on her shoulder.

I couldn't help but wonder what had happened to his mother when he was captured and if Arianna had filled that place for Val even when they were under Draconian's control.

Russ leaned against the doorframe, folding his arms over his chest. "It will most likely be Aurelia."

"Would they really make her one when I know her true name?" I looked over my shoulder at him.

He nodded. "I believe they will."

"Will we see her again if they do?" Samantha asked.

Arianna smiled. "They'll keep her busy, but I'm sure she'll make time for you."

Malcolm watched me stretch. "No nightmares last night?" It was still dark in the room, but his eyes glowed like a cat's.

"No." I rolled my neck. "Without Mavros here, I really haven't had many." I pulled my hand through my hair. "Just the one where … you know."

He stood up and glowered at me. "I'm not going to die. Not yet. Wish me luck."

"Good luck."

He disappeared.

"He's gonna find him." Cody rubbed my back.

I dropped my head into my hands. "I want him to. I really do, but I don't think he will. My dream—" I looked out the window, not seeing anything "—felt like a premonition. I know it's going to happen. I just hope I can keep Malcolm alive when it does."

I felt Cody sit up behind me. He wrapped his arms around me and rested his chin on my shoulder. He was warm and comforting. "Didn't realize." He kissed my neck. "Thought you were being pessimistic."

"Maybe I am." I folded my arms over his. "We'll find out when Malcolm comes back tonight."

He kissed just under my ear, and I leaned into it. "What're we doing today?"

"Studying." My voice sounded breathless.

"You sure?" He kissed me again, and I turned, wrapping my legs around his waist.

I ran my finger down his nose, then pressed my hands to his bare chest. "What did you have in mind?"

His hair was tousled, and his eyes looked mischievous. "Could just stay here all day." He tugged me closer and kissed my chin. "Keep your mind off things." He trailed his lips down my neck.

I closed my eyes and clutched his back. A soft moan escaped from me. I bit my lip and pulled away from him. "Dragons are always watching."

You could shut us out, Cash said. *You shouldn't, though.*

"I know."

Cody tilted his head. "You know what?"

"I was answering Cash." I kissed the tip of his nose.

He leaned back. "So, we're studying."

I lifted one shoulder. "We'll never be alone. We might feel like we are, but someone will always be watching me." I scooted onto the couch beside him. "Is this what you want out of life?"

He slid his hand over mine. "Just want you. I'll take the rest."

"You deserve better."

He traced his fingers along my cheek. "You're the best thing that's happened to me, Dacia. You're amazing, and I will take everything else as long as I get you."

I squeezed his hand. "Thanks, Cody."

He spent the day studying on the couch, and I sat at the desk. By the time Malcolm came back, my eyes were so blurry I could barely read the words in front of me.

"I'm sorry, Dacia." Malcolm sat on the couch with his head bowed over his lap. "I can keep looking. We don't have to give up yet. I'll search for another week. Then if I don't find him, you can take us to him."

"No." I got up and sat between him and Cody. "I don't think we should wait." I put my hand on Malcolm's arm. "I know you don't want to put me in danger. I don't want you in danger either. I think you should stay behind when I go."

His bronze eyes narrowed and became more dragon-like. "I won't put your life in danger while sparing mine."

"I didn't think you would." I tugged my hand through my hair and tried to figure out a way everybody could get out of this alive. "I guess we need to get everybody together and come up with a plan."

My room was too small for six dragons and six humans, but we all squeezed in anyway. Bryce, Cassandra, Samantha, and Dan crammed together on the couch. Cody stood by the window. Aurelia sat in Cookie Monster, and Malcolm sat at the desk. Val sat next to Arianna on the floor. Russ and Cash each leaned against the door. I paced.

"Dacia"—Aurelia's voice was soft—"are you sure this is what you want?" She looked at Bryce and Cassandra.

I stopped pacing for a minute and looked at everyone gathered in the room. As little as a month ago, I wouldn't have pictured us as friends, but now, I couldn't imagine my life without them. "Yes." I walked three steps to Cody and turned around.

"We have not been able to locate Argentum." Aurelia's gold skin shimmered like it did before she transformed into her dragon form. "The elders pride themselves on keeping secrets. They have been doing it for so long that they know no other way. None of them know where Argentum's lair is."

Malcolm watched me pace. "I've been searching for Dacia's scent, but he's not within a thousand miles of here."

"So, is Dacia going to have to go into hiding again?" Cassandra tugged on her sleeves, pulling them to her wrists. The blue of her sweater made her eyes even more striking than normal.

"No." I stopped moving. "I'm going to have to lead them to him." My voice sounded hollow. Even though I never wanted to see Argentum again, I was more afraid of guiding the other dragons to him.

Bryce leaned forward with his elbows on his knees. "How?"

"I've been in his lair"—I lifted a shoulder toward my ear—"so I can picture it and teleport back there again."

Cassandra tilted her head to the side and asked, "So why haven't you done that already?"

Cody's voice was a low growl. "Wants to eat her."

"Oh." She lifted her hand to her mouth. "Oh, right."

Bryce's mouth opened, then closed. He stared at me for a minute before he said, "And you're going back?"

"I've got to." I slid down the wall and sat on the floor. "I think it needs to be in the next couple of days. I don't think we should wait any longer than that."

"If you're sure this is what you want—" Malcolm rubbed his hands together "—we'll surround you when you teleport in. We can each lend you some of our strength." He looked at each of the other dragons, and they all nodded. "At the first sign of trouble, you can teleport out of there."

"And, what about you?" I stared at him pointedly.

He gazed back. The expression on his face was indecipherable. "I'm not going to die."

"Will you leave?" I stood up. "If things go bad, will you leave with me?"

His eyes softened. "For you, I can make that promise."

Aurelia's golden gaze flicked between the two of us, and I realized he must not have said anything to her about my dream. Her eyes settled on me. "The council wishes for us to return Argentum to them alive. However, if the choice is between saving somebody in this room or saving him, all of us will put your lives first."

Chapter 36

Another Sleepless Night

Cody breathed softly. He'd been sleeping for an hour or more, but I couldn't close my eyes. Every time I did, I pictured Argentum killing Malcolm. He was over two thousand years old, but that didn't mean he'd live forever.

"You need to sleep," Malcolm whispered from his post in the chair.

Not wanting to wake Cody up, I spoke into Malcolm's mind. *I can't.* I thought about Argentum killing him in my dream and accidentally sent the image to Malcolm.

He winced like I'd slapped him. *Not happening.* The words were snarled. He composed himself before saying, "I could help you sleep."

"Not yet," I whispered.

"You have an hour."

An hour came and went, but Malcolm didn't force me to sleep. He continued watching me. Concern softened his features, making him appear more human than I'd seen him before.

I had no idea how long it took, but I finally drifted off. Even though I was in Cody's arms, nightmares haunted me.

Wednesday morning, I stood in the center of a ring of dragons. I was exhausted but trying not to show it. I'd woken up with sleep-crusted eyes. All I'd wanted to do was roll over and doze off again, but it was time to face Argentum and end this.

Each of the six dragons put a hand on me. Their strength flowed into me, and adrenaline pushed away the fatigue. "He won't go easy," I said. "Please be careful, and if he looks like he's going to attack, just get out of there."

Cody watched us from the couch. His mask slipped enough that I saw the torment on his face before he slid it back into place. I held his gaze, hoping this wouldn't be the last time I looked into his sapphire eyes. Smiling at him, I teleported. The dragons' energy funneled into me. We stretched out and squeezed in.

The putrid aroma of the cavern assaulted my nostrils before my body solidified. Shadows engulfed us, and the steady lapping of waves was the only sound.

I transformed my eyes into a dragon's to penetrate the darkness. One of my comrades breathed in deeply enough for me to hear it, then moaned.

"You're blood's here." Val's whisper seemed deafening in the silence of the cavern.

The water rippled. *He's in the water.* My thought was panicky, but all the dragons received the message.

Turn invisible, Aurelia thought back.

I did as she said and watched as the dragons disappeared one by one. Aurelia seemed to stand alone in the chamber. She stared at the lake, watching Argentum's wave rush toward the shore.

He rose out of the water, like a leviathan. "What are you doing here, Aurelia?" He kept his head absolutely still, but his eyes scanned the area.

"The elder council would like you to come back with me for questioning." She seemed relaxed, almost nonchalant.

He pulled one foot out of the water, making the earth shake. "I thought you didn't lie."

"I am not lying." Smoke rolled out of her nostrils, but she showed no other signs of anger.

"I can smell the other dragons." He lowered his head and sucked in a deep breath. "I can smell *her*."

She stepped forward, moving slightly to the side to block me from him. "They are here. We are to bring you in if you do not come willingly."

A low rumbling sound filled the cavern. The sound grew, bouncing off the walls and ceiling. I clasped my hands over my ears, finally realizing Argentum was laughing. "You think that you"—he practically spit the word—"can take me in. Unless you brought the entire elder council with you, that won't happen." He pulled his other foot out of the water.

"Why?" Aurelia held her ground. "Why did you betray us?"

"The girl cannot live. Surely, you can see that." He shook his body, and water sprayed around the cavern. The splash marks showed where all of us stood. "She has the power to control all of us. We have a responsibility to keep that from happening again."

Cash growled. It wasn't a warning growl or an it'll-be-fun-to-scare-your-friends growl. It was filled with more than three centuries of rage and hatred. He turned visible and stepped forward. "We were under his control for hundreds of years, and you did nothing!" He strode toward Argentum, anger visible in the lines of his body. "You only care about yourself. The council is supposed to do what's best for all dragons."

Argentum whipped his head around, facing Cash. His lip lifted in a snarl, exposing his fangs. "Insolent, disrespectful whelp. What makes you think you can talk to me like that?" His neck and chest illuminated and fire spewed from his maw.

I threw a shield up, blocking all of us from Argentum's rage. The flames arced over our heads, lighting up the vast cavern. They crawled along the ground, charring the bones strewn throughout the chamber.

"Argentum, the council is debating your punishment." Aurelia's voice commanded attention. "Do you really want to amplify their wrath?"

His flames cut off. "Leave the girl here and go." Even though I was still invisible, he narrowed his eyes as if he could see me. "As soon as I'm finished with her, I'll come in. The council will thank me once it's done."

The air moved around me as the dragons stepped closer. One of them grabbed my arm, and energy flowed into me. I recognized it as Malcolm's. *I won't let him take you ... no matter what.*

Thanks. I hadn't even considered that they might. I trusted each of these dragons, and my main concern was keeping them safe. I lowered my shield, letting Malcolm's power amass inside of me.

A golden haze swirled around Aurelia as she transformed into her dragon. She was smaller and leaner than Argentum, but I wasn't about to count her out. "We will not hand Dacia over to you." She stepped toward him, and I prepared to block his flames again if necessary.

He lowered his head and prepared to breathe fire. Instead of putting a shield around us, I wrapped it around Argentum's head. His flames filled the bubble, reminding me of when I froze fire. Smoke filled the orb, choking out the flames. Argentum swung his head from side to side.

He jumped out of the water, running straight toward us. His rheumy eyes opened wide with fear. I held my shield in place and backed away. Malcolm moved with me, keeping his hand on my shoulder, lending me his strength.

Argentum slammed into an invisible barrier and bounced back. He crashed to the ground. The earth shuddered. I stumbled, but Malcolm held onto me, keeping me on my feet.

I strode toward the shield one of the dragons had erected, fitting the mask to Argentum's face, squeezing all the oxygen from it.

Argentum thrashed, tearing at his snout with his claws. He rolled on the ground. His tail whipped through the air. Then he slowed. His head slumped.

Chapter 37

Decisions

The dragons regained their visibility. Aurelia and Russ strode toward Argentum. Aurelia nudged his head with her snout. "Unless you want to kill him, release him." Her voice was soft, making it clear that she would stand by me no matter what I decided.

There was no choice for me. Two deaths on my conscience were more than enough. I knew I couldn't cope with another one. I dropped my hands to my sides and became visible, staring at Argentum's face. His eyes were rolled back in his head. His forked, black tongue hung out of his mouth. His yellowed fangs were chipped and cracked.

Malcolm clasped my shoulder, and the steady flow of his energy streamed into me. I felt like I'd had far too much caffeine. My heart raced, and my muscles shook. I pulled away from him. "Thanks. I'm good."

A gold haze surrounded Aurelia, churning and spinning. She emerged from it in her human form. Long, golden hair hung to her waist. Her skin shimmered slightly in the dim lighting left by Argentum's fire. She waved her hand, and the dragons other than Malcolm went to her. They surrounded Argentum, and each of them laid a hand upon the silver beast. He dwarfed them, but he hadn't so much as twitched since he fell.

"Take care of her," Aurelia said to Malcolm before they disappeared with Argentum.

Malcolm held his hand out to me, and as I slipped mine into it, I asked, "Where'd they take him?"

"To the elder council, I imagine." He teleported us back to my room.

Cody jumped up off the couch. Lines of tension disappeared from around his eyes and mouth as he took in my appearance. He brushed his hair back. "You're okay."

I nodded. "The others took him."

"So … is it done?"

I stepped up to him and wrapped my arms around his waist. He slid one hand into my hair and pulled me against him with his other one. I leaned into his embrace. "I don't know."

"He's powerful." Malcolm's voice was low. "He might be able to break free from the council or use his magic even from containment."

I dropped my head onto Cody's chest. "He'll hate me even more now."

"Silver dragons pride themselves on being just." The chair creaked, and I imagined Malcolm sitting in Cookie Monster, holding his head in his hands. "It isn't hatred that drives him. He believes he's doing what's best for the world."

I stepped back from Cody and turned toward Malcolm. He sat in the chair exactly like I'd pictured he'd be. "Well, that's just great."

"How's she convince him otherwise?" Cody asked.

Malcolm shook his head. "I don't know if she can."

When the dragons returned, I called everyone and asked if they wanted to come over for pizza. I wanted to talk to them, but I didn't want to do it in public. I thought it might be best to keep the Nephilim from knowing what had happened with Argentum. There was always the possibility they'd decide I was a danger to them again.

While waiting for everyone to show up, Malcolm went to Aurelia's room, and Cody sat on the couch, watching me pace. By some small miracle, I hadn't worn a path into the lavender carpet yet.

I felt Samantha's and Dan's auras. A few seconds later, the doorknob turned. I stopped and stared at it. As soon as they opened the door, Samantha dropped her bag and ran toward me, hugging me. "How do you keep walking into danger? I was so worried about you the whole time."

"It's not like I want to." I shrugged as she pulled away from me. "I'd like to have a peaceful … normal life."

"What happened?" Dan stepped up beside us.

I sat on the floor in front of Cody. "We'll find out."

The dragons came over right after Bryce and Cassandra showed up. Aurelia stared out the window with her hands behind her back. "We took Argentum to the elder council." She spun around. "They questioned him. Then they threw him in the dungeon." Her expression was caught somewhere between anger, disgust, and disbelief. "At one time, he was one of the best of us. He was just and honorable."

"I'm sorry, Aurelia." I stared at the floor.

She shot me a sad smile. "You are not to blame. Argentum made his choices. He feels that you are a threat to dragons, but he does not know you. He does not see what is in your heart."

"Yeah." I pulled my hand through my hair. "The Nephilim feel the same way."

Cassandra snorted. "If this is what good guys are like, wouldn't it be easier to deal with bad guys?"

"Sometimes, the lines between good and evil become blurred." Russ looked around the room. "Other times, who the good guys are and who the bad guys are depends on which side you stand on."

Cody snatched a piece of pizza. "Couldn't the Nephilim and elder council read her aura and figure out that she's good?"

"Yeah." Dan tilted his head as he looked at Aurelia. "Wouldn't that have been easier?"

"Woulda saved a lotta trouble." Cody shook his head and ate half of the slice in one bite.

Arianna nodded. "It would have, but none of the elders or leaders of the Nephilim are willing to get that close to a human as powerful as Dacia, not after Draconian."

"Will they let me go to him?" The idea stole the breath from me and sent a jolt of adrenaline through my veins. "If I opened myself to him, he'd be able to see that I don't want to hurt anyone." My words rushed out.

"No." Aurelia shook her head. "He could destroy your mind."

"He doesn't trust you." Malcolm looked like he wanted to protect me from some threat I couldn't see. His muscles were taut, and his face was strained. "He'd think it was a trick."

"This is no longer your fight." Aurelia sat on the floor next to me. "You need to let us handle Argentum."

Cody wiped his mouth on a napkin. "Is it over?"

"I hope so, Cody." Aurelia patted my shoulder, but she didn't sound convinced.

"Forgive me, Dacia." Tye focuses on the snow-covered ground between us instead of looking into my eyes. His shoulders slump forward, and the star-flecked night seems to swallow him up.

Unrecognizable mountains surround us, pine trees stretch toward the heavens, and in the middle of this beautiful scene, we face each other. I stand with my feet shoulder-width apart and my knees slightly bent. My arms hang loosely at my sides, ready to defend myself at any sign of trouble from him. "How can I? First, you were going to let them cage me. Then when that didn't work out, you were going to let Argentum eat me." The wind tosses my hair over my shoulders, and I pull it away from my face, tucking it inside my hoodie.

"I didn't know he wanted to kill you." He looks up at me, and his eyes are red-rimmed. "The others are hunting me. They'll kill me. Please … if you forgive me, they'll leave me alone."

I shake my head. He doesn't want my forgiveness because he feels guilty about what he did. He wants it for his own self-ish reasons. "How can I? You'll stab me in the back the first chance you get."

"No." He falls to his knees. "No. I thought you'd try to control all of us." Lowering his head to the ground, he says, "I thought that with time, you'd come to enjoy the peace of the sanctuary. I thought it was what was best for everyone." His head drops even farther. "I never wanted to see you hurt."

"Get up." A deep voice rumbles through the clearing, and a wizened man strides from the trees. Long, opalescent hair flows to his waist. Braids at his temples pull his hair away from his slender face. "You sniveling fool. The elder council impris-ons me for five minutes, and you run to this girl like she is your only hope." He narrows his hard, gray eyes, and there is no compassion in them. "Pathetic whelp."

Tye scrambles to his feet, careful not to look either of us in the eye.

The man strolls toward Tye, keeping his gaze on me. "You have caused me more trouble than any of your kind has ever been worth." He clasps Tye's shoulder, and Tye cringes under his grip. "Because of you, I've been hunted and imprisoned. You nearly stole my minion. And, yet, *you* remain free to terrorize the world."

"Maybe because I never threatened to eat anybody." I lift one shoulder and flip my hand up. "I don't want to hurt anyone."

Argentum squeezes Tye's shoulder. "I met Draconian when he was a starry-eyed whelp. All he wanted back then was to save the world. I hunted him when he allowed innocents to burn for witchcraft. He was like you, and in the end, you'll become just like him."

My mouth falls open. I have no idea how to respond. "No." I shake my head. "He was evil. I saw his mind. There was nothing good in him."

"There was." Argentum softens his voice. "You see. That is why I cannot allow you to live. I cannot make the same mistake again. I cannot permit the dragons to suffer because I stood by and allowed another human to become corrupted." Still clutching Tye's shoulder, he reaches his other hand toward me.

Pain erupts inside me, and I drop to my knees.

Argentum puts his hand on my head. "Humans are not meant to be immortal. It breaks something inside of you."

"I'm not—" I gasp through the pain "—immortal."

"You won't be when I'm finished."

"No." I shove his hand away. "Death said he'd see me again."

He snaps his fingers and points to the ground beside him. Tye runs to him, and Argentum clutches his shoulder again. "Presently."

I picture my dorm room and try to teleport to it, but my power doesn't answer my call.

"Don't fight, Dacia." Argentum's command takes hold of me, and my body goes limp. "This won't hurt for long. Once it's over, you'll finally be at peace."

I relax further. My eyes drift closed. His voice lulls me to sleep.

No! Tye's voice snaps me out of my stupor.

My head jerks back. I scoot away from Argentum, trying to call my powers to me.

He lifts his hand, and pain courses through my body. It flows through my veins like lava. Burning, searing agony. A scream tears from my throat.

"Wake up, Dacia." Malcolm's voice was a growl.

Cody clasped my shoulder. His eyes were wide. "Okay?"

I dragged my hands down my face. "This needs to end."

Chapter 38

I slumped back against the couch. I'd been dreading this call all semester. Thanksgiving was next Thursday, but there was no way I could bring all my craziness home. "Hey, Dad."

"Hey, Sweetie." He sounded excited to hear from me. "Are you looking forward to coming home next week?"

Tears welled in my eyes, and I squeezed them shut. "I don't know if I'll be able to. I've got so much going on right now." I choked out the last word.

"Don't cry." His voice was comforting, not angry. "I remember how overwhelming college could be. We hoped we'd see you, but do what you need to do."

I wiped my hand across my face, then dried it on my sweat-shirt. "I'm trying to get everything done. I just don't know if I'll be able to in time."

"Let us know as soon as you do." He paused. "And don't sweat it. We understand."

I hadn't expected this. I thought he'd try to talk me into going home. I thought I'd have to argue. I figured we'd both hang up angry. Instead, we talked about school, my life—the parts I could tell him anyway—Cody, and what they'd been do-ing for the last few months. It was nice to hear his voice and to remember that there was more to my life than magic, demons, and dragons. I hung up the phone, hoping I'd be able to go home next week to spend some quality time with my parents.

Cody, Malcolm, Cash, and I jogged around the indoor track at Lupine Fieldhouse. They let me set the pace, and I took it slower than normal. Last night's dream and this morning's conversation with Dad both weighed heavily on my mind.

"What's up?" Cody bumped his shoulder into mine.

Placing my hands on my hips, I slowed to a walk and tried to steady my breathing. "I wanted to go home for Thanksgiv-ing."

"So, go." He shrugged like it was that easy. "Argentum's imprisoned. What's stopping you?" He wiped the sweat off his face with the tail of his shirt.

"Bad feeling." I remembered last night's dream. "It's not over." I started jogging again. I didn't want to continue this conversation. I didn't want to consider that I could end up like Draconian. Had he really been decent at one point in his life?

The others caught up to me. Malcolm's strides were perfectly synchronized with mine. "What did you dream?"

"Can't talk and run." I shook my head and sped up.

He grabbed my arm and pulled me to a stop. I stumbled, but he caught me before he said, "Problem solved."

The ground near my feet held my interest while I told them about my dream. The lane of the track I stood in was gray, but staring down at it, I saw flecks of white, blue, black, and pink intermixed.

Malcolm placed his hand on my shoulder but didn't say anything until I finished and looked up into his bronze eyes. "Argentum wasn't wrong. Draconian wasn't always the monster he became, but even before madness and power corrupted him, he was never someone I would have sworn to protect. He was never the type of person who would go out of his way to help someone else. He always had selfish tendencies."

"You are nothing like him." Cash's voice was nearer to his dragon's, a deep growl that raised the hairs on the back of my neck. "Nothing."

"Maybe not." I moved to let a couple of girls run past. "But Argentum thinks I am, and I think he'll do whatever he can to keep me from following in Draconian's footsteps."

Malcolm stared at Cash for a minute before focusing on me. "We need to train."

"What?" Cody looked at Malcolm like he'd missed something. I assumed my expression looked the same.

Malcolm put his hand on my back and led me off the track. "We don't know where Tye is, and if he's working with Argentum, they can combine their powers to control yours." He nodded at Cash. "If we work together, we may be able to help you figure out how to prevent that from happening."

We went to the locker rooms, and I just pulled sweats on over my shorts and T-shirt. When we stepped outside, the cold air hit my hot skin. I lifted my face to the breeze, savoring the feeling. I was stuck in my head on the way back to my room. I must've replayed Draconian's death a thousand times. I'd killed him, and at one time, he'd been good. He'd probably even had people who'd loved him and supported him. What had changed him? Would it do the same to me?

We'd barely gotten the door closed when Aurelia teleported into the middle of the room. "Argentum is gone."

"Great." I set my bag down by the door. "I thought I'd have longer."

Cody squeezed my hand. "Better train now." He tried to conceal the worry on his face and in his voice. He sat down at the desk and pulled one of his books from his backpack.

"How?" I asked Aurelia. "When?"

She stood absolutely still. Her long, golden hair looked perfect, not one single strand was out of place. Her face was stony with wrath. "When his guard changed, they noticed he was gone." A muscle in her jaw ticked, and I wondered if I'd seen her this angry before. "The guards' memories have been searched, but we found nothing." She shook her head. "I warned them that he was too powerful. I told them he needed additional guards. I have to get back to see if I can track him."

"Be careful." I watched her disappear, hoping she would be able to find him before he found me. Then I turned to Malcolm. "Whenever you're ready."

"How do we do this?" Cash sat on the couch.

Malcolm positioned himself on the other end of it. "You're just going to lend me your power." He waved toward me. "Why don't you do ice, so we don't accidentally catch the room on fire?"

I stood in front of them and held my hand out in front of me with my fingers spread wide. Ice crystals manifested on my palm, drawing together until they formed a sphere. Malcolm's power tugged on it, and the ball flattened, molding to my skin. Frost crept up my arm, encircling it.

I tried to call my power back to me, but the ice spread faster, branching out, then merging together, leaving no skin exposed as it climbed my arm.

I claim you, I thought to my powers. Then I visualized sunny days and bonfires. My thoughts inadvertently turned to Mavros and the way he smelled, warm summer nights and sulfur.

The ice continued its trek, not diminishing in the slightest. It flowed over my face, blocking my air. My heart thundered, and my lungs burned.

"Enough." Cash's voice was muffled.

Malcolm let go of my powers, and I gasped for air. I leaned against the wall, shaking my head. "It was like it wasn't even there."

"Let me know when you want to try again." Malcolm tipped his head back and closed his eyes.

My powers surged inside of me, flowing through my veins, fueling me. They were like a living being, sharing my body, strengthening me. I pushed off the wall and stood in a defensive position. Holding my hand out in front of me, I thought of winter, snow, and cold again. This time I hung an icicle off of Malcolm's ear.

He laughed in surprise. Then the icicle shot toward me. I backed up, and it landed on my foot, thinning out as it covered it. The ice spread, and I shivered.

Once again, I thought of warm, sunny days. Then I reached for my powers. I was met by a vast, emptiness that scared me more than any demon or dragon I had faced. I dug inside, searching for even a tiny spark that I could fan.

Malcolm clutched the arm of the couch. He stared at Cash. Cash's violet eyes drooped. The frost climbed both of my legs, creeping over my skin and sweatpants, encasing me. Fear clutched my heart. If Argentum and Tye did this to me, I would die.

Ignoring the ice that consumed my flesh, I pressed my eyes closed and imagined my power. I pictured it as a massive serpent. Its coils rippled, making its pearlescent scales shimmer. The beast stared at me with copper eyes.

"You are mine," I said to it.

The viper buried its head in its coils. Ice spread over my body, sliding over my stomach and sending a chill through me. I filled my voice with command. "Look at me!"

The beast snapped its arrow-shaped head up and hissed, flicking its tail in warning.

I stepped closer to it. "You are mine!"

It stretched up, standing about four feet off the ground, and puffed its body up.

"Don't you know me?" I reached my hand out to it. "You are a part of me. You've always been part of me." Ice flowed up my neck, then glided over my lips before slipping down my throat. *You are mine.*

It slithered toward me. Its body looped around my leg. Its scales slid over my jeans as it ascended.

I gasped, choking on the frost. Coils tightened around my body, crushing my ribs. I lifted my hand to my throat.

The snake's head swayed, but it held my gaze. Leaning back, it opened its mouth and struck. Its fangs pierced my skin, sinking into my neck.

There was no pain.

The ice retreated from my throat, and air whooshed into my lungs. I sucked it in greedily. The serpent merged with me, and power surged through my veins. *You are mine,* the snake whispered.

I opened my eyes, and the ice sphere was in the palm of my hand. Malcolm smiled at me. "How'd you do that?"

"I claimed them, and they claimed me." I looked down at my hands, and for a second, I thought I saw the serpent slithering under my skin.

Cody watched me from the desk. "You were blue."

"I wasn't breathing." I lifted one shoulder to my ear, then looked at the door. "I need to talk to Diana." I wasn't sure how she'd react, but I'd put it off long enough.

"Why?" Cash leaned forward like he was ready to jump up.

I walked over to the window and stared outside. Snow swirled across the ground, piling in drifts. "It would be better to have them on my side than on Argentum's." I tugged my hand through my hair, turned around, and looked at all of them. "I don't want to give him the chance to make them worry that I'll abuse my powers."

"Shower before you come back." Malcolm flashed his fangs at me.

Cash tilted his head and sneered. "Or maybe before you talk to her."

"You could just say, 'Hey, Dacia, you stink.'"

"Hey, Dacia—" Malcolm smiled at me "—you stink, and Val will be back before too long."

"Fine." I grabbed my bathroom bag and tossed clothes into it. "I'll shower. Then I'm talking to the Nephilim."

Cody stopped me by the door. "Careful." He traced his fingers along the side of my face. His eyes softened, and he pressed his lips to mine.

I wrapped my arms around his neck, pulling him closer to me and deepening the kiss. Cody lifted me off my feet, and I moaned into his mouth.

Cash growled, and Cody set me down. He looked over my shoulder. "Sorry." Then he brushed my hair back and tucked it behind my ear. "Argentum's out there."

"I'm aware." I held the doorknob. "There should be enough eyes on me here to keep me safe. Have one of them"—I nodded at the dragons sitting on the couch—"take you if you're going to shower." I didn't want Cody to have to worry about his safety, but Tye knew how much Cody meant to me, so Argentum probably did, too.

Staring at the white and purple-flecked tiles, I walked down the hallway. Olivia and Diana followed behind me and stood guard outside while I showered.

When I finished, they were still standing there. "I need to talk to you," I said as I walked past them.

Olivia frowned at me, but Diana nodded and followed me. "What about?"

"In my room." I trailed my fingers along the wisteria vines painted on the wall.

When I walked in, Cody sat at the desk, watching the door. His hair was wet, and he was clean-shaven. Malcolm and Cash sat on the couch. I waved the Nephilim into the room. Malcolm nodded at them, and Cash glowered.

"So, what do you want?" Olivia folded her arms over her chest and leaned against the doorjamb.

I walked over to the refrigerator. "Drinks?"

Olivia glared at me, and Diana shook her head. I grabbed a bottle of water for myself and took a big drink.

"Any day." Olivia drummed her fingers on her arm.

I wanted to put off talking for longer just to egg her on, but it wasn't worth it. "Argentum escaped. He'll be coming after me, and I'd like your help."

Chapter 39

Olivia and Diana looked at each other, then at the dragons. When they finally turned back to me, they stared like I'd magically grown three heads. For half of a second, I wondered if I could. I bit back the smile that tugged at my lips. Now wasn't the time to try it.

"Why would we help you?" Olivia's lip curled up, and it was clear from her expression that I would never be anything more than vermin to her.

"Olivia." Diana's voice was filled with warning. She turned toward me. "Why is Argentum hunting you?"

"He's afraid I'll—"

"Fear." Malcolm cut me off. "She's powerful. He cares only for himself."

Diana stood with her hand on her hip and narrowed her sky-blue eyes at him. "That's a strong accusation to make about one of your elders. Isn't it?"

"Unfortunately, it is the truth." He pulled his gaze away from hers.

Olivia walked toward me. "Just throw her in the sanctuary and be done with it."

Before she even finished her sentence, Cash crouched in front of me in a defensive position. A low growl rumbled through the room.

Olivia rolled her eyes. "Oh, call your guard dog off." She waved her hand in the air and turned her back on us, walking to the door, making it clear that she wasn't afraid of Cash's wrath. "I'm just sayin' it would be best for everyone."

Cody scooted his chair away from the desk and stood against the wall so he wasn't between agitated supernatural be-ings.

"The fairies vouched for her." Diana's voice was soft, but the anger in it was evident. She turned toward me and attempted to smile. "What do you want from us?"

I chewed on my bottom lip. I wanted them to realize I wasn't a monster, that I didn't want to hurt anybody, that this wasn't my choice. The powers had been forced upon me, and I was doing the best I could with them. "I guess if you see him or Tye, try to keep them away from my friends and give me or one of the dragons a heads up."

Diana nodded. "We can do that."

"Thank you." I smiled at her.

Olivia opened the door and slipped out into the hallway. Diana stared after her. "I'm sorry for the way Olivia treats you. Dragons were not the only ones hurt by Draconian. She fears your power more than she will ever admit."

"I'm not like him." My voice was so soft that I barely heard the words.

Before Diana stepped into the hall, she said, "I know."

My muscles relaxed so quickly that I staggered back. My chest lightened, and I covered my mouth with shaking fingers. She would never know how much those words meant to me because I was too dumbfounded to say anything before the door closed.

Cody and I walked to Sedum surrounded by dragons. The Nephilim trailed behind us. Olivia watched me with narrowed eyes, but Diana smiled reassuringly.

Conversation filled the cafeteria, mixing with the smells. It was familiar and comforting. Sensing no danger, the dragons split off from Cody and me, going in search of meat.

"What're you gettin'?" Cody asked.

I looked at the options listed on the wall. None of the specials appealed to me. "Grilled chicken sandwich and a salad. I guess. What about you?"

"Oriental." He looked around the room. "You'll be okay?"

"Yeah." I strode away from him and tried to remember the last time I'd been alone. Even though I knew there were eyes watching every step I took, I felt invigorated.

When I got to our normal table, I looked at the two chairs that would remain empty. I set my tray down and strolled up to Diana and Olivia. They watched every step I took. The closer I came to them, the more Olivia's seafoam eyes narrowed. When I stood by their table, I swallowed over the lump in my throat and asked, "Would you two like to sit with us?"

Olivia stared at her spaghetti. She clenched her teeth but kept her mouth shut. Diana shook her head. "Not tonight. Thanks for asking, though."

By the time I got back to my table, the others had joined Cody. "What were you doing?" Cassandra looked confused.

"Trying to prove to Olivia that I'm not a monster." I plopped down in my chair and pulled my tray toward me. "Looks like it's not going to happen tonight." I stabbed at my salad, taking more of my frustration out on it than was necessary.

"What's it matter?" Bryce pinched his nearly invisible eyebrows together. "Who cares what they think?"

Cody draped his arm across the back of my chair and rubbed my shoulder. "Dacia does."

"Why?" Bryce looked genuinely confused. "You can't make everyone like you."

"Argentum escaped." I pushed my tray away and slumped back in my chair.

"No." Samantha covered her mouth and looked from me to Cody. He tilted his head in agreement.

"You'll capture him again." Cassandra sounded way more confident than I felt.

Holding my head in my hands, I said, "He wants to eat me."

"You've got them." She lifted one shoulder and pointed at the dragons sitting next to me. "You don't need the Nephilim."

"No, I probably don't, but I'd rather have them with me than against me." I spun my glass between my palms, watching the lemonade slosh up the sides. "Unless Olivia trusts me, I don't think that will happen."

"Have to eat." Cody pushed my tray toward me.

The chicken sandwich had looked delicious when I grabbed it. I'd added lettuce and tomato to it and had looked forward to eating it, but now my stomach rolled when I glanced at it. I pushed back on the tray. "Sorry, Cody, not happening."

He got up, kissed the top of my head, and walked away.

"What's he doing?" Bryce set his fork down and looked over his shoulder.

"Most likely?" I dragged my hands down my face. "Getting cookies."

"Why cookies?" Cassandra held her garlic bread in front of her mouth.

Dan smiled one of his amazing smiles. "They're her kryptonite."

"Don't exaggerate." Samantha laughed. "Only chocolate chip cookies have that effect on her."

When Cody came back, Cassandra smacked Bryce's arm. "Why don't you ever bring me cookies?"

"Aw, Baby—" he pulled her against his side "—you never have trouble eating."

She tried to jerk back from him, but he tugged her closer and laughed. "Ass," she murmured.

"Oh, Cassi, you know I love you." He kissed her on the tip of her nose before letting go of her.

Cody held the cookies out to me as he sat down. "Not fresh-baked but warm."

"Thanks, Cody." I broke one of the cookies in half and took a bite of it.

Cassandra watched me eat all of them. Her head was tilted slightly, and she looked like she wanted to ask something but didn't know if she should.

I wiped my fingers and mouth on a napkin, then said, "What?"

"Well, uh—" she rubbed the back of her neck and stared down at her plate "—you've got all these things you can do." Her hair fell in front of her face, and she gazed at me through it. "So, do you have a kryptonite?"

Dan smiled at her. "I asked that, too. That's how we came up with cookies." He held his hand up. "Fresh-baked chocolate chip cookies."

"Very specific." Bryce rubbed his hands together like a madman. "I'll have to remember that."

"Seriously, though." Cassandra leaned over the table. "Is there something we should keep away from you?"

I shook my head. "Demon venom is really hard for me to recover from, and I would do just about anything to keep my friends and family safe."

"Yeah." Samantha huffed. "Earlier this year, she killed herself."

Cody's face twisted with pain, but he didn't say anything.

"You killed yourself?" Cassandra's eyes widened.

I shrugged like it was no big deal. "Yeah."

"So how are you here?" Bryce held his fork in front of his mouth. Rice and meat dropped off of it onto his plate.

"Death gave me a choice." I stared at the center of the table. I didn't want to look into anyone's face. "I chose to come back. Aurelia had told me the world would need me."

Cassandra folded and unfolded her napkin. "How'd you do it?"

"I plunged a dagger into my heart." Phantom pains shot through my chest at the remembered action. "I was dead for about two hours."

"No more." Cody put his hand on top of my leg. His fingers trembled.

"If there's some everyday thing out there that would weaken me, I haven't found it yet." I spun my glass around again, focusing all of my attention on it. "If I use too much, too fast, I get exhausted. It happened when Cody and I were in the ca—"

"Dacia." Cody moved his hand on top of mine. "Too many ears."

Heat crept up my neck and onto my face. "Right. Sorry."

Cassandra leaned her chair back on two legs. "It would be so cool to have your powers, to not have to take crap from anyone."

My eyebrows lifted, and I said, "Really?"

"You didn't have to take crap from me." She waved her hand and laughed. "You could have turned me into a frog or something."

"Hmm." I rubbed my chin. "I haven't tried that before. Wanna be my guinea pig?" I couldn't help but laugh. "Literally."

"Ha-ha, funny." She looked at me like she wasn't quite sure if I was serious or not.

I lifted my hands, then stood up and grabbed my tray. "I never get to have any fun."

When I walked past Diana and Olivia, they were deep in conversation with a few other students. Diana glanced up at me and started to push her chair back. "I'm just going to my room," I said quietly enough that she would hear it but her companions wouldn't. "I have plenty of guards." I nodded at the five dragons trailing behind me.

She nodded and relaxed into her seat. *Thanks.*

We stepped outside. The heavy cloud cover kept the campus lights from dispersing. It was nearly as bright outside as in. The air was chilly, but for the first time in days, it wasn't windy. I shoved my hands into my pockets and trudged back to the dorm.

"So, when are you all going home?" Dan asked. "My parents want me back by Wednesday night."

Will he be okay? I sent the thought to all of the dragons.

Cody pointed at himself, then me. "We're staying." While Russ answered, *I will go with Dan. I will not let anything happen to him.*

Thank you. The relief in my thought was evident.

Samantha stopped and cocked her head. "Should we stay?"

I will keep Samantha safe. Arianna's lyrical voice answered my next question.

I shook my head. "You'll be safe, but I can't take this home." When I spun around to urge Samantha on, I saw movement in the trees. "Guys"—my voice turned into a fierce whisper—"we gotta get outta here."

The dragons immediately surrounded us. "What is it?" Malcolm's tone was feral.

"Bad feeling." I started jogging, and everyone else followed suit. "Something in the trees."

Cassandra didn't make it very far before stopping and grabbing her side. "This—" she gasped for breath "—isn't my thing."

Cash picked her up in a fireman's carry, and we kept going. As soon as we stepped through the doors, he set her on her feet. The air from the heater blasted down onto us, blowing our hair around our faces.

She ducked her red face to hide her embarrassment. "Thanks."

"What did you see?" Malcolm stood beside me, holding my upper arm.

Val stood on my other side, leaning his head in close and sniffing me. I'd gotten so used to him doing it that it didn't even bother me anymore. While the other dragons seemed human enough, he reminded me of a pet.

I rubbed my eyes and pinched the bridge of my nose. "I can't be sure, but it looked like long, silver hair."

Chapter 40

Ultimatum

Cody slept soundly. His breathing had evened out and the tight grip he'd had on me since lying down together finally relaxed. The glow from the campus lights crept in through a crack in the curtains. Malcolm sat in Cookie Monster, watching me watch him.

How can I beat him? I sent the thought to Malcolm without meaning to.

He folded his hands in his lap and gazed at them. *I don't know if any of us can. Aurelia is trying to get the elders to stand against him, but*—he pinched his eyes shut as if this was painful for him—*they have grown weak. For too long, they've hidden themselves away, thinking the legends of their great deeds would forestall any conflicts. None of us anticipated a struggle from within.* He looked up at me, and his bronze eyes were filled with regret. *I am sorry. You have seen nothing but the worst of dragons. We were not always this way.*

Maybe. I smiled at him, hoping to assuage some of his guilt. *I also got to see you and Aurelia. Arianna saved my friends when she didn't have to. Cash gave me a chance even though it went against everything he believed. Russ and Val have been honorable and trustworthy.*

He flashed his fangs at me. *And what was your first impression of me?*

I thought you were scarier than Hell.

I am. He allowed a little of his dragon nature to peek through. His pupils turned to slits, and his teeth lengthened. *And, even I don't know what to do about Argentum.*

Dread slithered up my spine, and goosebumps followed in its wake. As long as Argentum lived, he would be a danger to me, but I couldn't kill again. I couldn't.

"You don't have to do it, Dacia." Mavros stands with his back to me. The snow swirls around us. The lake is buried under drifts, and the tops of the mountains can't be seen through the clouds. Everything is gray and white.

I take a step forward and sink up to my hip in the snow. "If I don't kill him, who will?"

"Me." He turns around. His face is as beautiful as the first time I saw him. "Summon me. Order me to kill him. I will follow your commands. I will serve you for eternity."

I stop struggling to pull my leg out of the drift and stare at him. *Is he the answer I've been looking for? If I summon him to Earth, will he betray me?* "I want to trust you, Mavros, but can I?"

He walks toward me and extends his hand, helping me to my feet. He stands in front of me and brushes my hair back. His touch is gentle. "Only you can decide that."

"Even if I wanted to, I don't know how." I shiver, and he wraps his coat around my shoulders.

"The dragons can tell you." He steps back. "I only wish to spare you the pain. Can your conscience handle another death?" Wings sprout from his back. "The choice is yours, Dacia. I will not take that from you."

"Dacia." Malcolm's voice was low and urgent. He grasped my shoulder, shaking it.

I put my hand over his. "I'm awake. What?" I sucked in a deep breath and smelled warm summer nights and sulfur. I snapped my eyes open. Mavros' coat was draped over me.

"Is he back?" Malcolm growled. "What does he want?"

"Crap." Tossing Mavros' jacket to the ground, I sat up. "He wants me to summon him so I don't have to kill Argentum."

"Don't do it." Cody's voice was hoarse but adamant.

I sat with my elbows on my knees and my head held in my hands. "I didn't say I was going to."

"Thinkin' 'bout it." He ran his hand down my back.

I nodded. "Only because I don't want to kill Argentum." I shuddered at the thought of having more blood on my hands. "I can't."

"We'll find a better way." Malcolm walked to the window. "I won't make you kill him."

"I couldn't summon him if I wanted to." I leaned back into Cody's touch. "He told me the dragons could tell me how to do it if it's the path I choose."

Cody's chin was on my shoulder. He tilted his head and whispered, "Gotta be a better way."

"That'll have to be a last resort strategy." Malcolm pulled the curtains together, blocking out most of the light that had been seeping in. "We'll tell you if it comes to it, but for now, get some sleep."

Cody woke me up when he got back from his class. I'd only gotten a few hours of sleep because I was terrified of what I'd dreamt. Even though Mavros had chosen to go back to the Abyss, guilt still consumed me. If he hadn't fought Argentum's commands, I would be dead. I couldn't forget or deny that, but I didn't know if I could trust him enough to let him loose on the world.

Through Professor Granite's lecture, I doodled in my notebook. Argentum's human and dragon forms both came to life on my paper. The dragon had rheumy eyes, but the human's were clear, hard, and determined.

I stared down at the images, trying to figure out what to do. He wouldn't stop. I couldn't convince him I wouldn't become like Draconian.

Cody reached over and flipped the page. A clean white sheet stared back at me. He slid the pencil out of my hand and slipped his fingers into mine. He looked into my eyes, and if I didn't know better, I'd think he could read my mind.

I turned my attention to Professor Granite. He stood in front of the class, writing mathematical formulas on the whiteboard. As far as I was concerned, they might as well have been Greek. I hadn't been keeping up on my studies this semester, and it was beginning to show.

The dragons surrounded the four of us as soon as we stepped outside. The sky was a brilliant blue. White, puffy clouds floated across it. Melting snow dripped off the tree branches.

Val's arm bumped against me as we walked, and even though he was closer than the others, he was still vigilant. Like they'd done in the beginning, they didn't move aside for anyone. When we were all inside my room, they relaxed.

"Was he out there?" I walked over to the window and peeked through the curtains.

Cash shrugged. "We don't know, but we're not about to take any chances."

"Are the other dragons still watching over me?" I turned and faced them. "The four that saved me that day."

Arianna tilted her head to the side. "I don't see why they wouldn't be." She looked at her companions. "We have been kept separate from them for a reason."

Samantha cleared her throat. "I need to get food before class. Does anyone want to come with me?"

"It's food." Cody shrugged. "I'm in."

Dan looked at me. "I guess we better go with them."

"Yeah." I smiled. "Somebody's got to keep an eye on them."

The walk to Sedum started just like the one from class. Malcolm walked in front of me. Suddenly, his muscles went taut, and he growled. We stopped moving, and the dragons took defensive positions. I stood on my tiptoes and tried to peer over Malcolm's shoulder. When that didn't work, I ducked down and looked between his body and his arm. Tye strode toward us. He seemed relaxed and confident; the Tye I'd thought of as a friend.

He lifted his hands to shoulder height. "I'm not here to hurt anyone." He took a couple steps closer and stared into my eyes. "Argentum wants you to come to his cave tomorrow night."

This time all the dragons growled and flashed their inner beasts. Cash stepped forward. "That's not going to happen."

"If it doesn't, Argentum will bring the fight here." Tye dropped his head to his chest. "Innocents will suffer." He stepped back. "I made a mistake, Dacia, and I'm sorry. I thought you'd be like him. I see now that I was wrong."

I pressed my hand against Malcolm's back, trying to get him to step aside, but he didn't budge. "Let me read your aura, Tye. Stand with us."

"I can't." He shook his head and lifted his hand. "They'll never forgive me."

"Damn right we won't." Russ' voice was animalistic.

I raked my fingers through my hair. "But I will."

He backed away. "They'll kill me."

Knowing I was about to make everyone mad, I pinched my eyes shut and sucked in a deep breath. "Tell him I'll be there."

"No, Dacia." Cody grabbed my arm. "You can't."

I pulled away from him. "I have to. I can't let anybody else suffer because of me."

"He'll kill you." Dan's voice was panic-stricken.

I huffed and shook my head. "Thanks for the vote of confidence."

"Sorry." He squeezed Samantha's hand.

The dragons relaxed as Tye backed into the trees. We walked into the dining hall, but I'd lost my appetite completely. The smell of food made my stomach roll. I walked straight back to our table and sat down with Cassandra and Bryce.

"Not eating?" Cassandra pointed her fork at me.

"No." I closed my eyes and pictured Mavros like I'd seen him in my dream. "Not today."

"Everything okay?" Bryce asked.

I shook my head. "Nothing's okay." I pulled my hair back, clutching it. "I dreamed about Mavros and woke up with his coat covering me and my room smelling like him. If I don't go to Argentum tomorrow, he'll come here. I don't know how to beat him. I can't kill him. I can't."

"Oh." Cassandra set her fork down and pushed her plate forward. "So, what are you going to do?"

"Try not to die."

She moved next to me and put her hand on my back. "I'm sorry."

"Yeah." When Malcolm and Cash walked past, I patted the table. "Sit here, please." As soon as they sat down, I asked, "So, what does it take to summon him if I need to tomorrow?"

"We'll be with you." Malcolm cut into one of the bloody hamburgers on his plate.

I folded my hands behind my head and leaned back into them. "Tye didn't say I could bring you."

Cash lifted his shoulder to his ear. "He didn't say you couldn't either."

Cody sat down next to me and slid a plate of cookies in front of me. "They're fresh."

"Thanks." I smiled at him but didn't touch the cookies.

When Dan and Samantha came over, Cassandra moved back to her seat. She clutched Bryce's hand but never took her ice-blue eyes off of me.

Diana strolled toward us. Her hands were tucked into the pockets of her blue jeans, and she looked like she had just been told her best friend had only days left to live. She stopped across from me. "We will stand with you if that's what you want."

"No." I looked across the room at Olivia. "This isn't your battle."

"I'm sorry I tried to force you to go to our sanctuary." She lowered her eyes. "I'm sorry I couldn't see through to your soul. I should've realized how strong you were. I should've seen that your heart was pure."

"Thank you, Diana. That means a lot to me." I picked up one of the cookies and ripped it in half. A gooey ribbon of melted chocolate clung together, and my mouth watered.

Diana turned to go back to her seat. "Be careful tomorrow. Come back."

Chapter 41

Weighing My Options

Skipping class was never something I'd dreamed I'd do, but since coming to college and facing monsters, it was something I'd done all too often. Samantha wasn't happy about it, but I was skipping again. I needed to figure out how to stop Argentum, so when everyone finished lunch, Arianna walked to class with Samantha, and the rest of us went back to my room.

Aurelia teleported in as soon as the door was shut. I looked from her to the other dragons. "I contacted her," Malcolm admitted.

"How can I stop him?" I plopped down in Cookie Monster and dropped my head into my hands. "Please tell me you know a way."

Val sat on the floor next to me. Pulling his legs up to his chest, he laid his head against the side of my chair. His desire to be close to me didn't bother me like it had at first. While the other dragons acted like guard dogs, Val reminded me of a kitty that just wanted affection.

Aurelia perched on the edge of the couch as close to me as she could get and pulled my hand from my face, holding it in hers. "We can try to capture him again. We had been working with the Nephilim to figure out a better way to contain him. Though, it seems we are out of time." She leaned back, dropping my hand. "The elders are not being as helpful as they should. They fear that anything they say to the Nephilim will eventually be used against them."

"Maybe it should be." Dan climbed up into Samantha's loft.

The dragons' heads all snapped in his direction.

He set his jaw and spoke with conviction. "It might put a stop to other dragons doing what he's doing."

"Yes," Aurelia said, "but it could also lead to dragons being hunted and captured. After what Draconian did—" she shook her head "—the elders will not willingly let it happen again."

Cody leaned on my chair, making it rock back. "Capture's not the answer then."

"Probably not." Malcolm shook his head and smiled sadly.

"So … what do I do?" My voice sounded desperate and weak. The room seemed to squeeze in on me. The air thickened and became hard to breathe. I wrapped my hands around my stomach and leaned forward. My vision blurred, and my heart beat in my ears, blocking out all other sounds.

Cody knelt in front of me and put his hands on either side of my face. He rubbed his thumbs along my cheeks. His mouth moved, but I couldn't make out anything he said.

My lungs burned, and black spots dotted my vision.

Breathe! Aurelia's voice screamed inside my head.

I sucked in a startled breath, and the spots diminished.

Cody smoothed my hair back. "You okay?" He stared into my eyes, not letting go of me.

"Yeah." I placed my hand on top of his. "For now." I turned toward Aurelia. "Thank you."

She dipped her head but said nothing.

"Am I going to have to kill him?" The thought brought images of Draconian dying to mind, the feeling of his blood on my hands, watching the light fade from his eyes.

"We'll be with you," Malcolm said.

Cash put his hand over his heart. "I'll spare you from that fate if I can."

"If we do not end this, he will never stop hunting you." There was sadness in Aurelia's golden eyes like I'd never seen before. "How the mighty have fallen," she whispered.

"What about—"

Malcolm shook his head. *Keep it between us.*

Better to ask forgiveness?

He nodded his head slowly. "What about what?"

"Nothing." I pulled my hand through my hair. "Never mind." I didn't need to pretend to be flustered. I'd hoped for better news. "Do you really think it's the only way?"

Russ dropped his chin to his chest. "He's too strong to contain, and he's too stubborn to see past his righteousness."

Cody stood in front of me, facing the dragons, with his arms folded over his chest. "Gonna make her do it for you?"

"No." Aurelia stood. "She stands a better chance than any of us, but we will do what we can to spare her from that fate."

Expelling the breath I'd been holding, I said, "Thank you."

"I must go to the elders, let them know we are out of time, and hope they do the right thing." Aurelia turned from me. "Keep her safe."

After she left, Cody sat on the edge of the couch. "Need to do something."

"What?" I asked.

"Get outta here." He shrugged. "Keep your mind off things."

Everyone in the room stared at me. I felt them weighing my mood, judging my actions. Unstable, I was a danger to everyone. I sucked in a deep breath and focused on the blue of Cody's eyes. I'd never been able to capture the color in a drawing or painting, cobalt with aqua shooting through them like lightning.

He blinked, and I shook my head. "If I'm gonna keep my mind off things, I need to do something besides sit."

"Basketball, racquetball, sledding." Cody ticked choices off on his fingers.

Arianna cocked her head to the side, landing her birdlike gaze on him. "What is sledding?"

"Well, that decides that." Dan, still perched in Samantha's loft, smacked his hands together, then rubbed them excitedly. "Sledding it is."

The sky was a dismal gray. The clouds looked threatening. I couldn't help but wonder if it was my doing. Tomorrow I would go to my death, and this time, it would be permanent. If Argentum ate me, I doubted even Death could send me back.

I stood on top of a hill. We'd parked the cars, then the dragons had teleported my friends to the peak. Cassandra bounced on her toes. Her voice was high-pitched. "That was a-mazing! I never dreamed I'd do something so cool."

Bryce fiddled with his gloves loosening and retightening them over and over, fighting against the smile that tugged at his lips.

Cassandra grabbed his arm. "Wasn't that awesome?"

"Yes." He pulled her against his side, and a grin spread over his face. His pale green eyes lit up with amusement.

I dropped my sled and sat in it. Cody climbed on behind me and pulled me against him. Then he shoved off. We skimmed over the top of the snow, gaining speed as we zipped down the mountain, dodging trees and boulders. My hair whipped around my face, and a laugh burst from my lips.

Excited screams echoed through the valley, trailing behind us. We slowed to a stop at the bottom of the hill. Dan and Samantha slid beyond us. Samantha toppled out and lay on the ground, making a snow angel.

Arianna and Val were the next ones down the hill, then Cash. His gaze immediately went to me. When he saw I was okay, he smiled. Bryce and Cassandra bounced down the hill, ramming their sled into the back of ours. Cody jolted forward, holding onto me as we tipped over.

"Sorry." Cassandra giggled.

Malcolm's and Russ' were the last two sleds to reach the bottom.

"Now comes the worst part." Dan stared up the hill.

Val tilted his head. "What?"

"Climbing back up the hill," Samantha answered.

I held on to Cody's hand. "I'm not climbing." I pictured the peak, the trees that had been twisted by harsh winters and strong winds. The snow whirled around us, then we stood at the top, looking down the slope at my friends far below. The dragons grabbed their hands and teleported them to where Cody and I stood.

Bryce's legs wobbled. He stretched his arm out for balance.

I sat in my sled, and Cash put his hand on my shoulder. "Let me go first."

I lowered my head. It was hard to forget my problems while under constant guard, but I understood Cash's concern.

He pushed off. Cody and I waited about thirty seconds before I used my powers to help us race down the hill. About halfway down, we caught up to Cash. He looked over his shoulder and shook his head. A gust of wind hit his sled, speeding him down the hill.

When we came to a stop, Cash was in full-on guard dog mode. "Do you think he'll attack?" I asked.

"I don't know." He brushed the snow off of his legs. "He's lived honorably most of his life." Cody snorted, but Cash continued. "He believes he is now. If he attacked you today, that wouldn't keep in line with his character."

"Why so anxious then?" Cody held his hand out to me, helping me to my feet.

Cash stared into the trees. "Just a feeling."

The wind blew, knocking clumps of snow from the branches. I shivered but not from the cold. Whether Argentum attacked me today or I went to him tomorrow, I wasn't ready. I didn't know how to defeat him or if I could. "I need to talk to Sarah."

"Sure." Cody dragged our sled out of the way.

Cassandra and Bryce blew past us, quickly followed by all of the others.

Samantha got out of her sled and looked at Arianna. "So, what do you think about sledding?"

Val bounced up out of his sled. "I love it."

"It's not bad—" Arianna smiled "—but flying is better."

Cassandra gazed up at the sky. "I imagine it's amazing."

"There's nothing like it." Russ' eyes had a faraway look in them. "Soaring on the breeze, the wind against your face and wings, riding the updrafts. It's incredible."

We went down the hill several more times. If anybody else came out to sled here, they'd wonder why there were so many sled marks coming down but no tracks going back up the hill. When we finished, we threw all of the sleds in the back of my truck. Then Cody drove us to Sarah's office. Malcolm and Cash waited to show themselves until we were in the vestibule.

Alicia sat behind the desk, filing her fingernails. She looked up at me briefly, then waved us to the seating area.

I leaned my head in close to Malcolm and Cash and said, "I need you to promise me something."

Malcolm narrowed his eyes. "What?"

"You can go on up," Alicia said.

On the way up the stairs, I thought to the dragons what I wanted from them. I needed to make sure they were in on the plan before I talked to Sarah.

A fire roared in Sarah's office, making the room warm and inviting. Cody, Malcolm, and I sat on one couch with Cash and Sarah on the other.

"I haven't seen much of you this semester." Sarah held her mug between both hands as if savoring its warmth.

Guilt weighed my gaze down. I stared at the tan carpet. "I'm sorry. I didn't want to bring anybody else into this."

"So, this must be important," she said.

I tugged my hand through my hair and focused on her hazel eyes. "Tomorrow, I have to face Argentum or he'll come here. I don't know if I can defeat him."

Cody's hand ran up and down my leg. Whether it was to comfort me or to comfort him, I wasn't sure.

"If I don't come back tomorrow, the dragons have agreed to stage an accident to explain my death." I didn't dare look at Cody. His grip on my leg tightened, but he didn't say anything. "They'll make it look like I was in a car wreck and manipulate the memories of everyone so they think they saw a body. That way Mom and Dad won't spend their lives wondering what happened to me."

Sarah tilted her head to the side. Her eyebrows pinched together. "Why are you making contingency plans this time?"

"He's an elder dragon." I stood up and paced behind Cody. I needed to move around to keep from falling into despair. "Aurelia thinks the only way to get him to leave me alone is to kill him." I stopped walking and clenched the back of the couch. "I can't kill again." My voice caught on a sob. "I can't."

The rest of the day passed by in a blur. Time seemed to speed up more and more as my deadline approached.

All too soon, I lay down on the couch beside Cody. He wrapped his arms around me, holding me as if he'd never let go.

Light streams in through the curtains, casting a purple tint over the room. I lie in the middle of the bed, and Cody is propped up on his elbows above me. His eyes are filled with love and admiration. I cup his face in my hands and bring his lips down to mine. He presses delicate kisses on my mouth, then pulls back, staring at me like he's never seen me before. "I love you, Mrs. Hawks."

Hearing my new name brings a blissful smile to my face. I draw circles on his bare chest. "I love you, too, Husband O'Mine."

He lies down beside me, and I rest my head on his chest. He smells like a cold winter's day, crisp and cool. His hand trails up and down my spine. I pull the sheet up, covering us both.

I close my eyes and slowly drift off to sleep.

I stared at Cody, lying on the couch beside me, wondering if my dream was a premonition or if it had just been wishful thinking. I wanted to believe in it. If it was a portent, it would mean I would survive my encounter with Argentum and end up with the life I longed for.

I reached my hand up to trail my fingers along his jaw but pulled them back. I didn't want to wake him up. Sleep had removed the stress from his face and left him looking peaceful.

You need to sleep, Dacia. Malcolm's voice entered my thoughts.

I glanced over at him and nodded. *I know.* I lay back down and closed my eyes.

The cavern smells like blood and fire. Flames still blaze. Their light dances along the walls and ceiling. My dragon guards are strewn across the ground, their bodies contorted into impossible positions. Their lifeless eyes stare at nothing.

Argentum stands above me, holding me down under his massive paw. One of his claws pierces through my shoulder, pinning me to the ground. "This death and destruction were avoidable. Why did you bring them with you? Why couldn't you face your fate alone?" His voice is filled with profound sadness.

"You … didn't … have to … kill them." Pain makes it hard to say more than a word or two without gasping.

He narrows his eyes at me. "They came here to kill me … because of you. Now, you shall die." He lowers his head. Saliva drips off his fangs, landing on me.

I press my eyes closed and send up a prayer.

I jolted awake. My heart raced, beating against my ribcage, begging for release. I pressed my hand over my chest and took deep, calming breaths.

I can take the dreams away for the night. Malcolm's voice startled me.

I turned toward him and nodded. *Please.*

Chapter 42

Like A Lamb To The Slaughter

*S*tanding in my room, six dragons surrounded me. When I looked at them, I saw them lying on the ground in Argentum's cave. Their eyes were glassy, their lives extinguished. I couldn't allow that to happen. No matter what it took, I needed to keep the dragons safe. They'd lived too long to die for me.

Each of them placed a hand on me. Their strength flowed into me. Their powers felt as unique as their auras. Aurelia's energy streamed through my body, and I felt her shame and regret.

When she'd come to my room this morning, her dragon had been nearer to the surface than I'd ever seen it. She'd paced behind the couch. When she'd spoken, her voice was feral.

"The elder council decided the risk outweighed the reward." Her slender fingers had turned into taloned claws. "They will not share their secrets with the Nephilim." She'd stared at me with inhuman eyes. "They have sentenced you to death. Any dragons who choose to protect you will be on their own."

Cody had jumped up and grabbed a duffel bag. He'd thrown anything and everything into it. "We'll leave."

"We can't." I'd pulled the bag away from him. "He'll bring the fight here."

His face had twisted with agony. "Not if you're gone."

"We don't know that." I had walked to the window and looked outside. It'd been gray and dismal to match my mood, but there was still beauty. I hadn't been able to help but wonder if I left with Cody, would Argentum leave it this way? "I have to face him, Cody."

He'd crumpled, looking like a balloon that had been deflated. "I know."

He sat on the couch, watching me with his expressionless mask in place. Even though I couldn't see his fear for me, I felt it. It crept over my skin like a thousand spiders, filling me with dread and uncertainty.

Dan and Samantha sat next to him. Samantha chewed on her lip, watching me with wide, unblinking eyes. Dan smiled at me, but it was a mere shadow of what his smiles could be.

I pictured Argentum's cave, the dark, deep lake, the bone-strewn floor. My body stretched out and pressed in, brushing against the dragons', holding the seven of us together. The light shining in through my eyelids dimmed. The air grew cooler, and the sounds from the hallway became the gentle lapping of water.

While I changed my eyes into a dragon's, the others transformed into their natural bodies. The cave was just how I'd seen it last time, dark and damp. A swell tore across the lake, advancing toward shore.

"Too scared to come alone." Argentum rose from the depths, shaking his massive head. Water showered from his body. Thousands of ripples spread over the surface of the lake. "Maybe you aren't as formidable as everyone seems to think. Maybe I should just let you live." He sucked in a deep breath and shuddered. "If I hadn't tasted your blood, I might actually believe your pathetic act." He glanced into the darkness, then back at me.

I felt him tug on my powers, and the mighty serpent slithered under my skin. It lifted its head and hissed at Argentum before tightening its coils around me. *You are mine.*

And you are mine, I thought back.

"Argentum—" Aurelia stepped forward "—Dacia means you no harm. Give up this madness and return with us."

I stared into the shadows where Argentum had looked before tugging on my powers. Tye cowered in his dragon form.

Argentum tossed his head. "Return with you to be held captive for all eternity. I think not."

"It's no more than you wanted to do to her." Arianna's voice changed little between her human and dragon forms. The disgust in it would be hard for anyone to miss, though.

He stepped out of the water. "For the good of dragonkind. You want to cage me to save one insignificant, little human. I wanted to protect all of you!"

"She is not insignificant." A burst of fire erupted from Malcolm's jaws, evidence of the magnitude of his anger. "You know nothing about her and don't care to."

Argentum spread his wings, and water rained down on all of us. "I've seen what she'll become. The Nephilim have seen what she'll become. Yet you fools believe she'll always be what she is now."

"Have you forgotten what we stand for?" Aurelia narrowed her eyes at him and prowled forward. Her talons clacked across the rocky ground. "Since when do we sentence beings to death for what they might become?"

His chest puffed up. "Since we made the mistake of allowing Draconian to live."

I walked forward, picking my way over the charred bones that littered the floor. The cave air was cool and damp and smelled stagnant, but sweat beaded on my forehead. I tucked my shaking hands into my pockets. "I will never be like Draconian. Would Death have sent me back if I was going to turn into some monster?"

"Death cares about nothing but ferrying bodies to the afterworld." Argentum cocked his head, looking down at me like I was a bug.

I nodded. "And, yet, he gave me a choice."

"So, you think you're special?" He lunged at me.

Malcolm rushed between us. His black scales shimmered as he darted in front of me. Argentum roared. His fangs sank into Malcolm's neck, and a choked, gurgling noise spilled from Malcolm's mouth. Pain glazed his eyes.

Cash plowed into Argentum, knocking Malcolm loose. Black blood dripped from Argentum's fangs. Malcolm hit the ground with a thud. His eyes rolled back, and he didn't move.

Argentum swung his head around, snapping his jaws. Cash ducked beneath his maw, narrowly escaping Malcolm's fate. He drove Argentum away from Malcolm's body, and I ran to the injured dragon, praying I could save him.

I pressed my palms to Malcolm's neck, sending healing energy into him. The punctures pulled together, and his breathing eased. His bronze eye cracked open, then immediately closed again. "Save … your … energy." He jerked his neck away from my hands.

Cash howled in pain. Argentum stood above him. "You hated humans. You hated her. Why are you protecting her?"

"I'm protecting humans. You're killing dragons." He snarled. "Seems we're both confused."

Argentum raised his taloned claw.

"Stop!" Aurelia yelled. "Come with us, Argentum. End this the way you lived your life, peacefully with honor and dignity."

He growled at Aurelia and swiped his paw down. Cash rolled away but not fast enough. Argentum's claws tore through Cash's side. Purple scales drifted through the air, and Cash roared.

Aurelia strode toward them, but Argentum lifted his paw again. "I'll kill him if you come closer."

She skidded to a halt. "Stop Argentum. You will regret this."

"I regret every drop of dragon blood that gets spilled." He dragged a single claw along Cash's side. "So, give me the girl and end this."

My power writhed under my skin. I called it to me, sensing its enormity. "I'm right here, Argentum. Come get me if you're brave enough." I stepped to the water's edge, away from Malcolm, hoping he wouldn't get hurt worse.

Argentum strode through the lake toward me. Water splashed onto the shore. The earth rumbled under his footsteps.

"What are you doing, Dacia?" Arianna's voice came from behind me, but I didn't turn around.

Pulling my power from deep within me, I said, "It'll be okay."

Argentum's low, rumbling laugh filled the cavern. "Yes, once you're gone, everything will be all right."

If you need Mavros, draw on our strength, say his true name, and command him to come to you. Once he's here, bind him to you. Malcolm's voice was stronger than before, but I worried what drawing on the dragons' strength would do to him, what it would do to Cash.

I lowered myself into a defensive stance and watched every move Argentum made. His head sank to my height, and a blast of fire shot from his mouth toward me. I pressed my hands against the air, and the flames fanned out around me, like Moses parting the Red Sea.

Argentum took a deep breath, preparing to blast me with fire again. I threw my shield around his head, tightening it like

I'd done before. He stood perfectly still and tugged on my power, pulling it toward him, but I clung to it.

"Noooo." Val slid across the rocky floor toward Argentum. His claws scrabbled at the ground.

When he came to a stop, Argentum stomped on his chest. The air whooshed out of Val's lungs. Argentum snapped his jaws, and the shield disappeared. "You brought all these dragons with you, delivered them right to me so I could use their strength against you."

"A dragon as ancient as you should be able to fight a teenage girl on his own." I shoved my hands into the water and shot lightning into it.

He spread his wings and hovered above the lake. "If you want to kill me, you'll have to try harder than that."

"I don't want to kill anybody!" I clenched my hands at my sides. "I never have. Can't you see that?"

He perched on a ledge above the lake. I would've never noticed it. It blended in with the cavern wall. I narrowed my eyes, scanning the rocks, wondering if there were others that might give me an advantage.

"You say that now, but as the power rots your heart, you will change. You will thirst for blood, and you will be too powerful to be stopped." Argentum's chest expanded, and flames spewed from his jaws. Fire roared through the cave. I held my hands up, and ice rushed from my fingertips. The force knocked me back a step. The ice crashed into the flames, like a wave breaking on the shore. It devoured the fire.

Power flared beneath my skin, thrumming in my veins.

"Argentum!" Aurelia's voice rang through the cavern. "Please."

I lifted myself off the ground, hovering above the ice-shrouded flames.

"The girl must die!" Argentum shouted. "Can't you feel her power? It's coming to life."

The air shifted. From all directions in the cave, it was sucked into Argentum. His body expanded.

The ice collapsed into the lake and washed onto the shore in chunks. The wind tugged at the dragons' wings, pulling them like kites about to be launched into the sky. They braced their feet against the ground. Their talons gouged the cave floor.

I clamped my hands over my ears, trying to block the sound so I could figure out what he was up to.

Dacia. Fear tinged Malcolm's voice. *Summon Mavros. You must do it now.*

Mavros' unbidden image came to mind. He knelt before me like he had when I'd used his true name and asked what I commanded of him. I imagined myself ordering him to kill Argentum, but I realized the guilt would belong to me no matter what. Either way, his blood would be on my hands.

I blasted a lightning bolt at the wall just above Argentum. Rocks crashed down on his rough hide, but it wasn't enough to stop him.

Val lifted off the ground, sailing through the air backward toward Argentum. His face was panic-stricken.

"Transform!" I shouted.

A blue mist surrounded Val. Caught by the wind, it rushed toward Argentum, temporarily blinding him.

His outraged roar shook the cavern. Rocks jarred free and tumbled from the ceiling and walls. I shielded myself and the injured dragons.

Val plummeted toward the lake. I lifted my hand, stopping his fall, and pulled him to me. He cowered behind my legs, leaned his head against me, and whimpered softly.

Russ and Arianna transformed into humans. Arianna raced to me, grabbed Val's hand, and pulled him away.

Rage burned in my chest. Anger for what he was doing to my friends. Fury that he couldn't see past his prejudice. Lightning bolt after lightning bolt shot from my fingers. They collided with the ledge he sat upon.

The wind gusts ceased as he plunged from the rocky outcrop. He spread his wings and soared, landing in front of Aurelia. The ground shook in response. Rocks splashed into the lake and crashed against the floor. He lowered his head. "Can't you sense it?" A silver haze surrounded him. "She'll kill us all." The voice that came through the mist was more human than beast.

Tension eased out of my shoulders. As it did, the power in my veins diminished. It was still there under the surface but no longer crackling with purpose.

Arianna stood over Cash, healing his wounds. Val hid behind a boulder, watching every step Argentum took. Russ went to Aurelia's side, and Malcolm came to mine.

I nodded to the shadows. "Tye's hiding back there."

"I saw him," Malcolm growled. *Don't trust Argentum. This is too easy.* Even in my thoughts, his voice was feral.

I nodded and put my hand on his leg. Healing energy surged into him. "Save your strength, Dacia." His obsidian scales were hard plates ending in sharp points. His muscles rippled with every step. His talons clacked against the ground. He was an apex predator, bred for fighting, and Argentum had swatted him aside like he was a tiny housefly.

"I don't think I need to." I'd never felt energy like this before. Even so, I needed to make sure not to deplete my stores too much because Malcolm was right. This was too easy.

Just as the thought blew through my mind, Argentum knelt in front of Aurelia. His silver hair pooled on the ground at her feet. She stretched her paw out to grab him in her talons, and he latched onto her. Her eyes glazed over, and as Argentum transformed into his dragon, his laugh filled the cave.

Chapter 43

Bloodlust

To me! I shouted the command to the dragons. They responded immediately, surrounding me. I put one hand on Cash's neck and one on Malcolm's. Val, Russ, and Arianna each held onto me. Their power flooded into me like a tsunami. "Chaódis Skotádi, I summon thee. Come forth, and stand before me." The dragons turned their heads looking at one another, trying to figure out what I was doing.

Malcolm never looked away from me, holding my gaze with his, reassuring me this was the right thing to do, the only thing to do.

A black haze undulated through the air. It weaved and twirled in a mesmerizing dance. The vapor clung together forming Mavros. He knelt in front of me. A knowing twinkle sparkled in his obsidian eyes. "What do you command of me, my prothymós?"

I tilted my head, not sure what he'd said, afraid he would try to mislead me.

"It means liege," Arianna said as she let go of my shoulder. Her voice was laced with disgust.

I lowered my hand to Mavros. "Lend me your strength."

"I can kill him for you." Mavros slipped his hand into mine and stood. "I can save you the pain."

Malcolm stared at Mavros' hand in mine. "You must set ground rules, Dacia."

"There isn't time for that right now." Mavros had helped me. Would he try to defy me now? "Do not try to control me. Do not hurt any of my friends. Do not do anything that you know I would disapprove of." I turned toward Malcolm. "Good enough?"

"For now."

Mavros' power slammed into me. The serpent under my skin greedily sucked it in. It was dark and ominous, forbidding. The alien energy was like a hurricane blasting through me. I searched for the eye, hoping to find a calm inside this raging storm.

I strode out from between the dragons, holding fire in both hands. It burned blue and black. Mavros walked beside me. "Argentum, let Aurelia go." My voice sounded like me, but not. It was harsher, deeper, and had a violent edge to it.

"What will the fairies think of you now?" He shook his massive, silver head in revulsion. Raising his voice, he asked, "Do you now see that she is evil?"

"If summoning Mavros makes me evil, then we are the same."

He lunged.

Mavros knocked me to the ground. Argentum clutched Mavros' body in his jaws. Black blood ran down Argentum's jaws, sizzling as it dripped onto the rocks.

My eyes widened in shock. Had I just sentenced Mavros to death? The magic pulsed under my skin, seeming to have a mind of its own. Pain ripped through me as my body transformed. Bones broke and rearranged themselves. Leathery wings tore through my back. My neck lengthened. Long fangs jutted out of my mouth. Two more necks stretched out of my massive shoulders. I pinched my eyes shut. The influx of information made me sway on my feet. A tail swished behind me. Thick legs ended in wicked talons.

I turned one head, marveling at this new body. My flesh was mottled blue, and I looked like the demon version of Mavros.

I darted forward, and Argentum stumbled back. His eyes widened, and Mavros slid from his slack jaws.

One of my heads lunged for Argentum's neck. He dodged it but didn't notice the other head snaking up from underneath. I struck him. His blood poured into my mouth. I tore into his flesh with sickle-like claws, shredding his scales.

His tail slammed into me, trying to force my jaws from his neck, but I held on with razor-sharp fangs, digging in deeper with every movement he made.

His claws tore into my hide. Pain lanced through me. I snapped at his paw with another head.

Malcolm and Cash latched onto his neck.

Argentum's massive body collapsed. His blood coated my lips and ran down my throat. I savored the taste of it. Ancient power.

His strength waned, and my other heads sunk their teeth into his neck.

Instinct took over, and I tore at his flesh. With every drop of blood that ran down my throat, my power multiplied.

Malcolm nudged me.

I growled and snapped at him, protecting my kill. Flames exploded from my hide. The blue and black blaze danced along my body. Malcolm and Cash backed away; their eyes widened with fear.

"He is gone, Dacia. He cannot hurt you anymore." Aurelia's soothing aura calmed me, breaking through my bloodlust. "Let him go."

I stepped back and surveyed the cavern. Mavros lay crumpled on the floor. Russ, Val, and Arianna stared at me. Their eyes were wide. Purple and black hazes surrounded Cash and Malcolm. Tears lined Aurelia's golden eyes.

My body shrank, becoming my own. I fell to my hands and knees and retched.

Malcolm held my hair and patted my back. "You're okay, Dacia. It's okay." His words were laced with soothing magic.

My eyelids drooped, growing too heavy to stay open. I wobbled, and Malcolm caught me, clutching me against his body, mumbling indecipherable words in calming tones.

Fairies covered me from head to toe. Their iridescent wings fluttered incessantly, and they chirruped. Their voices were too high-pitched for me to make out what they were saying. Other conversations drifted over to me.

"She gonna be okay?" Concern clouded Cody's voice.

"She'll never forgive herself." Malcolm's words were clipped, angry.

Aurelia looked like somebody who'd just seen their puppy get run over. "We must help her."

Rayne hovered in front of my face. "Demon energy does not mix well with human power."

"I—" My voice was froggy. I cleared my throat.

"She's awake." Relief and fear seemed to mix together in Cash's voice.

"I didn't know." My words were barely whispered, but Rayne heard them. "I just wanted to save Aurelia."

"He held back." The other fairies flew off, becoming tiny lights against the cave's ceiling. Rayne landed on my chest and folded her arms. "Otherwise, you would be dead."

I pressed my eyes shut. When I opened them, my friends stood around me. Dragons, humans, and a demon. Mavros stood with his hands tucked in his pockets. He smiled at me and lifted his shoulder. "I couldn't allow you to die, not when I could save you."

"Thanks." My throat was scratchy and burned.

Cody sat on the ground and lifted my head into his lap. "How're ya?"

I looked at Rayne.

She hovered in front of my face. It looked like every beat of her wings took more energy than normal, and her tiny chin trembled. "You will be fine once the dragon blood is out of your system."

Dragon blood. I clutched my stomach as the memories flooded back into my mind. Rayne zipped into the air, hovering over me again. I rolled onto my hands and knees and heaved. Silver blood coated the rocks.

"Oh, my, God." I sobbed, clutched my hair, and rocked back and forth.

Cody rubbed my back, but I pulled away from him. "Don't touch me. You have no idea what—"

"It's okay, Dacia." He reached for me again, but I jerked away.

"It's not. I—" I remembered savoring his blood. I leaned over and threw up again. The room spun. My heart pounded against my ribs. The air rushed out of my lungs. I gasped.

"I can make her forget." Mavros' voice was low.

One of the dragons growled in response.

Do you want me to make you forget? He sounded like he genuinely wanted to help, like he was concerned for me.

Cody wrapped his arms around me. With his mouth right up against my ear, he whispered, "Breathe, Dacia."

You'll remember him dying, but you won't remember the bloodlust.

I sucked in a breath and choked on it. I stared into Mavros' eyes. "I don't know."

"What?" Cody asked.

I pulled out of his embrace and climbed to my feet. "Are you done with me?"

Rayne nodded. "Do not let the demon mark you again."

"I never let him mark me." I looked from her to Mavros. Once again, I wondered if I was an idiot for trusting a demon. "I don't know how he does it."

He knelt at my feet. "I vow to you, Dacia KayLee Wolf, I will never again mark you." He held my hands in his. "Please let me take the memory from you. Let me take the pain … like you took mine."

"Your demon is sincere." Rayne flitted by my face.

Cody brushed his thumbs along my cheeks. "If he can, let him."

Malcolm, Cash, and Aurelia stepped up beside Mavros."We can make sure he takes only the memories that will threaten to undo you."

I looked over at the other dragons, standing with my human friends. "What do you think?"

"None of us should remember that." Arianna shook her head.

The images came to my mind again, but the intense reaction didn't come along with it. "I'm sorry … for what I did … for not telling you." I remembered the look of disgust on her face when I summoned Mavros. "Don't hate me."

"Oh, Dacia." Her voice was soft. "I don't hate you." Her eyes darted toward Mavros. "I worry about you."

I felt a moment of remorse, but it disappeared quickly. "Somebody's controlling my emotions."

"Yes, Dacia." Aurelia waved her finger between her, Cash, and Malcolm. "We all are."

"Why all of you?"

Malcolm put his hand on my shoulder. "They are over-whelming, too strong for one of us to dispel on our own."

Mavros stood among the dragons, not looking out of place, not looking uncomfortable. He watched me carefully without making it obvious.

I stepped closer to him and reached my hands out. He held them tenderly. "Take the bad." I looked down at his thumb rub-bing my wrist. "I don't want to remember the taste of his blood. I don't want to remember the bloodlust. Just let me remember that he's dead and that you and the dragons helped me."

He nodded. "I would've done it for you."

"I know."

"Why didn't you let me?"

I pulled my lip into my mouth and looked at his feet. "If I would've commanded you to do it, it still would've been by my hand."

He touched my forehead with two fingers. "You are so strong, Dacia. I can't guarantee this will last forever, but hope-fully, it will last long enough to take the edge off and let you work through the pain."

A black mist floated across my vision. I saw Argentum fly down off the ledge. I summoned Mavros. His power flowed into me. I transformed into the demon beast. Blue and black flames danced along my hide. Malcolm, Cash, Mavros, and I cornered Argentum, and the four of us struck at once. Demon venom pulsed through Argentum's body. He weakened and crashed to the ground. His claws tore through my side. Malcolm struck, breaking Argentum's neck. My body became my own, and I collapsed from blood loss. The dragons brought me to the cave with the silver-haired fairies. They healed me and removed the demon taint from me. Mavros, my friends, and the dragons seemed to have decided on a truce. They all stood with me, helping me heal.

Mavros stepped back. "She needs sleep."

"Do not let her use her powers for a few days." Rayne hovered in front of Aurelia. "The demon's energy must be fully out of her system. Otherwise, it will taint her magic."

I nodded. "Okay. No powers."

"If you use them, find us immediately." She flew off, joining the others. "Fare thee well, Dacia."

I lifted my hand to wave and stumbled. Malcolm, Mavros, and Cody each lunged to catch me. The dragon and demon backed off, and Cody lifted me into his arms.

"Get her back to her room," Mavros said.

"What about you?" I mumbled.

Mavros clutched my hand. "I will not do anything you would disapprove of. I will stay close and watch over you."

"Thank you."

Malcolm clutched Cody's arms, and we teleported to my room. Cody laid me down on the couch and pulled a blanket over me.

Chapter 44

The serpent slithers toward me. Its once copper eyes are as black as the depths of Tartarus. Shadows ripple between its scales. *You are mine.* Its voice is possessive, dangerous. Not the comforting voice of the past. *You are mine.*

Fear claws at my stomach, and I step back. I glance over one shoulder, then the other. Darkness surrounds me, closing in. I transform my eyes into a dragon's, but there are only unending fields of ebony. A shiver creeps up my spine.

When I look back, the giant snake is gone. I press my hand to my chest, trying to calm my racing heart. Even though I can't see it, I know it's there, watching me, ready to strike.

I shuffle back and trip. I hear the serpent slide over the ground. The sound is like rustling leaves. Jerking my foot back, I search for the snake. I press my hands down behind me to push myself up, and the serpent coils around my leg.

As it moves along my body, the shadows clinging to it dissipate. It draws its head back and strikes.

Darkness burns away the light inside me. Anger and hatred fill me. My heart hardens. Shadows writhe under my skin. I look into the snake's onyx eyes, and the laugh that shatters the silence is maniacal.

My eyes shot open, and I jerked into a sitting position. The room spun around me. Malcolm darted over, kneeling in front of me, ready to face some unseen threat. "What is it, Dacia?" His voice was savage.

"I don't know." I held my head in my hands. "I feel like I forgot something, something that's important."

A shadow crossed his face, but he didn't say anything. Cody ran his hand up and down my back, trying to soothe me.

I got up and walked to the door.

"Where are you going?" Malcolm was suddenly in front of me, blocking my exit. "You need to sleep."

"No." I shook my head. "I need to pee."

"I'll go with you." He looked over his shoulder at Cody. "Don't leave."

I crossed my arms over my chest and tapped my foot. "What's going on?"

"I—" he rubbed his jaw "—I'm not sure how the Nephilim are going to react to you summoning Mavros."

Having Malcolm in my life made me wonder what it would have been like to have a big brother. He was protective, bossy, and always thought he knew what was best for me, but I couldn't imagine having gone through this without him, and I'd always owe him for killing Argentum. "Is Cash watching him?"

"Cash, Val, Aurelia, and probably Arion are all watching this room." Malcolm shook his head and dropped his chin. "Probably Mavros, too."

I grabbed his shirt sleeve and twisted him around. "Then let's go before I pee my pants."

As soon as we stepped into the hallway, Diana and Olivia came to attention. Diana strode toward me, and Malcolm held his hand out, effectively stopping her. She stood on her tiptoes, looking over his shoulder at me. "We need to discuss the demon."

"Not today." The warning in Malcolm's voice was evident. "Not tomorrow either."

"I don't know how long I can keep this from the council." Diana glanced at Olivia, and Olivia pretended to zip her mouth closed.

I pulled my lip into my mouth. "Sorry." I darted down the hall. "I really have to pee." I walked into the bathroom and stared into the mirror. Relief spread through me when I saw that my eyes were still green. I slumped against the sink and pulled my hand through my hair. Taking a deep breath, I walked back out into the hall.

Malcolm raised a single eyebrow at me. "Forget to flush?"

"Yeah." My shoulders slumped.

He stopped moving and wrapped his hand around the back of my neck, massaging it. "What's going on?"

"When I took control of my powers, I pictured them as a serpent." I looked down the hall at Olivia and Diana, but they didn't seem to be listening.

He followed my gaze. "They can't hear us."

"In my dream, my powers were corrupted. The snake … it was dark, menacing." I closed my eyes. "It attacked me …"

"And, you became like it." He finished for me. "So, why the act?"

I kicked at the ground. Lying was something I hated to do, but with my powers, sometimes it was necessary. I shouldn't have lied to him, though. "I wanted to make sure I was still myself." I pointed at my face. "My eyes are still green. The serpent's were as black as night."

"No magic." He stared at me, making sure I was paying attention. "None. Not for a week or more."

"A week?" My voice cracked. "The fairies said a few days."

His face was stony. "A week. If there is even a possibility that was a premonition, we're stopping it now."

I nodded and slunk down the hall past Olivia and Diana.

"Okay?" Cody asked when I walked in.

"Sure." I shrugged. "As long as nothing tries to attack me for at least a week." I lay down beside him.

"What?"

I waved my hand at Malcolm. "He can tell you." I kissed Cody's cheek. "Goodnight."

Sunday morning, I lay on the couch, snuggling with Cody. I'd been awake for an hour or more, but I wasn't ready to let go of him. I'd gone to fight Argentum yesterday, expecting not to come back. I'd thought I'd held Cody for the last time.

Somebody knocked on the door, and I huffed, preparing to roll off the couch.

Malcolm chuckled. "I got it. It's Cash."

"If I could use my powers, I might've known that." My words were mumbled, but I was sure he heard them.

As soon as the door opened, Cody sat up, taking me with him. The smell of warm cinnamon rolls wafted into the room. "You brought breakfast."

"I thought you might be hungry." Cash handed the box to Cody.

He grabbed it greedily. "Always."

"Thanks." I couldn't help but wonder if there was more to it than just being nice. The only times any of the dragons had delivered food to us was when we were hiding out in the cave.

Cash sat down in Cookie Monster and studied me. I set my roll down. I hated when people watched me eat. Staring back at him, I said, "What?"

"How are you doing?" He stared into my eyes, and I wondered if I should be concerned about the color of them. Were there black flecks in my irises, or were they still the same green they'd always been?

I shrugged. "All right. As far as I know, nobody is trying to kill me right now. It's been a while since I could say that."

Malcolm folded his arms along the back of the couch and leaned on them. The beads on the ends of his braids clicked together, and for the first time, I realized he must use magic to keep them silent when he wanted to go unnoticed. "I need to get out—" he grinned at me "—stretch my wings."

"Literally or figuratively?" I asked.

"Both." He pointed at my breakfast. "Eat, and don't go anywhere until I get back."

I rolled my eyes at him before ripping a gooey strip off and shoving it into my mouth. "Fly. Be free." I waved my hand at him, and he chuckled.

To Cash's credit, he tried not to make it too obvious that he was watching me. He leaned his head against the back of the chair, closed his eyes most of the way, and spent most of the morning surveying me through his lashes.

My power grew, filling every empty place inside of me, begging for release. I'd conditioned myself to use my magic to build my stamina, and now I fought to tamp it down. I paced behind the couch. I did jumping jacks, push-ups, and planks. I ran in place, did lunges, and tried several yoga moves. The energy surged.

"Dacia"—Cody reached up and grabbed my hand—"what's going on?"

I crumpled onto the couch beside him. "How'm I gonna go a week when I can't even get through one day."

"What do you mean?" Cash jumped up. He knelt in front of me and held my face between his hands, staring into my eyes. "You didn't use it, did you?" He didn't even give me a chance to suck in a breath before saying, "Did you?"

"No." I shook my head. "No."

He rocked back, letting go of me. "What then?"

I looked down at my hands. Power amassed in them, pulsing and flashing like a living thing. I felt it thrashing under my skin, begging for release. "There's so much. I feel like I'm going to explode."

"Give me your hands." He slid across the carpet, kneeling right in front of me, and I obliged.

The magic pulsed in response to his touch. He pulled on it, and it surged, charging from my fingers into his. The relief was instantaneous. Closing my eyes, I slumped back against the couch and let out a deep sigh. "Thank you."

Cash's pupils were enormous. A purple shimmer danced over his skin. He held his hand up in front of him and watched blue sparks flicker over his fingertips. "What a rush! Is that how it feels when you siphon some of my power?"

"I don't know." I shrugged. "It feels like a caffeine high. An adrenaline rush."

He closed his hands and snuffed out my magic. "As much energy as you transferred to me, someone's going to have to drain it a few times a day to keep you from unintentionally releasing it."

"Why?" Cody leaned forward. "When hiding, she went without."

Cash nodded at him. His eyes were still dilated, but he wasn't shimmering. "She was replenishing her magic then. She'd exhausted her supply, and as it"—he used air quotes—"re-filled, she was inadvertently using it to heal herself."

"Need to keep her safe then." Cody squeezed my knee.

Cash stood and walked to the window. "Even if she falls down and scrapes her knee, she will use her power whether she intends to or not."

"So … how long are you planning on keeping me locked in here?" I shook my head. The thought of being trapped in my room for a week or more was unbearable. "Now that Argentum is gone, I'd like to go home for Thanksgiving, and I need to make sure Mavros isn't stealing people's left shoes."

Cash cocked his eyebrow, and Cody snorted.

Mavros appeared in the middle of my room. "I believe that was a cartoon reference, but I'm not an alien, a dog, or an experiment."

"What are you doing here?" Cash narrowed his eyes at him.

"Proving to Dacia that I'm not stealing left shoes." He smiled at me, and it was breathtaking. "Or right ones for that matter."

I clasped my hands together in front of me. "What have you been doing?"

"Watching you." He leaned up against the wall, crossing one leg over the other. "The Nephilim are converging on the school again. It seems that more than just those two were keeping an eye on you."

My stomach plummeted. They'd probably force me to go to their sanctuary this time.

Cash rubbed his hand over his eyes, then pulled it through his hair. Purple and black strands stood on end.

"You knew?" Cody's voice was accusing.

Cash shook his head.

"You didn't?" Mavros asked.

"No"—I rubbed the back of my neck, hoping to loosen some of the knots in it—"but I guess it shouldn't surprise me. After all, I did summon a demon."

Mavros prowled toward me. "They won't back down this time." He knelt beside me and took my hands in his.

"You need to send him back in front of all of them." Cash's amethyst eyes softened.

"N—"

"You have to make sure they see you do it." Mavros squeezed my fingers. "I'll be fine."

Tears slipped from my eyes. I didn't try to hide them. "It's not right."

"It's okay, though." He brushed the tears off my face. "I'll still be here with you."

My eyebrows pinched together.

"My power lingers inside of you."

Chapter 45

Saying Goodbye

Malcolm came back late in the afternoon. He stood by the door and whispered to Cash. I didn't want to know what they were saying. I didn't want to hear that somebody wanted to kill me or cage me. I didn't want to hear that Mavros needed to be returned to the Abyss.

I rolled the dice three times and filled in twenty-five points for a full house. Then I handed them to Cody. "Your turn."

"Don't you wanna know?" He picked up the dice and rolled three fives.

I shook my head.

He rolled again and kept nothing. "Okay then." The third time he rolled, he said, "Ha! Yahtzee!"

"You could let me win. You know?" I batted my eyelashes at him. "I could've died yesterday."

He covered his mouth with his hand. "Oh, wow. You're going there."

"It was worth a shot. Wasn't it?"

He trailed his fingers along my jaw. "Let's not do that again."

"Well"—I raised my eyebrows and shrugged—"the way they're talking, it'll probably happen fairly soon."

Cody looked at them. "What's up?"

Malcolm came over and sat in Cookie Monster. He looked worn out. He scrubbed his hand down his face. "I'm sorry, Dacia."

I waved my hand at him to continue. There was no way I'd be able to talk over the lump that was growing in my throat and the pressure building in my chest.

"Mavros came to me after he was here." He looked down at the floor. His shoulders slumped forward. "I should've summoned him. I never should've let you. The Nephilim are planning to take you."

I slouched back and stared at the ceiling. "Tell Diana to meet me in an hour."

"Where?" Cash sounded defeated.

"Where—" I swallowed a sob "—where I sent him back before."

Cody wrapped one arm behind my back and one under my legs and pulled me onto his lap. "I'm sorry, Dacia."

"There's no other way." I pressed my face against Cody's chest.

The dragons, Mavros, and I stood on the mountain slope. The wind whipped snow up and threw it at us. Mavros held my gloved hand, rubbing his thumb along mine. Otherwise, he stood rigid, staring into the distance, waiting for the Nephilim to arrive.

They came all at once. Forty or fifty of them stepped through a portal. They stood opposite us, and Diana stepped forward. "Dacia, you need to come with us for your safety and the planet's."

"Why?" My voice was carried to them on the breeze.

The dark Nephilim from the side street stepped forward. "You summoned a demon. You cannot be trusted to remain free."

"She summoned him to help defeat an elder dragon that had been corrupted." Aurelia took my other hand in hers. "The dragons and fairies still stand with her. Her heart is pure. She plans to return him to the Abyss now."

"It's a trick," the Nephilim with the tattoo along the side of his face said. "She's standing with him, holding his hand."

Mavros looked down at me. "It's time, Dacia."

I bit my bottom lip, pulling it into my mouth, and shook my head. "I don't want to."

"I'll be okay." He slid his hand from mine and cupped my cheek. Even out here, surrounded by snow, his skin was warm. He kissed my cheek and whispered, "You can let me go."

I wrapped my arms around him, hugging him tightly, knowing this would be the last time I'd see him. "Thank you for everything." I pulled away.

He wiped my eyes. "It's been an honor, Dacia. Let me go."

My voice was soft. My words were only meant for him. "I'll never forget you."

"How could you?" His eyes sparkled affectionately.

Raising my voice so the Nephilim could hear me, I said, "Chaódis Skotádi, return to the Abyss."

His wings burst through his coat. He lifted into the air, transforming into a black mist that brushed against my cheek as it dissipated.

"That proves nothing," ponytail said. "She needs to come with us. She's proven she has no reservations about aligning with darkness."

Several of the Nephilim stalked toward us. Malcolm and Cash moved in front of me.

"Stop!" Diana yelled, but the Nephilim ignored her.

Cash's form rippled. A purple haze surrounded him. His dragon erupted from it. He roared, and the Nephilim stopped. "Leave." He whipped his head toward them, and his chest glowed from the fire within.

"Don't hurt them, Cash." I pulled my glove off, dropped it onto the snow, and pressed my hand to his side. "Please, don't hurt them."

Malcolm growled, and I turned to look at him. Scales lined his neck and face. "We made a vow to protect you. Our oaths are sacred."

I turned, looking at my guardians. All of them were caught somewhere between human and dragon.

"Just give us the girl," the tattooed Nephilim yelled across the clearing.

The snow in front of me seemed to explode, blasting up into the air. When it settled, four sets of footprints sank into the drift.

My heart pounded against my ribcage. The Nephilim rushed toward us, and I lifted my hands. I needed to do something to stop this, but I didn't know what.

The magic seemed to have a mind of its own. A barrier sprang up between us, blocking the Nephilim's attack. The Nephilim with the ponytail crashed into it.

"No." Malcolm sounded crushed. "Dacia, say you didn't." His scales retracted, and his bronze eyes filled with despair.

"I'm sorry. I can't let you fight. I can't let anybody die for me." Power like I'd only felt once before surged through my body. It boosted the shield.

Malcolm grabbed me, and electricity arced from me to him. He groaned but kept hold of me. We stretched in and pulled out. When he finally let go, we stood in the fairies' cave.

Malcolm fell to the ground. "Help her." His voice was a soft plea.

The fairies lit up the cavern. Rayne landed on my shoulder. Her lilac eyes stared up into mine. "What have you done?"

"I sent Mavros back to the Abyss." I pressed my eyes closed and rubbed my hand down my face. "I couldn't let the dragons and Nephilim kill each other."

She waved her hand, and the other fairies flew to her. "His power will corrupt you. You must resist using yours." The fairies converged on my body. Their bright, cleansing energy flowed through me.

They hovered in front of me, and my skin shone a brilliant white. "Thank you."

"You mustn't use your power again." Rayne's wings fluttered so fast they were little more than a blur. "If you do, we may not be able to keep it from spreading."

"I'll do my best." They flew off, and I knelt by Malcolm's side. "I'm sorry."

He pushed himself up to a sitting position. "We need to go back." He wobbled as he stood. I let him lean on me, fighting my desire to use my powers to help him.

The air grew colder, and I stood amongst ten dragons. I knew now who the footprints in the snow had belonged to. My unseen guardians stood between the Nephilim and my friends. The glow from my skin lit up a ten-foot area surrounding me.

Mara turned toward me. "The demon's taint has been removed from her." She faced the Nephilim. "You no longer need to fear her."

"If you advance, we will have no choice but to fight you." Aurelia's voice was a fierce growl. "Is it worth it to you?"

The six Nephilim from Althea stepped forward. One with short, dark hair pointed at me. "We will be watching you."

Several portals opened and all but Diana and Olivia stepped through them. Diana looked at Aurelia. "Can we catch a ride back to campus?"

Chapter 46

Thanksgiving

*M*y friends waited for us to return. Cody stood by the window, staring into the distance as if he could see what was happening. Dan and Samantha huddled together in Cookie Monster. Their faces were stony. Cassandra and Bryce sat on the couch, holding hands. They were the first to notice my arrival.

"You're all right." Relief filled Cassandra's voice.

I nodded at her.

Bryce's eyes widened as he took me in. "You're glowing."

Cody turned and looked at me. The stony mask melted off his face, and he let out a heavy sigh. He strode across the room and pulled me against him. One hand clutched the back of my head, pressing it against his chest. The other wrapped around my waist.

I held him, savoring his warmth and his strength.

"What happened?" Samantha asked.

I pulled against Cody's grip, but he clung to me.

"She sent Mavros back to the Abyss." Malcolm's voice sounded more human than it had on the mountain. "Then she held off the Nephilim's attack, and I took her to the fairies."

"The Nephilim agreed to let her remain free … for now," Aurelia said.

I stepped back, and Cody loosened his grip on me. I brushed my thumb along his cheek and held his face.

"Your eyes." He sounded hollow. "They're different. Why?"

I slid out of his arms, walked over to the sink, and stared into the mirror. Black speckled the green of my irises. "Because I didn't listen. I used my power to stop the Nephilim." I lifted my hand to my face, then spun around. "Will it go away?"

Malcolm shook his head. "I don't think so. I think that's why the fairies were so adamant that you don't use your magic again."

"What's going to happen to me?" Despair filled me, clutching my heart and nearly toppling me.

Aurelia strode across the room to me. She grabbed my hands. "As long as you refrain from using your powers, nothing will change."

Malcolm, Cash, and Aurelia crowded around my family's dinner table. Cody had ridden back to Bittersweet with me, but I'd dropped him off at his house with a promise to let him know if anything happened to me. As much as I wanted him by my side, I was glad he was with his family.

Turkey with all the trimmings covered the table. Pies sat on the counter. For six humans, there would've been plenty of food, but each of the dragons could easily devour several turkeys without even putting a dent in their hunger.

Trying to blend in, they put a little of everything on their plates. None of them had ever celebrated the holiday before, and they wouldn't be now if they weren't trying to make sure I didn't use my power. They took turns draining my magic every few hours. By claiming it, I seemed to have unlocked unfathomable depths of magic. I could tell the dragons were concerned, but none of them would confide in me.

While we ate, my parents asked me how school was going. They discussed the weather and how weird it was to be empty nesters. Their eyes never met the dragons', but they watched them.

After dinner, my guardians thanked my parents for letting them join us and insisted on clearing the table and washing the dishes. Mom, Dad, and I sat in the living room with the TV off. Logs sat in a fireplace that I couldn't ever remember being used. Family photos hung on the walls along with a picture of the mountains I'd painted in high school. The blue couch and loveseat were the same ones we'd had since I was six. The room held memories, both good and bad.

Mom leaned forward and whispered, "You and Cody are still together, right?"

"Yes, Cash and Malcolm are just friends." I looked toward the kitchen sure they were listening to everything we said. "Their families don't celebrate Thanksgiving, so I invited them to come with me."

"They're a little intimidating." Dad didn't bother lowering his voice. "They look like they'd break someone's kneecaps if they stepped too close to you."

I laughed, but I'm sure it sounded as fake to my parents as it did to me. "Okay, Dad."

"We know—" Mom's gaze darted toward the kitchen "—they're not human."

Dad's face paled, and he coughed. "Caitlin, I thought we weren't going to talk to her about this."

She fixed her pale green eyes on him. "If we don't, we're going to lose her, too."

"What—" the word caught in my throat "—what's going on?"

Dad seemed to shrink in on himself, but Mom sat rigidly. She nodded toward the kitchen. "We know your friends are more than they appear to be. We know there's more to your life than you can tell us, but I want you to know that we're here for you."

I stared at them with my mouth hanging open. "What are you talking about?"

"Dacia." Dad's voice was stern. "Don't act stupid."

I jumped up. Magic flared along with my anger. Suddenly, three dragons stood in the living room with me. Malcolm grabbed hold of my hand. "Too much," he said through gritted teeth.

Cash stood in front of me, blocking my parents from my view. He slid his fingers through mine. "Dacia, take a deep breath. Let it know you're not in danger."

I closed my eyes and tried to calm myself. "How can you say you're here for me?" Tears threatened to spill, but somehow, I kept them contained. "You've never been there for me."

"Oh, Dacia." Mom's voice was heartbroken. "We thought that if we ignored it, it would go away."

I pulled away from Malcolm and Cash. "Why would you think that?"

"It worked for me." Mom stared at the beige carpet.

Aurelia's head snapped toward Mom. "What did you say?"

"I had magic when I was little." She looked up, and her eyes were lined with silver. "Every time I used it, my parents punished me." She clutched Dad's hand. "I thought that if we pretended you didn't have it, it would vanish like mine did."

"Oh, Mom." I sat down and buried my face in my hands. "I wish you would've told me."

"We see that now," Dad said.

Malcolm knelt beside me and put his hand on my knee. "Your daughter is one of the most powerful witches I have encountered in my life. We"—he pointed at Cash and Aurelia—"came with her to keep her power siphoned while she's here. She must not use it for a few more days."

"What are you?" Mom asked.

Aurelia's voice sounded threatening. "Are you sure you want to know?"

Mom nodded, and scales appeared along Cash's neck and jaw.

"Dragons," Mom whispered.

Dad looked at her like she was crazy. When he turned to me, fear widened his eyes. "Are you safe with them?"

"Safer than I am anywhere else."

Cash huffed, and smoke rolled out of his nostrils. "She freed us from a madman, and we vowed to protect her."

Mom nodded, then focused on me. "What happens if you use your powers?"

"She may fall to darkness." Aurelia placed her hands on my shoulders and drew out more energy.

My eyes grew heavy. "That's enough." I yawned.

"Does Cody know?" Mom looked at Dad, and guilt marred her features.

Aurelia positioned herself next to me on the loveseat. Cash and Malcolm sat on the floor on either side. All of them were there if I needed them.

"Yes, he knows." I told them some of the things I'd been through since starting college. I didn't tell them about killing myself or nearly being killed. I didn't tell them I was a murderer. I tried to keep most of the terror from showing through, but there were several times throughout my tale when one of the dragons took hold of my hand to siphon off my power.

My parents didn't interrupt until I mentioned Arion.

"You flew on a pegasus?" Mom sounded awestruck.

A smile tugged on my lips and somehow made me feel lighter. "It was amazing. He's magnificent."

When I finished, both of my parents walked over to me. The dragons made room for them. "We are so sorry." Mom pulled me into her arms. "I had no idea. I thought your magic would disappear like mine did."

Dad wrapped his arms around both of us. "Thank God you're safe. I don't know what we'd do if we lost you, too."

"I'm sorry about Jonathan." I sobbed. "I never meant to hurt him."

Mom pulled back and stared at me. Her eyebrows were pinched together. "Honey, we never blamed you. The coroner said he died of asphyxiation, but there was no smoke in his room. They ruled it a SIDS death." She wiped the tears from my cheeks. "I never knew you blamed yourself. I'm so sorry."

"We were in a dark place." Dad's voice was full of remembered pain. "We should've realized you'd think it was your fault, but we couldn't see past our grief and our fear. We were so scared something would happen and we'd lose you, too."

Chapter 47

The Demon Within

The sky is lit with millions of stars. They twinkle against the velvet backdrop. Arion's fur glimmers. His wings are spread wide as we glide through the air. The wind blows my hair straight back behind me. I stretch my arms toward the heavens, and a joyous laugh tears from me.

This.

This is what makes all the trials worth it. This is why I'll keep fighting monsters. This is why I'm glad my powers hadn't disappeared like Mom's.

Arion suddenly jerks to the side. I lose my grip and plummet through the night sky. Arion dives for me. Tree branches scrape my arms, legs, and face. My power surges inside of me, but I refuse to use it.

The ground rushes toward me, and I squeeze my eyes shut, not wanting to see the end. I hit Arion's warm body, and my back cracks.

I woke up in Malcolm's arms. "I can't feel my legs."

"Dacia." The relief in his voice was clouded by fear. "I tried to stop you." He lowered his head in shame. "I was too late."

My heart pounded against my chest. Then it plummeted like I had. "What's going to happen to me?"

Tears filled his bronze eyes. "I don't know."

The End

The best thing that you can do to support an author,
especially an indie author, is to leave a review.

Not only do your reviews help new readers find us,
they help the algorithms guide more people to our books.
In turn, that makes it possible for us to keep writing.

Positive reviews bring a bright spot to our day,
and reviews with constructive criticism help
us figure out how to make our books better.

Acknowledgments

If you made it this far, thank you. I hope you enjoyed reading my books as much as I've enjoyed writing. I never expected to finish writing one book. let alone four. And, I'm almost done writing the fifth.

Writing the books isn't as hard as doing all the rest of the work. Editing, proofreading, formatting, writing the acknowledgments (and hoping nobody inadvertently gets left out), designing the cover, and waiting for the sales to come. I'd add marketing, but I haven't tackled that beast yet. I'm hoping to get there soon.

Thank you to Jeff for having faith in me and most importantly for loving me. Thank you to Jami and Jesse for being the best kids a mother could ask for. You both make me proud every day. To my parents, Jim and Vicki, for being amazing. And to my brothers, Jason and Zach, thank you for the expert help with the monsters and how to slay them.

A special thank you to Stone Sour and Shinedown for providing much of the music I listened to while writing this.

Thanks to all the people at 20BooksTo50K®. Without them, I doubt I would have ever tried self-publishing.

To everyone who enjoys reading my books:

Thank You!

If you liked this story, you can join my mailing list.
Drop by my website MandiOyster.com
or if you have any comments,
shoot me a note at mandi@mandioyster.com.
I am always happy to hear from people who've read my work.
I try to answer every email I receive.

If you liked the story, please write a short review for me.
I greatly appreciate any kind words, even one or two
sentences go a long way. The number of reviews a
book receives improves how well a book does.

Facebook: https://www.facebook.com/MandiOysterAuthor
Instagram: https://www.instagram.com/mandioyster/
My web page: MandiOyster.com

About the Author

Mandi Oyster lives in Southwest Iowa in the middle of an enchanted forest where unicorns, fairies, and dragons abound. At least, that's what she assumes when she looks out into the trees. Her husband, two kids (when they're not away at college), four cats, and two chinchillas share the house with her. 

Besides being an author, she also runs her own editing business and works full-time as a digital prepress technician for a local printshop.

You can find her online at:
https://www.MandiOyster.com
https://www.facebook.com/MandiOysterAuthor
https://instagram.com/MandiOyster/

The Story Continues in ...
Dacia Wolf
AND THE
DARKNESS WITHIN
Book 5